I0647957

BELOW 200

A Novel

ALSO BY RONALD ALEXANDER

The Final Audit
The War on Dogs

BELOW 200

A Novel

Ronald Alexander

 Hollyridge Press
Venice, California

Hollyridge Press
P.O. Box 2872
Venice, California 90294

Cover Art © Photographer: Vitaly Valua | Agency: Dreamstime.com
Book Design by Rio Smyth
Author Photo by Cynthia Smalley
Manufactured in the United States of America by Lightning Source

Publisher's Cataloging-In-Publication Data
(Prepared by The Donohue Group, Inc.)

Alexander, Ronald D., 1942-
  Below 200 : a novel / Ronald Alexander.

  p. ; cm.

  ISBN-13: 978-0-9799588-1-6
  ISBN-10: 0-9799588-1-4

1. Gay men--Fiction. 2. HIV-positive gay men--Fiction. I. Title. II. Title:
Below two hundred

PS3551.L35755 B45 2007   2007940985
813/.54

        14 13 12 11 10 09 08   10 9 8 7 6 5 4 3 2 1

For

Angelo Cottonaro
1947 - 1989

Robert Larsen
1956 - 1995

No man, for any considerable period, can wear one face to himself, and another to the multitude, without finally getting bewildered as to which may be true.
—Nathaniel Hawthorne, *The Scarlet Letter*

The power of the newest drugs, called protease inhibitors, and the even greater power of those in the pipeline, is such that a diagnosis of H.I.V. infection is not just different in degree today than, say, five years ago. It is different in kind. It no longer signifies death. It merely signifies illness.
—Andrew Sullivan, "When AIDS Ends," *The New York Times Magazine*

Below 200

ෲෲෲ Part I ෲෲෲ

Chapter One

THE FIRST THING I did after I tested positive was quit my job, and when I called Mother to tell her, she yelled at me as if I'd forgotten to take out the trash. "Chris, you've flipped your lid," she said. "You're making more money than your daddy ever dreamt of."

He worked in the brick factory, firing the kilns. It's the only place left in New Harmony, unless you're a farmer. From our house on the southern edge of town you could see the six, square chimneys, poking thirty feet in the air and sending out gray smoke, but beyond the city limits the kilns themselves were visible—brick igloos, arranged in the open as if in a small native village.

There were twelve kilns in all that Daddy tended by himself, walking the cinder pathways that linked them, shoveling coal into the small openings, keeping the fires constant and even for three days until the bricks were baked. He said that winters were the easiest because it was like working in front of a large fireplace: the front of his body at least kept warm. And in January, when it was zero and the bitter winds blew, he could duck into the heated maintenance shed for a few minutes to thaw. But during the summer, when it was ninety in town and humid, the heat at the plant blistered his skin and there was no place for relief.

I can still see my dad's shiny, red face and the swelling under his watery eyes. It didn't take a ton of New Harmony bricks to fall on me.

There was nothing for me in town. I wasn't going to stay around and learn to make bricks and look like an old man at forty and die from emphysema before I was seventy.

I studied accounting, and then after graduating in 1980 I moved here to Chicago. That's when I went to work at J.W. Bradley—as a receivables clerk. I worked my way up to one of the two supervisor positions, and to hear Mother talk, you'd have thought I was Donald Trump.

"Life's more than money," I said. She grew up during the Depression. When I finally let it out that I had taken a job in a flower shop, she made a snorting noise.

"Why do you want a sissy job like that?" she said. She can't say the word *homosexual*. Anything sexual upsets her.

⊱•⊰

I enjoyed the flower shop. For the first time in my career, I looked forward to work. From the moment I stepped inside each morning, until I locked the door at night, the colors cheered me and the fragrances warmed me. At Bradley, I felt like a cat running with a pack of feral dogs. There were only two other employees in the company that I knew for sure were gay, and they called the one, an older man about fifty, *Dan the Dream* because he was so obvious. The other worked in the mailroom and kept to himself; I saw him sneaking into the gay bookstore on Wells Street one Saturday night. When I first started at Bradley I told myself I'd pay off my student loan and leave, but they kept advancing me and giving me raises, and I got hooked. And they wouldn't just let me do my job; they wanted me to hang out with them, drink with them, and chase women. They expected me to go to their parties too. That's how I became friends with Cynthia—the shampoo girl in the salon where I got my hair cut. I complained about having to go to my boss's New Year's Eve party, wondering if I should go alone or not at all, and she offered to be my date.

My boss repeatedly asked me to play golf. What a waste of a day. When I mentioned to Mother that I golfed with the Accounting Manager, she must have told everyone in New Harmony, because when I went home one of her friends from the quilting club came over to the house, and said: "Your mother tells me you play golf." That amused me, since I spent most of my time in the rough searching for my ball. And there wasn't enough money at Bradley to make me wear one of those ridiculous golf ensembles. Sometimes, it embarrassed me to be seen with Stanley at the golf course, even though I owed a lot of my success to him. When he got a promotion, he moved me up. He's a tall, heavy man, and he wore plaid, double-knit slacks and bright sweaters. One Saturday he wore a canary yellow knit cap with a green pom-pom, but I made so much fun of him, he never wore it again. I told him that he looked like a clown when he got into the golf cart, and truly, he reminded me of a Shriner racing around in one of those tiny cars at the circus. Stanley really liked me. He slapped me on the back, and squeezed my neck.

I worked at Bradley for almost seven years. After I resigned, a fellow from the bars offered me a job in the flower shop that he'd opened. Joey's family had money, and I assumed that he didn't have to work, that the shop was a diversion. At first, the idea of me working with flowers sounded absurd, then I decided it would be liberating to do what I wanted for a change. There wouldn't be pressure to socialize, and no one would force me to play golf or waste an evening pretending to be interested in women. I've always liked flowers, especially wildflowers, although I didn't know much about them. Learning the names of different varieties and how to arrange them in bouquets turned out to be challenging—but extremely satisfying. I suppose I sound like one of those ads: *Enjoy the exciting and challenging career of Ikebana in your spare time.*

The week I started—it was ten days till Christmas—another person from the bars came into the shop. He was a partner in one of Chicago's biggest law firms and used to try to pick me up in Equinox. He was tall, blond, and Waspy: not my type. Whenever he spotted me in the bar, he stood close and stared, giving me his best cruise with his stomach sucked in and his shoulders reared back, until I'd walk away to the back room or up in front to try to lose him in the crowd. Then, before I'd know it, he'd be back—this time standing next to me. Not talking or anything, just looking over, and then taking a swallow of beer, then looking over again. One night I left and went home early. It got so bad I stopped going to the Equinox on Friday nights for a while. When I finally did return, there he was following me around again. I weaved my way through the crowd, past the coat-check room, and I could practically feel his breath on my neck. Most people would get the hint. I surely wouldn't be chasing after someone if they ran from me. So, I turned around, and said: "Look it's nothing personal, but I'm not interested. Sexually I mean. Okay?" I didn't tell him that I liked younger, darker boys, that I liked Italians and Puerto Ricans.

"So?" he said, in a haughty tone. "What makes you think I'm in-terested in you?"

"You've been chasing me around this bar for months," I said. "I never figured you wanted financial advice."

"Dear boy," he said, "your imagination is playing tricks on you." He huffed off and, after that, didn't bother me. If I'd see him out, he'd act like he didn't see me—until over a year ago at Ron MacNeil's Labor Day party. When Darren walked over, Ron started introductions.

"Chris, you know Darren Wedgewood, don't you?"

Before I could open my mouth, Darren said: "Chris and I are old friends."

He was so drunk he had trouble standing up straight. He's one of those too-tall types. About six foot seven. In the bar he stood out like a cactus on the desert. He towered above me, weaving back and forth, holding his drink at shoulder height, and tipping it sideways so that I thought he would spill it at any minute. I stuck out my hand, but he didn't offer his or respond. He glared. For a second I wondered if he was going to throw his drink on me. Ron picked up on the vibes and like a coward ran off to make sure the caterers had enough champagne on ice.

"So, how's the world of litigation?" I asked, as if we really were old friends.

He kept staring at me with opossum-like eyes, shifting his weight from the balls of his feet to the heels and then out of nowhere said: "Would you care to join me in the bathroom for a toot?" He was the last person I would have figured to have cocaine. I had classified him as the sloppy drunk. I knew I had a problem, but was still planning to deal with it later, so we made our way through the crowd to the bathroom on the first floor—just off the den. The line went all the way back to the French doors that led to the terrace. Darren grabbed my arm and tried to wink. "VIP lounge," he said.

We went through the living room, up the stairs and down the hall to the master bedroom. Now excited about the prospect of doing some, I already planned to call Arvo and arrange for more. The door to Ron's bedroom was locked, but Darren didn't flinch; he fumbled around in his pocket and brought out a set of keys. He put them close to his face, separated a gold one from the others, and poked at the lock. The key wouldn't go in so he took it out, turned it right side up, and tried once more. This time he unlocked the door, and we slipped inside. The select group did their drugs in the bedroom—with an endless supply of porno showing on the video.

Darren had a brown glass container that held two grams, and he put a capful up each nostril, and then handed the bottle to me. I was high instantly and couldn't wait to get back downstairs and see how the crowd looked now. There had been this one great-looking boy with black curly hair and a beefy body, who I'd been watching, and now that I'd had some drugs I wanted to go up to him and start a conversation.

"Let's get a drink," I said, to Darren. "Thanks for the coke." It would have been impolite to ask if he had any to sell.

"By all means, old chap," said Darren. He had a habit of lapsing into a clichéd English accent and, as I found out later, persisted with it when he was plowed.

When we got back downstairs, the crowd had doubled in the time since we'd been away. I didn't see the cute one right away, but as we got close to the front door, Arvo came in with his latest boyfriend—a cheeky-faced blond that I classified as from the Westside and probably Latvian or Lithuanian.

I pushed through the people to Arvo and said: "Where have you been? The party's great. I need a couple of grams." I didn't waste time with Arvo, trying to act as if we were best friends the way some people do. He'd gotten me high many times so I'd buy. Besides, he had come to the party to work. Whenever I called his place and asked if he planned to go the bar, he'd say: "I got to work, don't I?"

Arvo gave me his slyest, most charming smile and raised one eyebrow; he'd had his eyes done a year ago. Where he found the doctor, I don't know, but he had these two crescent-shaped, keloid scars about an inch above his eyebrows. The effect was hideous when he smiled. He had a mocking gaze and wore makeup that made him look like Little Richard. I got my coke from him and lost Darren, not intentionally this time but it was just as well, and went looking for the boy I'd seen. But I saw someone else with better definition and a more muscular ass. And I didn't see Darren again that night.

When he came in the flower shop that first week, stomping snow off his shoes, he pretended not to see me. He had on sunglasses, most likely because he was hung over. I'd heard he was really into the coke now. I could only imagine what it would be like to get him for a lawyer. Some poor, unsuspecting victim needing a good defense—and he goes to court with Darren who's high or fighting a hangover. He stayed by the front window looking at some arrangements, still ignoring me, so I went up to him.

"What can I help you with, Darren?"

He slid his glasses down on his nose, peered over them at me and said: "Chris, old bean. I say, whatever are you doing in here? Don't tell me J.W. relieved you of your command? I've done some legal work for the firm; perhaps I could put in a good word for you."

"I resigned," I said. "What do you need?"

"Resigned. Hmm. Curious." He slid his glasses back. "I'm having a Christmas party and I need tuberoses. I'm decorating with poinsettias, holly, and tuberoses."

I didn't know tuberoses from tea roses, so I went in back to call Joey on his car phone. I wasn't about to let Darren know how ill equipped I was to be selling flowers.

∾•∾

Mother came up for Christmas a week later. I'm sure she wanted to get a firsthand look at the shop and find out what I was really up to, but she claimed to be coming to spend the holidays with my sister and me. Mae was staying at my place for the time being, but it was a couple of days till she revealed the reason: Charlie had punched her again during an argument. I hoped she was finished with Charlie. Irish men don't respect women.

I drove to O'Hare to get Mother, wishing I could tell her I was positive; it would help explain so many things. Even then, I tried not to be morbid about my health, and I knew I'd done the right thing getting tested. The articles I'd read stressed that there was no need to panic—there were treatments now available to help infected persons live longer and healthier lives.

The day I went in to get my results, I could barely speak. As a child, I'd been a hopeless hypochondriac and as an adult I have only slightly overcome my irrational fear of doctors. When the receptionist smiled and wished me good morning, I searched her face for an indication of my fate and managed to squeak some sort of reply. She asked me to wait, and after forty-five minutes of agonizing in a corner chair, while the sick and emaciated paraded in and out of the office, she directed me to an examination room behind the reception area. The room was cold: the stainless steel examination table would probably have fogged over if I'd blown my breath on it. I heard people walking back and forth in the hallway outside, and after fifteen more minutes of waiting, I heard a clipboard being taken from the holder on the other side of the door. A moment later, Dr. Townsend came into the room.

"As I suspected," he said with no preamble or indication why he had suspected anything, "your test came back positive." Although I realize that tens of thousands of others have gone through that moment, I hope their doctors were at least somewhat sympathetic. Dr. Townsend scribbled on his clipboard. "We'll start you on a protocol of AZT and possibly ddI," he said.

I couldn't understand why, even before he did blood work, he was so eager to put me on AZT. I'd read that if your T-4 cells were in the 400 or 500 range, they were recommending AZT, but Townsend didn't even know what range my cells were in. I said: "I'll take care of myself." I didn't tell him I did coke occasionally because I was determined to stop. "I'll practice safe sex." I believed that if I cleaned up my life, I could stay healthy. "I'll get plenty of rest, work out regularly, and eat right. I've stopped smoking." And I had, except when I slipped and did coke. "Maybe I could try eating macrobiotic?" I made the mistake of phrasing this as a question.

Dr. Townsend seemed wired. He isn't old, he looks my age, I guess he's in his thirties, but he wears a hairpiece and has startled, blue eyes. "That's denial," he snapped. "Sleeping and going on a macrobiotic diet isn't going to cure AIDS."

I knew better than to be honest with Mother. She let me know at every opportunity that anything dealing with homosexuality offended her. For a while, after Daddy died, I considered telling her, but Mae talked me out of it. She said there was no reason. I lived in Chicago and Mother lived in Ohio. It would only upset her. Mae is even more intimidated by her. Mother makes hateful comments when she's provoked; I guess I inherited her tongue.

One weekend when I was home from college, Mother was doing my laundry and found a picture in my shirt pocket that I had cut out of a gay magazine. It was a muscular man lying on the beach and covered with a tiny towel. *Troy.* That was his name—or the name they gave him in the magazine. I've always been fascinated by pornography. During my adolescence, these magazines were the only evidence I had that there were others like me in the world. Later I realized it was more complicated. I also feared being intimate with people. On cocaine, I preferred pornography to the real thing. Mother handed me the picture that time, she had the saddest expression, and said: "We don't have to tell Daddy about this."

I missed a chance there, I suppose. But I didn't have the courage to confront the issue. I said: "Oh this. I cut it out to show a girlfriend of mine. As a joke." Neither of us ever mentioned it again.

Another time Mae told me Mother confessed she had been having terrible dreams. "Like what?" Mae said. She'd gone home for the weekend and this conversation occurred the very minute she had stepped through the front door and into the living room.

"I was at a church supper," Mother said, "and I saw Chris across the room talking in a group of people. I went to see him, and when I got close, he was carrying a purse." Mae laughed and told Mother not to worry—because I didn't carry a purse. It's funny really. So she knew, but went on pretending that I had girlfriends. She told the ladies at the quilt club that Cynthia was my fiancée and had our picture—when Cynthia went with me to an AIDS benefit—on the mantle. I was thirty-one years old, and Mother still hoped I'd get married.

When I got to O'Hare she was waiting outside. She looked very pretty, standing there in the snow. She was wearing the blue, wool gabardine coat, trimmed in fox with a matching hat, that Mae and I gave her for her birthday. I don't approve of people wearing fur, but Mother had always wanted a fur coat so this was something of a compromise. Mother doesn't look like a woman in her sixties. My father was ten years older. In that respect, I'm like him: I prefer them young. I'm never ashamed to introduce Mother to people. She may have grown up in a small town, but she's stylish.

"You're alone," she said, as she climbed in the car.

"You've got all my presents in that little shopping bag?" I said.

"I thought maybe Mae would come with you." She leaned over to kiss me on the cheek.

"Mae's working."

"And Cynthia? Is she working too?"

"Cynthia? She took the day off to register at Marshall Fields. Didn't I tell you? She's getting married. In June—"

"Christopher," she said. "You let her get away."

"Cynthia and I are friends," I said. "We don't have a romantic relationship. Why do you insist on making it more?"

"Don't try to tell me she feels that way."

She wouldn't talk for the rest of the way into the city. I couldn't wait for Mae to get home from work so Mother could start on her. Since Mae had been staying with me, Charlie had called every night—at five-minute intervals in the evening until she'd answer. I told her to ignore it and let the machine pick up, but the ringing bothered her so much that she would finally answer. I'd leave the room, so she could have some privacy, but my apartment is small; I used the front room as my bedroom and had put Mae on the hide-a-bed in the den. The mattress is fairly firm, but while Mother visited, I planned to let them have my bed.

I really shouldn't have taken the time to drive to the airport—I had to get back to the shop—but Mother didn't like to take taxis since the time the driver had taken her and Dad all over the north side of Chicago, up to Evanston and back again before depositing them at my doorstep. It was the last time Dad was able to travel and the memory of his struggle stayed with her. She was practically crying by the time I got home. Dad looked so tired. He said, "The cussed little foreigner didn't even understand English." What upset him was that the man had driven the entire time without taking the automatic transmission out of low gear. Mother said that Dad and the driver had almost gotten into a fight, because the driver kept saying: "It is the characteristic of the car, the characteristic of the car." Mother said when the driver stopped at a light, Daddy abruptly leaned across the front seat, and she had a vision of him clamping his hands around the driver's neck and smashing his head repeatedly against the steering wheel. All he did though was reach over and put the transmission into drive. Then the rest of the trip the driver kept saying, "I thought it was the characteristic of the car, the characteristic of the car."

❧•❧

There were only three more days till Christmas, and the shop was full of customers when I got back. Joey was even working. "Doll, where have you been?" he said. "It's madness." He asked me to check the order of twenty poinsettias for the Comfort Inn, and said that Norberto was going to squeeze in an extra delivery.

Norberto, the new delivery boy, was a muscular Puerto Rican barely out of high school. He would have been my type except for two things. He was living with a girl, and they had a child. Three things. Joey was hopelessly infatuated with him.

Joey was sweating heavily. He was an intense person and had a serious Quaalude problem at one time, but had been in a twelve-step program for two years now and was sober. Really, he had traded his drug problems for an eating disorder. His weight had ballooned to 250 pounds at least, and since he was far from tall at 5'7", it showed. A month earlier he had joined Overeaters Anonymous. I didn't even know there was such a group. Before Joey joined, it had been all women.

"You had a call, Chris," Joey said. He gazed at Norberto who was bent over in the cooler rearranging vases of roses. "Someone named Darren Wedgewood with a severe accent. Australian or something. He left a number, but wouldn't leave a message. He said he'd try you at home." My first thought was that Mother would answer my phone and interrogate him.

"Can you handle things for awhile?" said Joey. "I'm going to help Norberto with the deliveries, otherwise we'll never get everything out." He didn't look me in the eye, and it was no use to object. We both knew he'd be busier at the shop and that Norberto could handle the deliveries. Norberto backed out of the cooler and closed the heavy door. The wind was blowing furiously, it was about twenty degrees outside, and not much warmer inside, and Norberto, dressed in a tank top and the new 501's that Joey had bought for him, looked happy as a prom queen. He smiled repeatedly at Joey showing his crooked teeth. He knew it was going to be a good Christmas. Joey, crazy for this boy, was absolutely no help in the store, I was getting calls from Darren, Mae was staying with me, Mother was in town, and I had two canker sores in my mouth.

COUNTRYSIDE

The hardwoods retain red and yellow leaves, and a midday sun warms the November air. I drive past the gravel road that traces the edge of Dooley's Creek because the entrance is overgrown with brush; this old way has been replaced a few miles to the south by a wider, paved highway, which cuts through the hills in a straight line. I park on the weedy shoulder, and we set out on foot. I carry the basket of sandwiches and wine, and he takes the wool blanket, and when we arrive at the pasture, I see the hay barn and silo at the top of a rise in the distance. The old structure has been repaired and painted: the Amish farm here these days, having come from Pennsylvania in search of cheaper land. Except for a territorial sparrow overhead and the field of grazing Guernseys, we are the only visible living things and we follow the edge of the clearing for a while, before moving back into the brush at a bend in the creek. Brambles and briars snag our clothing, but spotting the faded red covered bridge ahead I move faster, stepping not so carefully through the growth until I stand at the opening, staring up. We walk side by side across the planked floor to the other end, where leafless blackberry vines make this impractical, so I lead the way—looking back now and then to make sure that he follows closely. We walk alongside the stream and come to the field of rattling cornstalks enclosed by a rusted barbed wire fence. Here, in a splash of sun with the fence at our backs and the noisy creek in front, we spread the blanket and put down the basket. This is the countryside that sustained me in childhood. We stand motionless and silent. He steps forward to enclose me in his arms. The sky is clear and pale, and a breeze unloosens a flurry of leaves from the surrounding trees when he kisses me.

ꙸꙸꙸ Chapter Two

EVEN BEFORE WE SAT DOWN to our turkey dinner, Mother brought up the year that Daddy surprised me with an electric train and got an entire miniature kitchen for Mae. Then Mother shook her head and said Christmas wasn't much fun without children.

Mother was right. Christmas Day was especially disheartening at my apartment. Mae worried about Charlie, I worried about Mother being there to pass judgment, and Mother missed Dad. There is something depressing about the picture of three adults sitting around a Christmas tree, distributing presents. I had given in to Mae's pleas, though, and bought a real tree and put it by the window in the corner of the dining room. My apartment is on the second floor of an old frame building in the DePaul area; it's like an attic with the ceiling sloping to the outer walls, so the windows are rather small. But the people in this mixed neighborhood get heavily into Christmas decorations. The old man next door, besides outlining his entire house in gaudy lights, had installed a Santa display complete with sleigh and reindeer on his roof, and if you got right up next to my window and looked up, you could see Santa's arm and Rudolph's nose. His place had more candlepower than the city tree at Daley Center.

Still, I had difficulty keeping an image of over-the-river-and-through-the-woods in my mind. When I was a child and Mae was a baby, we spent Christmases at Grandmother's. She died before I turned seven so I don't have many personal memories, but I've heard the stories from Mother about how she cooked dinner for more than ten people on a coal stove. I don't feel that thirty-eight is so old, but when I think about my grandmother's coal stove and the outside toilet, I realize that it is. When dating, I preferred to think of the guys I went out with as getting younger. It wasn't so shocking that none of my dates had heard of Tallulah Bankhead or seen *The Women*, but these days they hadn't even heard of Sylvester.

Mae and Mother were busy in the kitchen, at the back of the apartment, when the doorbell rang. Cynthia said she would stop by in the morning so that we could exchange presents. I had asked her to spend the day, but mainly as a courtesy since I knew she was spending Christmas with her fiancé and his parents in Melrose Park. I tidied the room by collecting the bits and pieces of wrapping paper in an empty box, all the time wondering how Mother would act now that I'd told her about Cynthia's marriage plans. There was no chance of Cynthia bringing Louie along. A couple of months earlier she told him that I was gay. Since that time he'd avoided me. He'd been surprised by the news, primarily because he suspected that we were more than friends; he's one of those straight men who don't believe it's possible for a man and woman to simply be friends. He believes one or the other will develop sexual feelings. When I want to I can camp it up, but most people never suspect that I'm gay, and it upset me that Cynthia told him, because it was none of his business. I kept pestering her to give me his reaction, so she finally admitted that he said, "Gay people are sick."

Half of the homosexuals I know believe it is abnormal themselves. And why not? Growing up listening to the things people say about homos and fags and queers. Stanley said that homosexuality was an aberration, and I never felt the same about him after that. I looked up the word to make sure; it means more than a deviation from the norm in a statistical sense. It's a negative word. I've read that ten percent of the population is homosexual or has tendencies, so I should have asked him if he felt that blood type B positive was also an aberration, because ten percent have that type.

I ran downstairs to let in Cynthia. She remarked that it was freezing outside, and that it smelled delicious as we came up the stairs and into the middle room where the tree was. Hearing us laughing and talking, Mother charged out of the kitchen. I hadn't mentioned Cynthia.

"Thought that was your voice, sweetie," said Mother, drying her hands on her apron. "Chris didn't tell me you were spending Christmas." She hugged Cynthia, and frowned at me. "Set another place, Mae."

"I can't stay, Mrs. Hale. I stopped to wish you a happy Christmas and drop off Chris's gift." She handed me the white package tied with red ribbon, and smiled.

"Cynthia, not more Chrysler stock. You shouldn't have," I said, and glanced at Mother, who was biting the inside of her cheek.

"Give me your coat," Mother said. "You have to stay and have eggnog."

"I don't know if I'd let her have your coat, Cynthia. She may not give it back," I said. Mother shot me another grim look. I wondered if she would say anything about Cynthia's wedding plans; it would be just like her to ignore the subject. After she and Mae went into the kitchen to get the eggnog, Cynthia sat on the couch next to the tree, and I searched among the presents for the small box with the gold earrings that I'd chosen for her.

We started talking about the first Christmas that we knew each other, and how she'd gone back to Ohio with me for the holiday; it surprised me to realize that it had been so long ago. It was Dad's last Christmas, and he adored Cynthia. He never missed an opportunity during those three days to tease her.

Mother came back in with the eggnog as Cynthia and I were laughing about the tavern in New Harmony that we'd gone to. Bing's Place. Mother sat next to the tree and smiled as I told the story about the intoxicated couple who got into a fistfight and were thrown out on Christmas Eve. The woman, short and fat, was dressed festively in red and green, but her husband had on soiled, mechanic's coveralls. "They should have named the town New Disharmony," I said, and we all laughed.

The Christmas that Cynthia went home with me, Daddy had a new set of dentures. He'd had false teeth for as long as I could remember, but always complained about how they felt and had products to make the plates fit more comfortably. He enjoyed sitting, crouched on the floor, and carving the high spots down with a pocketknife then using a pink, putty-like material to build them up again. While Mother worked on her quilt, he whittled his teeth. It was one of his many obsessive qualities, if I could call it a quality. After I introduced Mother to Cynthia, she sat in the rocker and chatted about the drive down and how pretty Ohio was, how it wasn't flat like Illinois. Her chair was next to a heat register, and when she swiveled to the right to put her feet closer to the heat, she saw a set of dentures on the register. Dad had put them on the vent to dry after one of his meticulous, reworking sessions. Cynthia's mouth gaped open when she spotted the dislodged teeth, and almost immediately Mother noticed where she was looking. At this exact moment, Dad walked slowly out of the kitchen with a grilled cheese and bacon sandwich in his hand. He was out of breath—the process of making a sandwich had exhausted him— and by the time he got to the floor by Cynthia's chair he practically fell into his usual crouched position on the rug. No one said anything as Dad stretched over to pick up the teeth, slid them into his mouth, took a bite from his sandwich, and then, while chewing and gasping for air, said: "Dale Hale. Call me Dale."

I mentioned the false teeth incident, and Cynthia and I laughed. Hearing us, Mae came in from the kitchen, and I asked if she remembered the time Dad left his teeth on the register. Mae said that wasn't half as funny as the time he put them in the oven to dry and forgot them. She described the two pink puddles on tin foil and the dots of teeth that now pointed in every direction. I laughed harder, relieved to have a distraction from my feelings about Cynthia's marriage plans. Then I saw Mother's pained expression.

"I'm sorry your dad and me weren't sophisticated. We tried to be good parents," she said. "We did the best we could." With that, she stomped from the room. Mae rolled her eyes at me, and Cynthia said she had to go because she was late to pick up Louie. I knew we hadn't done anything wrong. And my parents did not embarrass me.

Once, when I was ten or eleven, I went with Daddy to the grocery store and he ran into a redheaded, bearded man that he worked with at the brick plant. Daddy got involved in a long story about his champion Blue Tick coonhound and why he had named him *Humphrey*. "There ain't nobody in the whole damned county as smart as Hubert H. Humphrey," said my dad. Then he went into the details of a recent hunt (when Humphrey went in the opposite direction from the other hounds to tree three coons while they were busy treeing one) to prove his point, and the redheaded man shifted back and forth and looked around for a distraction. Then, I was embarrassed. I wanted to take my dad by the sleeve and rush him off. But his teeth didn't embarrass me.

After Mae pleaded, Mother came out for dinner, but wouldn't talk. She managed a smile or two when she opened her presents, but made an excuse about having a headache and went back into the front room to lie down before dark—and it got dark early. When Mae went to bed too, I thought about sneaking out for a drink, but told myself only losers frequented bars on Christmas night. At times like that, I wished I had a lover. But I'd never had a relationship that lasted more than a few weeks in my entire life, let alone someone who could be called a lover. I always got rid of them. After awhile, I didn't want to have sex with them anymore; I didn't even like for them to touch me. Besides, I couldn't see myself setting up housekeeping with the guys I was attracted to.

So far that day, I hadn't thought much about what it meant to be H.I.V.–positive. But, sitting in the den alone with the television on, I couldn't help it. Thus far, I hadn't told anyone about my status. I wasn't about to tell anyone gay. I'd seen the gossip start all too quickly. I was fine. I hadn't told Mae or Cynthia. The newspapers make it sound far worse than it is—like the minute someone tests positive they're doomed to an early, horrible death. No reason to scare Mae or Cynthia. I was fine.

∾ • ∾

Mother left for home on the morning of the thirty-first, and Mae went to stay with a girl friend from the office until she could find an apartment. I told Mae she was welcome, but in truth I was relieved to have back my privacy. And after Mother left, I stopped chewing my nails.

I sometimes thought it would be more natural for people to act as animals do, and break all ties with their young at an early age. I've seen mother cats hiss and swipe at their kittens after only six weeks. Yet here we humans were, pretending we still had emotional ties—when the truth was we no longer had anything in common. I had even less need of a mother, because she'd been totally unable to prepare me for the life into which I'd been born. And I didn't need advice on raising children.

Ron MacNeil was hosting his annual New Year's Eve party—traditionally even more outrageous than the Labor Day party. Sometimes, Chicago seems like a small town. I knew I'd see the same people that I saw at every other party in town, but still looked forward to it with excitement. I also worried, because I understood that I shouldn't drink or stay out late. But I needed this party. I needed this chance to forget about everything that was going on. I needed the chance to relax after Mother's visit.

Stanley called and invited me to his New Year's Eve party in the suburbs. "You and Cynthia won't even have to drive back afterwards; you can sleep in the guest room. We won't even tell anyone you're not married." I thought that when I quit Bradley, I would also be able to quit lying to people, to quit making up excuses about my plans. "We're going to stay in the city," I said. "She's making dinner at her place. We'll probably have some champagne and go to bed early. I'm not crazy about New Year's Eve. It's not my favorite holiday."

I got to Ron's house at nine-thirty, while the caterers and bartenders were still setting up. The bartenders were shirtless, like Chippendale dancers, and I recognized one as a guy I'd dragged home from the Loading Zone on at least two occasions. He was a little nelly, but had an incredible body and in the darkness of the bar—and with a cocaine high raging through my body—he'd looked pretty good dressed in tight jeans and a tee shirt. Ron had the front downstairs bedroom set up as a coat room, and I gave the boy my jacket and scarf and slipped the claim number in my pocket before going over to the bar to say hello.

"Happy New Year, Chris. You're my first customer. Champagne?" He leaned across the bar and puckered his lips.

I kissed him quickly and said: "Happy New Year, Mike."

"Mark," he said.

He constructed two glasses, inserting the tops into the plastic bases, and without looking at me said: "You never called." I didn't remember promising to call, but perhaps in a weak moment I had. He pulled the cork and poured.

"Things got crazy," I said. "My sister was staying with me, and my Mother has been visiting. You know how it is when family is around. It sort of cramps your style," I laughed, and Mark smiled.

"Not really," he said.

"Excuse me," I said.

"I wouldn't know how it is. Parents cramping your style, that is. I came out in high school. My parents have always been very supportive." He took a sip of his champagne and looked at me as if we were in a game of chess.

"Well mine, it's just my mother now…my mother doesn't know."

He gazed at me, reached for a pack of cigarettes, and pulled one out with his forefinger. He tapped the filter on the edge of the bar, then put the cigarette in his mouth and lit it. "All mothers know," he said. "How old are you? Don't you think she wonders why you're not married?" I glanced around to find a convenient way of excusing myself. More people had come in, but no one I knew well enough to talk to.

"I guess she knows—she just doesn't want to know officially," I said.

"I took a man to my high school prom," said Mark.

"Where did you grow up? Denmark?"

"That's funny," he said, inhaling deeply on his cigarette, but he didn't laugh.

Then I saw Ron on the balcony above the living room, heading toward the stairway, and I excused myself to wish him a happy new year. "Later," I said.

Mark inhaled again. "Don't let it be too much later," he said, and winked. I thought he winked, but he got smoke in his eye, so I wasn't sure.

I caught Ron at the foot of the stairs. Ron had vision. His house was practically toppled when he found it, but he had gutted it and rebuilt it, and a few years ago, *House Beautiful* featured it as one of the best renovations of 1985. The two-story living room had a cathedral ceiling, and the second-floor bedrooms had interior windows—each affording a view of lower area. At parties, you could stand upstairs and see who came in. Problem was, Ron threw so many that the carpeting was already worn and the furniture was soiled and nicked.

When entertaining, Ron consumed enormous quantities of white wine—he preferred red, but said it was dangerous to serve red at a party for faggots—and he told loud, tedious jokes, with a breath that reeked of cheese and alcohol. As I approached, he started: "Chris, a Christian, a Jew, and a Moslem are riding on a plane, and there's this fly—" I showed my teeth in a fixed grin while others roared without effort at his punch lines.

Ron said he had a surprise for later in the evening and told me not to leave early. His surprises had become legend and something of a cliché. The latest porno star on the scene would make a surprise appearance at one o'clock in the morning, and then strip.

Before the party, I vowed not to do cocaine. I wanted to prove that I could have as much fun by having a few drinks. I went to the upstairs bar—so I wouldn't have to continue the strange conversation with Mark—and made my next two drinks soda water. Eventually, though, as more guests arrived, I became aware of people disappearing into the bathrooms—in pairs. I trembled. The determination that I had collected in my brain, short-circuited. The thought of doing a line or two crept in, then the more I watched them slip into the bathrooms or go into the master bedroom, the more I saw people coming out with big smiles on their faces, the more I felt my own face dropping. I approached two guys that I knew bought coke from Arvo, and asked them if they'd seen him come in. One of them said he thought Arvo had gone to New York for the holiday, so I hurried off to look for others who might be able to confirm or deny this. After fifteen or twenty minutes of searching, it occurred to me that I might be unable to get coke. I should have been relieved, but became obsessed. I went to look for Ron to ask him if anyone had brought blow to sell. I worked my way through a mob that was increasing by the minute, but couldn't find him. As soon as I got to one end of the house on the ground floor, I would head back the other way to the other end of the house on the top floor. The crowd grew, and it became impossible to move quickly through the house.

"Have you seen Arvo?" I asked Lenny, a hairdresser, notorious for his use of drugs.

He put his hand on my ass. "Nice booty," he cooed.

"Thanks," I said, moving out of his grasp. "I'm looking for blow."

"I could spare a snort. Would you be eternally grateful?"

"I was looking to buy."

"Can't help you there. Would a toot tide you over? Get you through the famine?"

"I suppose," I said and smiled, not wishing to appear unappreciative. "But you haven't seen Arvo?"

"Honey, the only time Arvo takes off his heels is when he puts on his boots to step on his coke. If I were you, I'd pass on his shit. Unless you prefer speed. Have a taste of mine so you'll know what to look for."

I followed Lenny to the bathroom and stood at the back of the line, but he took my arm and we went to the front. "We're going in next. Want to come with?" he said to the boy first in line, who immediately agreed, apparently feeling it was better to do someone else's drugs when able. Lenny pounded on the bathroom door and became generally obnoxious until it opened and three boys came out giggling. The three of us went in to take their place. Lenny gave me a couple of big snorts and then insisted on a kiss of appreciation. He pursed his lips like a guppy and I thought to myself, please don't let it be a wet one. But he went immediately for my throat pushing his tongue into my mouth.

The boy who had been invited in with us was more cooperative when it came his time to get a kiss, no doubt having ulterior motives. Actually he was attractive, though a little on the thin side, and Lenny broke from their embrace and studied him silently for a few seconds before taking out his bottle of blow again. As Lenny unscrewed the cap, he looked at the boy's head. "Your hair's thirsty; you should use conditioner," he said to him. "But let's get married anyhow."

I saw my chance and took it. I thanked Lenny and slipped out the door, then apologized to the first fellow in line. "They're not finished yet."

The gloom lifted at once. I felt great, but the old joke is true. After coke, you feel like a new man, and then you feel like a new man who wants more coke. I spent the next fifteen minutes searching for Ron, Arvo, or anyone who could put me in touch with more. If only I hadn't found any; if only I'd gone home and gone to bed. That's the best thing that could have happened. But, eventually, Arvo showed up. When I saw him, I pushed through the crowd as quickly as possible. Several of his regulars clustered around him: they hadn't connected with him at home, or had run out and needed more. I slipped him two hundred dollars for two grams and turned away, but he took hold of my arm.

Arvo amazed me. I'd known him for five years and he'd never had a regular job. He used to sell grass and MDA, but it was the eighties now and he had switched to cocaine and ecstasy. It also amazed me that he never did drugs himself. I'd known of several people who had tried to sell and eventually got addicted to the point where they did all their profits. I knew of one dealer who consumed two ounces one night with a hustler, then shot himself in the head with a .38 revolver. He'd been the sweetest guy before he started using. Successful dealers don't sample the merchandise.

Arvo said: "You know my friend Tim, don't you?"

Of course, I'd seen him with Arvo. Tim, a stocky blond with green eyes, wasn't my ideal, but was cute in a puckish way. He had red cheeks that made him look seventeen or eighteen, but he could easily have been older. He had a way of ducking his head before he looked a person in the eye—sort of like a dog that has an unpredictable and sometimes brutish master. Arvo had referred to Tim as his boyfriend on previous occasions, but this time he said friend.

Still holding my arm, Arvo turned so that Tim couldn't hear. "I'm supposed to meet someone."

"Here?" I said.

"Tim's hot, don't you think?"

"He's cute. Yes."

"It would be a huge favor if you would sort of watch after him."

"You mean for a few minutes, an hour? What?"

"Tonight. The whole night. I could throw in a couple of G's for the entertainment?" I glanced at Tim. There were already two older guys moving in. "He thinks you're handsome," said Arvo.

"Tim thinks I'm handsome? He's mentioned me?"

"He says he's straight. He likes girls, but he thinks you're hand-some. He thinks you're straight acting. I didn't tell him what a woman you really are," he said.

"Thanks a lot, Arvo," I said. Then, I looked over at Tim again. This time he looked back and smiled.

"Big legs," I said.

"That's not all that's big," Arvo said. "Deal?" He furtively slipped me two more Snow Seal packets, opening his palm quickly so that I could see them, before pushing them into the back pocket of my Levis.

"Tim, stay with Chris. I'll be back later," said Arvo. Tim didn't look disappointed.

Arvo didn't wait for an answer from either of us; he plunged into the crowd like a politician, and I took his spot next to Tim, who turned his back on the two that appeared to be competing for him. He put his hand on my back and patted, then moved in closer as if for protection. I asked him if he wanted to get a drink, and he ducked his head and gave my lat muscle a squeeze. We made our way among the people and approached the downstairs speakers. The dining room had been cleared for dancing, and the bass was so cranked it vibrated my body as we passed. I saw a bar friend at the edge of the dance area, and when he saw me, he blew a kiss. When he spotted Tim he dropped his jaw and licked the air with his tongue, and as we passed behind, my friend leaned over without breaking his dance rhythm and yelled. It was impossible to hear, so I mouthed "what?" He yelled again, dancing still faster, and this time I made out the word *adorable.*

At the bar, Mark was pouring drinks as fast as he could set them up, and had worked up a sweat. Our eyes met, and he pointed at one of the cocktails before pushing it across the bar surface in my direction. I asked Tim what he wanted and leaned in to tell Mark that I also needed a Screw Driver. He glanced at Tim and gave me a good-natured smile. Then Tim and I went back into the living room where it was quieter. We talked for an hour at least, and I forgot about the coke. Tim told me his Dad had kicked him out of the house for staying out too late, but after he got a job at Jiffy Lube, he'd let him move back home. It was an okay job, Tim said, but he wanted to go to DeVry Institute and study electronics. He said he was always pretty good in science. This felt like a date—an unusual situation for me—and it wasn't depression but more a feeling of fatigue that reminded me of the cocaine in my pocket. I suggested going to the downstairs bathroom, but when we arrived the line stretched to the library, so we decided to try upstairs. That line turned out to be worse, and that's when Tim suggested we go to my place.

"What about Arvo?" I asked. "Are you sure?"

"He won't miss us," said Tim.

We got our coats, with everyone else checking theirs, and slipped outside. We walked over to Clark Street to get a cab. The temperature sign at the Continental Bank read sixteen degrees, but there wasn't any wind, and I was so high that I wouldn't have felt it anyway. Our breath swirled in the cold and Tim, who had impressed me as quite shy, now chattered nonstop. He told me he had played hockey in high school, said he loved to skate, and made me promise to go ice-skating with him in Lincoln Park sometime. It was only eleven o'clock, a record for me: I'd never left a New Year's Eve party before midnight.

When we got to my house, we were careful not to make noise, because I'd been invited to a party that my landlords, Angelo and Clinton, were having. They lived in the main unit, and had been lovers for thirteen years, but weren't people I chose to spend time with. Their friends were unattractive couples who sat around discussing theater and opera. In my quieter moments, when I wasn't being dragged around by my dick, I enjoyed talking about movies and I even liked some classical music, but I couldn't help who I was attracted to. Tonight I wanted to be alone—with Tim. Besides, they would know we were doing coke and wouldn't be able to resist a chance to lecture; Angelo and Clinton were recovering alcoholics who had started AA after Angelo, the younger of the two, had fallen out of their Jeep on the way home from the bar one night. He had bottomed out at the corner of Fullerton and Sheffield.

I slid my key into the lock silently—since I hadn't bottomed out I didn't want to subject myself to their finger wagging—and motioned for Tim to step into the entryway. The door into Clinton and Angelo's apartment had frosted glass, and I could see shadows and hear people laughing in high-pitched squeals. Clinton was in drag—his New Year's Eve tradition. He wouldn't tell guests who he was planning to dress as before the party, and I overheard him once tell Angelo that the mystery guaranteed a good turn out. Last year he'd dressed as Cher, and when I stopped in for a drink, he asked me if his ass was flat enough to do her convincingly.

The stairs creaked as we climbed, but I'm sure we weren't heard with the noise from their party. I had a twenty-dollar bottle of champagne in my fridge. After peeling off the foil, I brought the bottle and two glasses into the den, where I'd sent Tim, and put them on the coffee table. Before opening it I went into the living room to turn up the heat, then after I heard the furnace kick on, I changed into a pair of gym shorts and found a pair for Tim. Back in the den, I tossed them to him, uncorked the champagne, and poured. He took off his Levis in front of me, and I felt a twinge in my groin seeing his chunky, muscular legs. He also had a rounded, athletic ass. Nothing turns me off faster than a guy with a good upper body and skinny legs. I've heard them called counter queens because they only look good behind the counter.

Since my middle rooms are the warmest in the winter, we were comfortable on the couch right away. I emptied one of the packets of coke on the glass table. We did some and talked. We just talked, although Tim sat close. He wore Canoe cologne; no one I knew had used Canoe since high school. It didn't even look like Tim had to shave very often, but in my euphoric mood this only increased my attraction to him. I verified his age, twenty, but he looked younger, and as was so often the case when I was with someone quite young, I began to make conversation as the older, wiser, more worldly person. Well I was more than a whole decade older; I had to be wiser. It occurred to me on a number of occasions that there was something legitimate about my desire for younger boys—something that wasn't exclusively sexual. A desire to experience fatherhood perhaps, a desire to teach, a desire to be looked up to…I don't know. There was no doubt that the sexual attraction was enhanced by the fact that I was in charge, that I was in control—and wasn't being pursued. Sitting there, I thought about Darren and imagined that if Tim were to chase me as blatantly, I would probably run in the other direction as fast. Like that joke about the country club, I didn't want to have sex or be lovers with anyone who'd have me.

Tim and I didn't have sex that night anyway. We talked and snorted and talked some more. I massaged his neck and shoulders and we held hands; we rubbed each others stomach to compare firmness and flatness, but we didn't kiss. Tim didn't like to kiss. I'm sure I could have given him a blowjob or something, but it didn't seem necessary. It was more like we were having a date.

He told me that he thought I was straight. When Arvo first started taking him to gay parties, he'd been surprised that they weren't all pussies. I liked his compliment. He used the word pussy like Mother used sissy. He also told me that I had a great build and wanted to know how often I worked out. I made some comment about how my torso was too short, my legs were too long, and I'd never been able to develop decent abs. I rejected the compliment as I did all positive remarks. I hated my body. His was potentially much better. He had wide shoulders, a small waist, and big legs from his years of hockey—

and football, which I learned he played as well. Tim was a jock. I'd never been good at sports. I suggested we work out together sometime and got excited thinking about how great he would look after he lifted for a few months.

We did the coke I bought, and one of the two grams Arvo had given me—the other I'd already hidden away in my dresser for another time. Tim said he had to go home, but we promised to get together soon.

"Remember you promised to work out with me," he said and disappeared through the door.

I thought about trying to sleep. Depression had started to hit. I thought about the gram I had hidden and decided to turn on some porno and do the last of the coke. I also thought about what staying up all night and doing drugs had done to my immune system, but that didn't stop me from pouring the white powder from the final packet onto the glass table. At that moment I wished I had two or three more so I could really make a night of it. Or a day of it. In spite of the fact that the house next door was only three feet away and that little light came in, the morning rays of the sun filtered into my kitchen from the back window, which looked out over the alley.

I put in the tape and settled back. I was too high to get an erection. I chose the film of the two steroid bodybuilders. The bigger one puts his partner across his lap and spanks him, then fucks him.

CONNECTIONS

We stand in front of the Van Gogh self-portrait. Misting rain and somber fog have driven us inside the Art Institute, where the voices of school children echo in an adjoining gallery. He doesn't notice; he's staring at the painting. His eyes and Van Gogh's the same—fervid and green—and this connection, I decide, accounts for his concentration. The children, perhaps a dozen of them, appear in our room, prancing and laughing until the teacher hushes them and herds them into a group. I watch over my shoulder, but he doesn't avert his gaze from the painting until they're gone. Then he tells me how Van Gogh cut his ear on Christmas Eve after a quarrel with Gauguin, who lived with him in Arles. One theory, he says, holds that Van Gogh suffered aural hallucinations: a voice told him to kill his friend. I watch as my friend's eyes travel the canvas. He recounts: Gauguin left their yellow house to go to a brothel, and Van Gogh followed; Gauguin heard footsteps and turned to confront Van Gogh holding a razor; Van Gogh regained his senses and then ran home and cut off the offending ear. I listen as he shows me with his index finger the angle of the cut—from the top of the lobe to the halfway point of the outer ear. He continues studying the painting, and I look at his ear, smooth and intricate. He tells me that after the incident, children taunted Van Gogh and threw cabbage stalks at him when he walked through town with his paints, and that the townspeople even signed a petition to have him locked up. What did Van Gogh and Gauguin fight about? I ask. My friend smiles and turns to me. We stand close. I can hear his breathing, but only our shoulders touch. No one knows, he says. Maybe Vincent was in love.

ဿဿဿ Chapter Three

BUSINESS WAS SLOW during January. Joey said things would pick up in February, before Valentine's Day, but it didn't bother him, because he only came in for an hour or two a day. I opened at seven every morning: Joey's idea. He said some customers liked to stop in on their way to work. I argued that people wouldn't buy flowers on Halsted Street, and then drag them onto trains and buses, when they could buy them in the Loop on street corners.

One girl did stop in early; she marched in wearing sneakers with pom-poms and carrying a shopping bag with her work shoes. She unfailingly bought the stalest arrangement. First thing, she'd ask about the price of some flowers, then point out that were practically ready to throw out. I tried joking with her, but she had no humor, which matched her lack of taste in flowers. I told Joey that we only had one customer, who spent three to five dollars, and I suggested that we open at nine. He refused.

Norberto came in at ten with flowers from the mart, and after we put everything away and cleaned up, we had time to talk. No matter where I stood he moved in close. In the black, deerskin cowboy boots that Joey had given him, we were the same height, and I found myself staring into his green eyes and at his cocoa-colored skin and thinking only of his peppermint-scented breath.

Joey spent several thousand on him for Christmas, counting the toys for the kid and jewelry for the girl friend, but Norberto gave me these details, not Joey. Joey pretended the relationship was business.

Norberto had his hair cut at the salon where Joey went and now wore a trendy haircut—long in back, short on the sides, with neatly trimmed sideburns—but before Joey started the makeover, Norberto had an unsightly patch of curly hair on his chin and a scrawny moustache. I had to admit—when Norberto asked me how he looked—that the improvement was outstanding. For a while, I couldn't pinpoint the difference. One morning he seemed brighter and happier, but I didn't figure out that the facial hair was gone until Norberto actually said something. He also confided that Joey was going to have pictures done to get him started modeling. Joey told him he'd get Skrebneski to take the photos, and Norberto kept asking if I thought "Bictor" Skrebneski was good. I assured him that he was the best, but privately doubted, even if Joey was prepared to spend that kind of money, that he could manage to get him.

Except for his crooked teeth, I didn't see why Norberto couldn't model; he had an interesting face with good bone structure, and the ethnic look seemed to dominate the men's fashion magazines. He had a great build too, and it had improved since Joey bought him a membership at the West Bank Club and made sure that they worked out together daily. Joey had slimmed down and firmed up too, and I attributed that to the incentive that Norberto provided.

Norberto said that Joey had come over to his crib for rice and beans that his girlfriend made, and then he and Joey had gone out to the clubs while she stayed home with the baby. Norberto wanted me to see his daughter. I was flattered, and though I didn't approve of his treatment of his girlfriend, I kept quiet.

"Joey wouldn't want me to spend time with you," I said.

"He wouldn't have to know, man," said Norberto. He winked, took hold of my upper arm, and squeezed my triceps muscle. "Big arms, man," he said.

The idea of intrigue gave me a rush, and though it would have been selfish to mess up Joey's thing, whatever it was, I considered it. The more time Norberto and I spent at the shop together talking, the more I became attracted to him. Most of the time, as I got to know someone I became less attracted to them. Like Tim. We worked out twice in early January, but because I trained in a straight gym I introduced him as my nephew since he looked so young.

In the daylight he didn't look as good. He had short, stubby, pink fingers and his nails were grimy from the Jiffy Lube. He also wore cheap gym shoes. Really I hadn't seen him accurately that night. When I was high those things didn't matter. Cocaine forced me, allowed me, to lower my standards. Tim called, once to tell me that his father had thrown him out again and that he was staying with Arvo, and then twice more to ask me to work out, but I gave excuses. There was no point. Nothing would develop. Besides, with Tim at Arvo's it would be too easy to get coke.

Since New Year's Eve I hadn't touched cocaine. I stayed home every weekend, because I knew if I went out, I'd see a dealer, like Arvo, and buy some. Like Pavlov's dog, I salivated when I walked inside a bar.

Saturday nights especially made me lonely. With a lover I could have enjoyed staying in and renting a movie, but by myself I worried. Cynthia and I went out one Saturday, when Louie had a friend's bachelor party to go to, and we saw the Woody Allen film where the man kills his mistress; afterwards, we stopped in Periwinkle's for coffee. I missed her and didn't think she would be happy with Louie. She was aware of my feelings about him, but as always on the few times we now saw each other, we avoided discussing him.

Weekends alone took away my courage. Going to bars had become a way to forget about Bradley. I never confided in anyone about my homosexuality, even though dishonesty and secrecy are counter to everything that I believe in. I needed my job. One time I saw *Dan the Dream* in Equinox, but I left before he had a chance to see me. If he had, I would have told him that I'd gone in by mistake. I also worried about straights who came into the bar, but I rationalized that if they were in there they were at least sympathetic. Except for those paranoiac moments, talking and camping with other gays in the bars was a pressure release valve—and something I now missed on my weekends alone.

When I realized that I wasn't handling cocaine, I told Cynthia, and a few times—after I'd been up all night and was thinking about suicide—I called her. I didn't believe I could really kill myself, but I thought about the concept of suicide. She stayed on the telephone with me for an hour and a half once. She told me to eat, suggested a hot bath, and reminded me that I'd feel better as soon as I slept, but mostly she just talked. Another time she rushed over and sat up with me on Sunday morning. Since Louie, I hadn't called her. Cynthia knew my darkest side.

That night at Periwinkles I wanted to be sexually attracted to her. She looked so beautiful that if I could have snapped my fingers and been straight, I would have. I couldn't help thinking life would have been, would be, easier. We sat at one of the uncomfortable wooden booths waiting for our cheesecake, sipping cappuccino.

"You remind me of a girlfriend in high school," I said.

"You never mentioned that before."

"Colleen Dimitrius. Blonde and pretty with a wonderful sense of humor. I was infatuated with her." I averted my eyes and took a careful slurp of cinnamon-flavored froth.

"You went out together?"

"She'd gone to school in Switzerland and moved to town after her father bought the New Harmony State Bank. Her father thought she was too wild in Switzerland. When she first came she didn't shave her legs and everyone made jokes about that. What is it about hair with Americans? Half the guys I know now even shave their legs. Straight ones too. They always find some excuse to shave their legs, swimming or bodybuilding or something. Even I think muscular legs are sexier shaved."

"I think it's silly," said Cynthia.

"After Colleen started shaving, she asked me out one weekend. To the drive-in. Back then, in our town, no girl ever asked a guy out, but now, it's probably not so unusual. I almost couldn't answer I was so surprised. After I said 'yes' I worried the whole week and got so nervous I wanted to call her and say I was sick. But I didn't. I didn't even have to ask to borrow Dad's car, because she had her own. She had the first foreign convertible in New Harmony—an Austin-Healy. I wouldn't let her pick me up. I was afraid Dad would say something to embarrass me and really I didn't want Colleen to see our house. She picked me up in front of the post office."

"How did the date go?"

"Humiliating."

"I'm sorry."

"She was all over me and I couldn't get excited. I even tried to imagine her getting screwed by the entire Prussian army. Finally, I got hard when I pictured her having sex with Steve Schroeder—captain of the football team and class president. But I was ready to quit when she was just getting started. She asked me out a couple of times after that but when nothing spontaneous happened, we became friends. We dated the whole senior year; we liked each other's company."

"And that's why she reminds you of me? Because we're friends?"

"Not only that. Cause I know we're compatible, and I think you're beautiful—like Colleen."

If I were attracted to women, she would have been perfect. For months I lay in bed thinking about her, trying to get an erection, but I couldn't. Then, the minute I'd think about Steve Schroeder, how his Levis fit his calves, how he looked in his football jersey with his bare stomach showing, and his big arms with that one vein that ran down the surface, I immediately got excited. I'd read that teenage boys go through a homosexual stage, but this was no stage. I knew I'd never really enjoy sex with Colleen or any other girl for that matter.

"If I were straight, I'd marry you," I said. "We'd have more fun than you and Louie. I'm sorry, I didn't mean that."

"I know what you mean," said Cynthia. "I consider it a compliment."

We talked for a long time. I certainly didn't plan on telling her I was positive; I didn't plan on telling her I was afraid I was going to die; I didn't plan on telling her I was as scared as when I lay in bed in high-school trying to get turned on thinking about Colleen. I wasn't sure a person should trust anyone with that kind of information. I didn't plan on getting emotional and teary-eyed there in the restaurant. It was quiet and I don't think anyone else noticed, but I did tell her. Cynthia didn't say anything at first; she just reached over and held my hand.

"You'll be okay," she said, at last. "Everything will be fine."

IN CONCERT

The fifth is his favorite of all the Tschaikovsky symphonies. He described this moment for me—the *Andante maestoso* section of the *Finale*—in the dress circle during intermission. The orchestra is playing *pianissimo*; there's only a vibration in the violins, a whisper in the reeds, a rumble in the bass viola. The acoustics in Orchestra Hall are legendary, he says, and we sit in darkness at the rear of the balcony, among the purists, where the sound is crisp and resonant; the tuxedoed conductor and musicians in black and white are illuminated in a distant square. I study the curves of cream and gold, the backdrop of towering pipes, the dots of light arching the proscenium, the red velvet of the seats. The maestro makes a sudden stab with his baton, signaling the transition to the coda, and the white head in front of me jerks. The motto theme is urgent now, no longer in the minor, but in the major. He rests his hands on his knees, leaving the armrest for me, and glances over to make sure I'm focused on the tonality, appreciating the bassoons and clarinets. On stage, elbows and arms slash the air; cheeks bulge; fingers dance. The timpanist strikes his kettledrums with wooly mallets; trombonists saw space with their slides; the conductor rises and crouches on the podium, swerving left, hovering over the strings, then twisting to point at the horns. But I turn to watch him, to see him. I consider the olive burnish of his complexion, the curve of his eyelashes, the serious ridge of his brow. He places his hand on my arm, looks at me, and raises his eyebrows. These are the final measures. *Fortissimo. Allegro vivace.* This is fate. The psychological reversal. He puts his mouth next to my ear and whispers. Defeat turning into triumph.

ಬಬಬ Chapter Four

MOTHER WAS DELIGHTED that I'd be spending a few days with her in Ohio on my way to Florida. The weather in Miami had been beautiful, according to CNN, which I watched nightly before leaving. Thus far, February had lived up to its reputation as Chicago's worst month, weather-wise, and one week before Ron MacNeil's Saint Valentine's Day Massacre party, I persuaded Joey to let me have two weeks off. For the money he paid me, I should have quit. Personally, it aggravated me that with all the real things I had to worry about, I was taking this job so seriously, especially since Joey didn't. All my life I'd had trouble changing directions; once I started something it had to be finished. Mother and Dad tattooed that rule on my brain. Daddy boasted that he worked at the brick factory for over twenty years before taking a single sick day. No doubt, that made it especially hard when, toward the end of his career, just getting ready for work sent him into fits of explosive coughing to clear the green phlegm from his lungs.

Joey didn't want me to leave—he gave me a dose of Jewish guilt—but I appealed to his more generous nature. If I went to Ron's party, I would end up doing cocaine and I couldn't stand another trip to my own special hell.

"I'm having a problem," I said. "I have to get away."

"I'll take you to a CA meeting, doll," said Joey. "There are some numbers there; you might find a husband."

I told him that after I got back I'd like that, but truthfully the idea didn't appeal. I'd heard jokes about people telling the same dreadful stories, week after week, and how the meeting was more depressing than the cocaine problem itself.

I took my car in for a tune-up and oil change and picked it up as soon as the dealership opened so that I could leave before rush hour. It infuriated Daddy when I bought my first Honda. It seems like yesterday that I pulled onto the Dan Ryan Expressway and drove home for the weekend to show it off. It was my first brand-new car, and what a kick I got. I was high and hadn't even smoked a joint. I squeezed the steering wheel, watched the tachometer as I shifted, and admired the orange color of the dashboard lights, which reflected my warm, sunny mood.

Dad's oxygen tanks were lined up behind the headboard, and he had difficulty getting out of bed, even for short periods. In my worst moments, I felt satisfaction seeing him so helpless. As if I'd won. But no one should suffer. He wouldn't get out of bed to look at the car. Dad was in the Navy during World War II, stationed on a supply ship in the Pacific; he couldn't yell anymore, but still had to gasp for air after he finished telling me about the Japanese.

"We beat the bastards, then built them up stronger." His eyes bulged. Feeling pleasure at his condition was a victory by default.

"Hondas are made in Ohio. In Marysville, Dad."

"Don't make no difference. They're the bosses. Don't you have pride in America?" he said.

I didn't bother with my arguments about quality or warranty, or style for that matter. He'd never change his mind—and he hadn't even heard of Lee Iacocca. But a couple of days after I got there, I went into his room and caught him out of bed, hunched over—because it made breathing easier—and looking through the window. "Should you be up, Daddy?" I said.

"You never said what color, " he said. "I wanted to see what color you got."

I wished I could have taken him for a ride. Cars were one thing my dad and I had in common. We loved cars. We used to go the showrooms to see the new models as soon as they came out. On Sundays we'd drive to the outskirts of Cincinnati to see them; New Harmony only had a Ford dealership and that was mostly tractors. "If you could drive it, you might like it," I said.

Dad didn't say anything about that, but his eyes puddled; I would be willing to bet it didn't have anything to do with his emphysema. "It's a smart green," he said.

I avoided going home unless Mae or Cynthia went along. And it got worse after Dad died. Mother nagged when Mae and I visited, but when Mae took Charlie home, Mother didn't make a single unpleasant remark. You would have thought she'd brought home Prince Charles. It didn't matter that he mistreated Mae; Mother knew Charlie was undependable and that Mae was always upset about something, but it was always Mother who made excuses for him. She was the same way with me; if I took Cynthia home, Mother treated her like royalty.

The Chicago-to-Indianapolis stretch of I-65 has flat farmland unfolding ahead, as far as one can see. It takes three hours, but with no scenery and few radio stations, I usually put in a favorite tape to make time pass. Once you get past Indianapolis, onto I-74, and closer to Cincinnati, it's hillier and more scenic. I looked forward to the drive to Florida, especially through Kentucky and Tennessee after my visit with Mother, but those three hours between Chicago and Indianapolis were the worst. The sky was cadaverous gray and overcast; rain would have been an improvement. But it didn't rain. The fields were frozen and lifeless. It isn't prosperous farm country—the houses and barns need paint—but in the spring, with green shrubs and flowering fruit trees, with the fields full of new corn and wheat, a person doesn't notice the shabbiness. That day though, there was nothing to hide the worn out barns and the dilapidated houses with their crookedly-hung storm doors and windows and the rusted cars parked in the yards, close to the highway, with *For Sale* signs on the windshields.

How many more times I would make this trip? Would I live to see forty? Who had infected me with the virus? As if knowing how and when it happened would make a difference. I couldn't change things now. I had been safe for a long time. If only I had always been safe. But I hadn't lived in a bubble.

I put in *Pictures at an Exhibition*, determined not to spend any more time thinking about something, which I couldn't change. Then I pictured the Pacman virus, chomping through my veins, devouring the T-cells that blocked its path.

❧ • ❧

I spent three days in New Harmony before getting back on the road. Mostly, it was a pleasant visit. Mother had cleaned out the attic and found an old picture album that I hadn't seen in years, and there was one picture of me at three sitting in between Mother and Dad. I had a big smile, Mother looked beautiful—her hair was done in one of those short, fifties hairdos—and Dad, in a suit, looked as handsome and prosperous as a banker. I had to admit I looked happy, but anyone could see in my eyes that I was going to be gay. Naturally it's not the color or how big the pupils are or anything like that. It's more the shape of the eyes and the way the lids droop, doe-like. They reflect confusion about how aggressive the kid is supposed to be. The eyes are soft. And in little girls that are lesbians, the eyes are harder, tougher. I know I'm onto something. A person can tell by children's eyes if they're going to be gay—if the person knows what to look for. Just like when I heard my voice on a tape recorder. I wondered why other people didn't recognize I was gay when they heard me talk.

Daddy saw it in me. He saw something and, in the deep part of his mind, knew. That's why he was so cold with me, why he never touched me, why he had trouble looking at me. He loved coon hunting. Of course, I had to take care of his dog; Daddy liked having a coonhound, but didn't accept the responsibility that went with it. I fed Humphrey and cleaned out his kennel and pulled off his ticks. My reward for tending to his dog, Daddy said, was that I could go hunting with him and his buddies when I got older. And before Dad got really bad with emphysema, when he was still in his forties, I did go with him a few times. Daddy belonged to a coon-hunting lodge and felt the same way about that lodge that Stanley feels about his golf club. Dad had also promised to buy me a hunting rifle. At the time, the idea of a gun scared me, but I didn't say anything. He'd have shook his head, called me a pansy-ass, and been on me for forgetting to feed Humphrey or whatever else he could think of. I heard older boys at school talking about how guns kicked back, how the recoil could injure a person's shoulder, but I was ashamed to tell Dad that I was afraid of guns. I wasn't a chance-taker: when other kids bent their knees over the limb of a tree or the top rung of a swing set and dangled upside-down, all I thought about was how badly they'd be hurt if they fell.

Raccoon season is in January. The last time Daddy took me with him and his friends, there were several accumulated snow falls on the ground, although a thawing spell had turned the top layer to ice before it turned sub-zero cold again. The paths along the edge of the field became packed, like dry ice, from several nights of hunting, and the ground squeaked under my boots, as we moved out of the clearing and into the woods. Mother had bundled me up like Nanook of the North, and when Humphrey and the other dogs caught the scent of a coon and began to howl and chase through the woods on its trail, I pretended that I was in the Yukon, alone with my pet wolf, White Fang. I hung back as far from the others as I could, to make my fantasy seem real. I did love being out past my bedtime, bundled against the cold and tromping over the snow with my breath pluming out before me.

The dogs got steadily more excited as the trail became fresher, and we moved still deeper into the woods listening for the direction of their baying. The wind pushed wickedly at us from behind, and since the dogs were down-wind, we had trouble at times hearing them. As I said, I deliberately stayed at the back, but when the hunters increased their pace so as not to lose the dogs, I worried about being left. My imagination had been so active that being alone in the dark woods—especially with the weather engulfing the trees and brush so furiously, frightened me. I moved to catch up, and then we all caught up to the dogs. They had been following the coon into a gradually deepening gully and we now found ourselves surrounded—by a steep slope of timber on the left and an overhanging rock wall on our right. Instead of barking up a tree, though, the hounds were directing their attention to a place in the ground: the coon had taken cover in a rabbit hole. Six or seven of the hounds, including Humphrey, lunged hysterically at the hole, and were digging to make the entrance larger, but it didn't look like there was any way they were going to get the raccoon out. It was Daddy's idea to use barbed wire.

We had climbed over a broken-down and rusting wire fence, not too far back, and Daddy sent two of the hunters back to strip off some of the wire, while he and the other men made a fire under the rock cliff. It was at least a twenty-foot drop from the top of the cliff to the base—where they built the fire—and the concave shape of the rock made a natural draft for the smoke. I was excited that we were going to hang out around the fire instead of continuing on through the woods, and when the two came back with the wire, the fire was going so strong and lighting the area so brightly that we didn't have to use flashlights.

Daddy made a poker-like tool out of the barbed wire and began to ram it into the hole to reach the coon. Every once in a while he'd pull the wire out, and about the third time he did, the men started yelling because there was a piece of fur caught on one of the prongs. The hunters pushed closer, urging my father on until at last there was blood on the wire and more fur. When Daddy hesitated for a moment and just stared at the hole, one of the men—a shaggy blond whose hair stuck out from under the flaps of his hunting cap—took the tool from my father's hand, and continued the angling action with more enthusiasm. He swore and cussed, his face streaked with perspiration, until the barbed wire actually dripped blood. The whole idea of hunting coons was to sell the pelts, I thought, so I didn't see how this one was going to look very good if they did finally drag the animal from the hole.

We must have been there at least thirty or forty minutes more, while several of the men took turns with the wire, but Daddy seemed subdued now, and stood away from the fire with his arms held limply at his sides. I sat on a fallen tree, watching the men at the hole and looking over at my father from time to time. Then, I caught him looking at me. He averted his eyes and said nothing.

After awhile even the dogs became bored, and despite the blood and fur, the men couldn't manage to get the animal. It got late—the hunters sat around the fire gossiping and telling jokes. One man (everyone called him Slats) talked about the woman who tended bar in Bing's Place, and I knew who he meant. He said her "pussy snapped pretty good for a fat woman." Daddy didn't show much interest in the jokes, but stood when the blond man dragged the raccoon out of the hole. It wasn't dead yet, but close. Everyone huddled around my father to slap him on the back and offer congratulations for his idea, but all Daddy said, without emotion, was that the pelt was ruined, but the tail might be okay. The coon was still breathing—its eyes were glassy—and that's when Slats smashed its head with a rock. The fire had died down; the dogs were sleeping at the edge, near the warmth of the red coals, and didn't stir. We roused them, crushed out the remains of the fire, and headed back through the woods and home.

I didn't sleep well that night. I dreamed. I saw the raccoon's snarling face as it burst from the hole with scared eyes and black lips, curled back to reveal its bloody fangs. The next day I told Dad that I wasn't going to go hunting again—and that I didn't want a gun. Using his most sarcastic tone, he said: "I suppose you'd rather sew dresses." Then he strode from the house, slammed the back door, and flew down the back steps. I didn't care. He didn't ask me to go hunting again.

Mother put away the album and turned on the television so we could watch the eleven o'clock news before bed. She had an opinion on most every story and seemed to feel a need to help me understand or put each into proper perspective. "Do you think your daddy ever got away with writing bad checks?" she said. Then: "Well, she had no business being in his hotel room at three o'clock in the morning," and "It's always the U.S. that has to foot the bill for the world's messes." There had been an AIDS protest march in Dayton; they showed the protesters chanting and carrying posters with slogans like: *APPROVE DDC NOW* and *STOP* AIDS *SUFFERING*. There were gay and lesbian couples holding hands or with their arms around each other, shouting and yelling, and I waited for Mother's remark, but this time she was quiet. I was sure Mother could hear me swallow. Our silence became the most powerful communication we'd had. Maybe she was afraid to say anything because of how I might respond. After the protest story, they followed with an item on a ten-year-old boy who had contracted AIDS from a transfusion of tainted blood; they called him an innocent victim of AIDS.

"That's so sad," said Mother, but she didn't elaborate.

CONSERVATORY

Dieffenbachia, ficus, schefflera, dracaena marginata: infinite variations of green. We exhaust our minds, matching mottled leaves and slotted shapes with botanical names on the lettered plaques, spiked into the ground at the base of each plant. I take a breath of musky air. We're alone in glass and iron: it's Sunday morning in the Conservatory. The suspended sprinklers yield unexpected drop of water; some splash our arms and faces; others roll across the surfaces and off the tips of tropical spears, fanned overhead in a jungle canopy. We round a corner, enter a new wing, and see an elderly couple ahead, stooped over the soil. The man steadies himself with his cane and turns to the woman, twisting from the waist as if a corroded spine prohibits his head and neck from moving independently from his torso, and when the woman cants her head and attempts a smile, it is only the right corner of her mouth, which moves. Seeing us, the man touches the brim of his hat. His skin is pink as if it has been scrubbed too hard with a stiff-bristled brush, and there are splotches of red on his cheeks. He twists again and probes the ground with his cane, and then offers his arm to the woman—but it is obvious that she is the one who is helping him. The synthetic sheen of his maroon shirt drapes his body shamelessly, and his checked trousers, I imagine, cover bruised and atrophied legs. They disappear around a leafy turn, and we step into their place to look at fragile, speckled orchids. Beyond the square, glass panes, lies Lincoln Park, its ground covered with frost, and there is nothing but bare, black earth to indicate where rows of vibrant, red cannas stretched to the fountain last summer. Inside this world without seasons, my lover looks ahead. He twists and reaches out to me with an upturned palm; his movements are easy and spontaneous. The sun angles through the glass, filters through the fronds of a tall palm, and falls across his outstretched arm. I memorize the network of beryl veins on his biceps and forearm, certain now that the shelter of glass and iron cannot assuage the blue from fading. I step forward. He rests his hand on my shoulder, and we walk on together without speaking.

ೞೞೞ Chapter Five

THERE WERE HUNDREDS of lounge chairs arranged in rows that led to the water—suntans on an assembly line—but most of them were empty because of the overcast skies, and I was disappointed not to see one single boy with a good body. There was only a hard-core sun-worshiping queen, dark as a chunk of polished walnut and wearing a thong, dancing trancelike in the sand by himself. I walked down the beach, twenty or thirty yards from him, and put down my towel. After ten minutes or so of lying on my back, eyes closed, basking in the occasional patches of sun, and enjoying the sound of the surf, I sat up to read. The exhibitionist had halved the distance between us, but I was determined to put him out of my mind, and so, took *Notes from Underground* out of my bag. Gradually though, five or six pages into the book, I became conscious, first of the fact that he was dancing toward me and then that he was looking at me, indeed was performing for me. After he kicked the first bits of sand on my towel, I gathered my things and started for my room.

Originally, I'd planned to stop in Atlanta for a night, to check out the bars and boys, but I suspected they'd be blond and hillbilly, like me, and I decided to drive straight through to Florida. I needed to warm my blood and knew that I'd find an abundance of Cuban boys in Miami. The drive through Florida did restore my spirits; the sunny weather contrasted so dramatically with the murky grayness of Kentucky and Tennessee, and I put down my window to allow the fragrance of orange blossoms to fill the car. I knew that I would be on my own; Paul was the only person I knew from Florida, and I hadn't been in touch with him for years, but that made the prospect of going out more exciting. All those smooth-talking Latins. The closer I got to Miami, the harder I pressed on the accelerator.

Joey told me about a restored hotel on the ocean that wasn't expensive—in the Art Deco District of South Beach—and I'd called ahead to make reservations. I decided that if I didn't like it, I'd change to another place, but Joey had assured me that the location was "to die for" because it was close to the 21st Street gay beach. When I arrived, an hour after sundown, the streets were jammed with tanned, prosperous-looking people, but I was drained from driving and lay down for a nap, thinking I'd get up later and go out for a drink. It's probably good that I didn't wake up; I wouldn't have enjoyed myself if I were overtired.

I took the long way back from the beach, past the bookstore where I'd gotten my novel, so I could get a gay newspaper. Drops of rain began to hit my face. Perhaps the weather was a blessing. Too much sun was bad for the immune system they said.

My room was freshly painted, a cheery shade of pink coral, and newly decorated. Not fancy—the furniture looked like the office variety—but the bed was firm and I had a view of the ocean. I lay on the bed and began to leaf through the pages to decide what bars to try that evening. I fell asleep and napped for almost an hour, but woke when the rain splashed from the windowsill onto the back of my neck. It wasn't a downpour outside, but it kept me in the room. That's when I thought about Paul Peyton.

We met in a Cincinnati bar when we were in school. I sneaked away from college on weekends to go to a club that operated on a three-deck riverboat. The boat, a fake, paddle wheel steamboat that was really diesel-powered, attracted gays from all over the Midwest. It disembarked at 10 P.M. to cruise up and down the Ohio, and then docked twice during the evening (first at 1 A.M., to let some people off and others on, and again at 4 A.M.). Being on that boat with all those boys was unbelievably exciting for me; growing up, I couldn't have imagined there were that many homosexuals in the whole world, and to find so many that were normal like me was comforting. I even made a few friends. Not guys I hung out with, because I'd only see them on weekends then go back to college on Sunday afternoon. If I didn't meet anyone with an apartment in Cincinnati, I slept in my car. There were times when I met someone who lived in a dorm at one of the colleges in town, and since they didn't have any place to go either (if the attraction was strong enough) we'd get together in my car or his. Many times I was too eager and ended up with boys who weren't really my type. Some of them would come after me, when they saw me weeks later on the boat, and I tried to be friendly while letting them know that sex wasn't going to happen a second time. Almost exclusively, if I got loaded on beer and pot and went home with someone, I never wanted to trick with them again. Paul and I became friends under different circumstances, and as a result, remained in touch for several years. He came to Chicago twice to attend dental conventions, but I hadn't seen or heard from him in a long time, and we no longer sent each other Christmas cards.

Paul used to have a successful practice in Miami, so I took the telephone directory out of the desk drawer and turned to the *Dentists* section of the yellow pages. Since I had nothing to do, and because I found the number right away, I started to dial, then hesitated. Was I making a mistake trying to get in touch with someone I'd known so casually so long ago? After two rings, a girl answered.

"Is Dr. Peyton in?" I asked. There was no response. Nothing. Had I dialed a wrong number?

"Who's calling?" she asked.

"Chris Hale," I said. "Paul and I were friends in Cincinnati. I haven't talked to him for a while and—"

"Hold on," said the girl, and I heard a click followed by music. If I hadn't already given my name, I might have hung up, because I now had serious reservations about having bothered. He's too busy, I thought. He has a life and friends that I know nothing about. He won't remember me. Then a man's voice, a gay voice, came on the line, but it wasn't Paul's.

"May I ask what this is regarding?" the man asked.

"Paul and I were friends once, in Cincinnati," I said. "We haven't seen each other for a while. I'm calling to say *hello*. If this isn't a good time…" Silence. Was this a jealous lover screening his calls?

"I'm sorry to tell you," he said, finally. "Paul passed away last March." I didn't say anything for a minute. There was no mention of AIDS, but I knew. Paul had died of AIDS. The man didn't sound sorry to give me the news. As a matter of fact, his tone was elated. I didn't know this person, so don't ask how I know he enjoyed relaying the news that Paul was dead, but he did. If I could have seen his face, I'd have seen the trace of a smile.

I apologized for having bothered him and hung up. I lay motionless on my bed. Depression is too strong a word for what I felt. *Sadness*, maybe. *Fear*, for sure. Paul and I were on the boat the night of the raid. The Coast Guard escorted us back to the public landing where television news cameras and city police were waiting to put us in paddy wagons and take us to jail. Their excuse: a liquor violation. The City of Cincinnati claimed the boat was under their jurisdiction because it docked within city limits, but the State of Kentucky said the Ohio River was part of Kentucky, not Ohio, and the Coast Guard said the river was under federal control. Neither Paul nor I had been subjected to harassment before—though gay bars were raided with regularity back then, and anyone took the chance of exposure if he went into one.

Paul and I stayed together that night. Luckily, we had jackets so we were able to cover our faces from the TV lights. My moment of homosexual discovery had been more stressful than this, because then I was completely alone and believed that I was the only person in the world that had been so afflicted. With Paul, a straight-looking, straight-acting college student studying to be a dentist, I didn't feel bad. I looked at him and realized that I was all right too.

After they fingerprinted and questioned everyone, they put us in cells. Paul and I sat on the cold cement floor in the corner. I smiled and held out my hands, palms up. "Do you think the stain will wash off," I said, "now that we've been caught in a place where men dance with men?"

During the night, one effeminate queen, dressed in a hand-knit, aqua sweater, screamed and camped almost nonstop. "Don't beat me officer," she said. "I'm sorry I'm a faggot. I'm sorry I suck dick." There was one young cop, hot-looking too, who stayed in back by the cells—more I think because he wanted to, not because he was needed—yelling at everyone, raking his billy club across the bars, and unquestionably fascinated by the whole scene. He yelled at the queen to "shut up before he got something in his mouth he didn't like." Paul pointed out the cop's expression and said, "You could tell he was aching for a homosexual experience." We both laughed and continued watching the boy in the sweater, and then Paul put his face in his hands and didn't look up for several minutes and when he did his eyes were quite red and moist. I couldn't find the words to comfort him, but after a few more minutes of silence he wiped his sleeve across his face and said, in a voice now edged with anger, that he was leaving the Midwest as soon as he finished school. He said he was moving to San Francisco, but ultimately he ended up in Florida after meeting a student from the University of Miami.

We spent all night in the cell. Next morning, someone, perhaps the man who leased the boat, posted bail and Paul and I went for breakfast. Then we went to a motel on Victory Parkway. We watched a television news report, and were relieved to find that we hadn't been filmed. Suddenly, without saying a word, Paul took my hand and led me to the bed. We lay down and put our arms around each other and stayed just like that. We didn't have sex and we didn't take off our clothes. We fell asleep, holding each other.

That night in jail, we hadn't slept. They kept the lights on—"to keep us from butt fucking," the cop said—so Paul and I told each other our life stories. We talked about how we coped with being gay, what our parents expected from us, and how difficult we found it to be around straight college buddies. How they all wanted to double date, how they were getting engaged and married at a time when we had reverted to high school behavior: having crushes on pretty boys and looking for lovers. I suggested that we had been arrested because we suffered from arrested development. Paul said the experience would build our character.

I'm sorry I didn't stay in touch. It would have been fun to meet for a drink and talk about that night. Part of my life was gone with Paul. A part I couldn't reclaim.

ֆ•ֆ

The desk clerk told me that Club BUZZ was the place on Thursdays. It was an old theater, abandoned for several years until an enterprising New Yorker turned it into a scene. Most nights were straight, but Thursdays and Sundays were gay.

Tired of loafing in my room, I showered early and left. One bar in my newspaper ran an ad claiming that they had the "hunkiest strippers in south Florida." The dark boy pictured was exceptional: thick, sneering lips and rounded, pumped pecs. I made a note of the address, but didn't need the number; I identified the place by the loud music blasting as I drove by.

There were three old men inside, each seated alone at a straw-covered canopy bar in the middle of the room, watching a flour-white stripper on a platform at one end of the dance floor. Tinny, flat music echoed off empty walls while the stripper, who wore a gold lame G-string, stomped his dirty feet. I'm sure he considered himself an exotic dancer, but it looked as if he were trying to kill cockroaches.

In the vicinity of BUZZ, the *No Parking* signs had so many restrictions, a lawyer couldn't have figured them out: *No parking between the hours of 4 A.M. and 6 P.M., except on alternate Tuesdays, when the moon is full, and the marlin are jumping.* The third time I drove past the BUZZ marquee I saw a tall, blond in white pants and cowhide boots at the entrance. He was a muscular boy with ham hock legs and a small waist, and despite his blondness, my heart rate quickened. I anticipated a great night and was glad now to be early, because the line the desk clerk described hadn't formed. He said they made guys wait outside and only let the *hottest* men inside. I checked my hair in the visor mirror and wondered if I'd worn the right clothes: black jeans and a long-sleeved black shirt over a tee shirt—in case I was asked to dance. Somehow, even in February, black seemed out of place here. I went to bars to meet men, yet didn't want to be conspicuous. I walked down the wide sidewalk, past several crowded restaurants; everyone else seemed to be dressed in turquoise or yellow or pink.

Outside BUZZ, ropes had been set up to hold back the crowd, but when I approached, the bouncer—a bodybuilder dressed in a one-piece jump suit unzipped from his neck to his navel—unhitched the rope and waved me past. Arrogance is required demeanor for doormen at these types of clubs, and he took great care not to make eye contact as I walked past and into the lobby. With a snap of his head, he flipped his shoulder-length hair around so that it came to rest on the right side of his chest.

Inside, the theater seats had been removed from the main floor, and the perimeter of the club terraced up with banquettes of cocktail tables and booths, separated from the huge dance floor by railings. Madonna tumbled from an enormous sound system, which, since few people arrived this early, reverberated off the walls in a kind of vicious inner ear torture. At the two front corners of this main level there were stairs that led to a mezzanine and balcony, and I chose the one on the left to make myself familiar with the layout. Most of the original seating remained in the balcony, but had been cleared from the mezzanine to make room for tables. From this vantage, patrons could sit quietly with cocktails and look down upon the dancers. The place was a smaller version of the theaters-turned-clubs that thrived in New York: Studio 54, The Saint, Palladium. In some of those clubs, the rear balcony was pitch black, so that people who wanted to, could go upstairs and have sex. Sucking off a stranger in the dark was no turn on for me, but judging from the crowds I'd seen in New York, many others didn't agree.

There was a service bar on the topmost level. The bartenders wore tank tops that read BUZZ BOY and I went to the one with big pecs on the right side. He set my gin and tonic down on the napkin without a word, so I left and went down the front stairs and to the lounge area off the dance floor. I'd only just sat down, when the blond I'd seen outside came over and fell back into the opposing sofa. He smiled—it was more a leer—and opened a copy of *Gay Scene* that he had taken from the coffee table between us. He had muscular forearms with amazing vascularity and I was embarrassed to look directly at him, but I did manage to smile back. After a time he glanced up and yelled over:

"What's up, dude?"

I always felt stupid making small talk, especially with guys who used words like dude, but I yelled back some kind of friendly acknowledgment, then looked at my watch and asked him what time the bar got crowded.

"Twelve-thirty or one," he yelled, over the music.

I nodded, and he slumped back with his legs spread. A short time later he stretched forward, tossed the magazine on the table, and stood to come over and sit beside me. He had ashy blond hair, a great tan, and teeth so perfect and white, I decided that they must be caps. He gave me a sidewise look and put his hand around my upper arm.

"Big arms," he said. "How old are you?"

"Not as big as yours." I felt my face coloring. "Thirty-seven," I said. "How old are you?"

"Old enough to know better, and too young to care," he said, cackling a bit crazily. He kept looking at me. His eyes were vivid and blue, but without shards of green or flecks of amber or touches of violet, and this flatness, this monochromatic quality, made me feel as if I were looking into the irises of a wax sculpture. I peered around to check out the club, and he said: "You're in pretty good shape for an old guy."

"Thanks, I guess," I said. Then he grabbed my wrist and looked at my watch.

"Are you late for an appointment?" I said.

"I was seeing if you were wearing a Rolex." He laughed crazily again.

"Are you a hustler?" I said.

"I prefer to call myself an Entertainment Engineer," he said, with a wink and a rather vigorous elbow jab.

Hustlers have always fascinated me, but I didn't recall ever meeting one quite so comical. "Do you charge by the hour, like a consultant?"

"Two hundred an hour. Hors d'oeuvres, not included," he said. "Pardon me while I go expand my client list." He stood up, stuck out his hand. "Name's Tulsa, dude. I'll catch you later."

I sat there for a while longer before taking another tour of the club. It was filling fast. That's when I saw Darren from Chicago come in through the door in the front—wearing a suit made him stand out more in case his height wasn't enough. He hadn't seen me yet and I was considering turning in the other direction to avoid him, when he started over. In a way it was good to see a familiar face, even his, and he'd been cordial the last time we met and I didn't feel he was interested in harassing me sexually anymore, so I thought I didn't have anything to lose.

"Christopher, old bean. What brings you to Florida? Sabbatical?" said Darren.

"Yes, the pressures of the flower shop were getting me down," I said.

He sucked in his cheeks, peered over his glasses at me, and smiled crookedly. Then he scanned the club slowly, moving his head in a 180-degree sweep. "The good news is, this bar is open till six. The bad news is, there's no decent after-hours place in Miami. Except for a raunchy bookstore in Coral Gables," he said.

"Six A.M.? Doesn't anybody work in Miami? This is Thursday. It's a school night, Lulu." I checked Darren's eyes to see if the pupils were dilated.

"We don't have school. What the fuck do we bloody care?" He had lapsed into his accent again; evidently he was still watching Ronald Coleman movies on cable.

"I drove straight through from Ohio," I said. "I've only been here one night. There's no way I'll be able to stay up till six." I considered saying more or yawning widely to make my point, but wanted to be somewhat subtle.

"Libation?" Darren checked my glass, but before I replied he added: "Drink. Cocktail. Libation."

"I know what libation means, Darren," I said, and stuck out my tongue to show how presumptuous I thought he was. I tipped my glass to get the last bit of ice, and we made our way to the bar. He hadn't taken the hint. Maybe he didn't have coke.

"Where are you staying?" He leaned back against the bar and peered at me. I told him about my hotel, where it was located and all, and he looked shocked. "My God, that place is dreadful. Why ever would you wish to stay there? I'm at the Grand Bay in the Grove. Top drawer. Holy shit," he said, looking over my shoulder. "Who the fuck is that?"

I turned. Tulsa was walking through the crowd in our direction. "The blond?" I said.

"No, the skinny one with the pizza complexion and the overbite," Darren said with a sneer. "What a delicious fucking body."

"Name's Tulsa," I said. "He's a hustler."

"I had no idea you had a taste for hustlers."

"It's an acquired taste. Like Scotch," I said.

"Introduce us."

"What's in it for me?" I teased.

"A toaster," he said. "Here he comes."

"Tulsa, I'd like you to meet a friend of mine. This is Darren. He has a Rolex. Tulsa loves jewelry," I said. "Especially watches."

"Darren Wedgewood. My family's in the china business back in England. Pleased to meet you." I had jokingly once asked Darren if he was any relation to those Wedgwood's and he had pointed out that his name was spelled differently. The next thing he said convinced me that he was high. "You're a big boy," he said to Tulsa. "Do you have a big cock too?"

"Like a jackhammer, dude." Tulsa winked at me. "Are you rich?" he said to Darren.

"Very. May I buy you a drink? Or would you like something a little stronger?"

"Like Sterno?" I said. Tulsa cackled, but Darren ignored the remark.

"Follow me," Darren said, taking Tulsa by the elbow.

"Not without my buddy." Tulsa hung his arm over my shoulder.

"Of course not. Of course not. I don't have it on me, though. We'll have to go to my hotel." With that he handed Tulsa at least two, maybe three, $100 bills. I could see there was more than one, but I couldn't see how many. "Here's a deposit," he said.

I thought we'd run to the toilet, do a hit, and that would be it, so when Darren took off toward the front door and Tulsa followed, my initial urge was to stay behind. The A-crowd had started to arrive, but at the same time, I felt a sense of loss knowing that Darren had coke. "I'll stay here," I said. Darren didn't want me along. That's when Tulsa yelled:

"Come on, buddy. I ain't going without you." He turned, walked the distance between us, and pulled me along with him to the front door. In his hurry to get out, he knocked a drink from one boy's hand and sent liquid splashing on several others which prompted them to chorus: "Asshole." I didn't like leaving the club so early—and in such a conspicuous manner. Darren tore open the back door of a waiting cab and motioned for Tulsa and me to get in. "Grand Bay, in the Grove," he said, "and step on it."

"Step on it?" I repeated. "Darren, you forgot to say `and follow that car.'"

"We're going to party hearty," Tulsa yelled, letting out a scream like a rodeo cowboy. The driver did a U-turn and headed down Washington Avenue. As we passed my car parked at the curb, I wondered if it would be all right for a few hours. Our driver, an older Spanish man, watched us in the rear-view mirror.

Darren hadn't said anything, since ordering us into the cab, and Tulsa sat quietly at last with a self-satisfied, almost simple, smile. I looked over at Darren, just a peek from the corner of my eye. He had an odd expression: there was no animation in his face and the corners of his mouth turned down, like maybe his blow had worn off and he needed more right away.

"Eddie Fineman's birthday is next Saturday," he said, in a soft voice.

"From Equinox? How old is he?" Darren didn't answer; he stared out his side window. "Is there a party?" I said. Eddie had always owned the hot clubs in Chicago. Equinox had been around for several years now and was his most popular business venture thus far. For a while it was the only place to go. Then, it was so in straights started hanging there too, but I never liked it as much as when it first opened, when the gay drug crowd hung out there, doing MDA, acid, ecstasy, and of course, coke. Eddie was there every night snorting up a storm, taking every willing boy he could get his hands on into his back room office for cocaine and a blowjob. He bragged that his record was twenty-six in a single night. He and Darren had been tight; drugs make for strange alliances. I'd heard Eddie was sick.

Our cab headed across the causeway; Miami's skyline of brightly lit, colorful skyscrapers stretched along the shore. "He'll be forty-nine, but he won't see fifty. Dementia," said Darren, staring ahead. "What do you get a person who doesn't remember you? What kind of gift is appropriate for someone who doesn't know his own name? For some- one who shits his pants and wets the bed and weighs 125 pounds and looks like an old man?"

"How about a case of Depends?" said Tulsa, with a chuckle. I smiled in spite of myself and looked over to see how Darren took the remark. He smiled a little too. "God, it's getting gloomy in here," Tulsa went on. "I need a drink. Are we almost there? Let's liven this group up."

"I say old sport. Quite right, you know." Darren was back, with the accent. "Life is for the living. Eh what?"

He spent the rest of the trip to the hotel talking to Tulsa in the accent—and as if I weren't sitting between them in the middle of the seat. It was classic: "My family has a home in the Hamptons. You sim- ply must spend a week there with me this summer. We can fly on my father's Falcon Jet. Where are you from? How long have you lived in Miami? How do you like it here?" Darren was a male pigeon, strutting with his chest out.

By now BUZZ was probably teeming with boys from more tropi- cal latitudes. What was I doing with anal Darren and this blond? I made up my mind to have a little blow, excuse myself, and get a cab back. I'd let the two of them party. I felt better when we pulled up at the hotel entrance, having decided to do this, and took note of the fare when Darren paid so I'd know how much the trip back would cost.

Seeing the opulent lobby with the vases of exotic flowers made me wish for a better hotel. In the elevator, Darren swooped over to Tulsa and tried to kiss his neck.

"I don't kiss," said Tulsa, stepping out of the way.

"How intriguing," said Darren. The 8 lit up, there was a flat bell sound, and the doors opened. Tulsa and I traipsed down the hall after Darren to a room at the end. And what a room: the bathroom had his and hers vanities, the bedroom had a king-sized bed, and there was a lounge area with sliding glass doors that led to a terrace overlooking the bay. A room like this figured to cost at least two hundred, maybe three hundred a night.

Darren tossed his silk jacket on the bed, went to the walk-in closet, and returned with a plastic Glad bag full of cocaine. Tulsa was bent over and rooting around in the mini bar for a drink—the first thing he'd done was grab Darren's keys to get the little refrigerator open—and as Darren walked past, he bent his head and stuck his tongue out like he was lapping at Tulsa's ass, then gave me a nod and fanned himself with his right hand.

I followed Darren and sat in one of four chairs encircling the glass coffee table in the lounge area. "Are we filming the sequel to *Scarface*?" I said, as Darren dropped the plastic bag on the table.

"Put out some lines, Chris, while I slip into something more comfortable." He pulled out his wallet and took out an American Express card—one of those platinum, Optima cards of course—and tossed it on the table next to the coke, then went to the bathroom. I opened the bag and gathered some of the powder on the credit card and put it in a small pile on the glass. Just thinking about doing the coke had my heart racing and I couldn't resist sticking my wet finger in the bag to get a taste. Tulsa came over, stirring his tall drink with his finger, and let out another whoop.

"Holy shit. Think we got enough?"

I smiled and kept on chopping until it was smooth, then drew out three large lines on the glass. Darren came back in the room in a silk robe—all he lacked was a cigarette holder and an ascot. "Really, Chris. Lines, not squiggles." He took the bag from me and plunged into it with the Optima card, drawing out at least two grams that he dumped on top of my lines. Then, he licked the card's edges. "Don't leave home without it," he said, gesturing grandly with the card before dropping it on the table.

He dipped down on his knees and began mixing the powder as if he were making icing for a tiered wedding cake. He made three foot-long lines, and like a magician pulling out a bouquet of flowers, produced a gold tube from his robe pocket. He handed the tube to Tulsa, who did one foot-long line in the right nostril and another foot-long one in the left. It affected him immediately, and he took off his tee shirt and unbuttoned his fly and sat in the chair next to where Darren crouched on the floor. Tulsa knocked his knee against Darren's shoulder.

"Take off my boots," he said. Darren turned and pulled them off one at a time, so slowly that I thought he might start licking them. When he was finished, Tulsa got up and walked barefoot and shirtless onto the terrace. "Let's check out the view," he said. Darren followed him outside and I helped myself to the remaining line of coke.

I didn't move from that spot for at least an hour. I sat back, did some coke whenever I wanted, and watched an even more aggressive Darren paw at Tulsa. He'd already spent several hundred dollars on his prize. Darren reminded me of a horny dog that keeps sniffing another dog's butt and trying to mount it, only to be repeatedly tossed off. Only Darren kept struggling to peel off Tulsa's Levis. First, he followed him outside, then inside, and then back outside again, but Tulsa kept his pants on. When Darren finally produced a jock strap from his closet, Tulsa agreed to put it on and take off his Levis, but he made Darren leave the room while he changed—though he insisted that I stay.

"Go in the bathroom and wait until I call you." Tulsa's teasing was starting to excite me. He stood up next to my chair, just about a foot away. I knew he was interested in me, but over the last few years cocaine had become such a mental thing for me that I preferred fantasy to anything physical or real. I grabbed Tulsa's leg just above the knee— to make him feel I admired his build—and said something flattering about his quadriceps. He flexed and gave me a wink. "You can come back in now," he yelled. "But you have to crawl." Tulsa fell into the chair across from me again, threw his head back, and made a short, low howling noise. "Check this out," he said to me.

Darren entered the room standing. "You don't listen very well for a rich guy," said Tulsa. "Get down on the floor and crawl here. I have something to show you." Darren dropped to the carpet and scurried over like a child on his way to a box of newborn kittens, but in his haste, caught his knee on the edge of his robe and ripped the fabric. He sat upright, quickly took it off, and tossed it on the bed with his sport coat. The instant he got to Tulsa, he wedged himself between the coffee table and Tulsa's chair there on the floor. He buried his face in Tulsa's crotch and grabbed himself with his hand. "Put both your hands on me; I don't want you to touch your cock," said Tulsa. Darren mumbled something, but I couldn't understand him with his mouth full. He was holding onto Tulsa's biceps now and slurping in his lap. He mumbled again.

Tulsa grabbed a handful of Darren's hair and jerked his head up. "We can't understand you, man."

"I said," Darren was no longer using the accent, "you're like a big football player."

"You like football players?" Tulsa pushed his head back down. "First and ten, again," he cackled.

SEICHES

The lake is black; the moon has disappeared. The shoreline and the city lights stretch to the south; the waves slap in darkness against the quarried rocks. Without this stone barrier that terraces down to the water, the lake would nibble at the shore and erode the beaches, claiming parkland and swallowing large chunks of pavement. During gale-force winds, when the water invades the harbor, capsizing boats and flooding roads, newspaper headlines announce that we've held back Lake Michigan too long from its natural boundaries, but when calm returns and the water retreats, it's as if the stories never appeared. This morning, before sunrise, it's cold and calm. Behind us cars drive down Lake Shore Drive, past Lincoln Park, at the start of rush hour. We try to count the high-rise buildings, using the differing tones and intensities of light to distinguish them from one another, but we lose track and conclude that there are thousands, each with hundreds of apartments. I like the contrast of all those cellular lives against the two of us sitting in spacious emptiness on the rocks. In bed I awoke to the touch of his hand on my forehead as he smoothed back my hair; he wanted to see the sunrise. He grew up near the Atlantic, and our predawn visit prompts comparisons to the ocean; it amazes him that this is fresh water, and that he can't see across to the other side. I explain changes in air pressure, how dangerous seiches are for sailors, how they can occur without warning. I provide details of winter storms and describe the great waves that splash onto the Drive and freeze, making travel hazardous. I tell the story of the loaded freighter on Superior, bound for a steel mill on the lake's shore. I use my hands to show how the ship seesawed up and down until its cargo of coal slid to one end, sinking the ship, killing everyone. I'm unable to remember the boat's name, but I tell him that someone wrote a song about the men, who were entombed forever in an icy coffin on the bottom of the lake. Suddenly the sky has grown lighter, and I realize that I've been doing all the talking; he's just watching me and listening. In my desire to make him aware of the lake's treachery, I may have given the wrong impression. I look out across the water. A band of orangey red now delineates the horizon. It grows thicker and deeper in color until the space above it takes on a rosy hue, which gives way to purple then to blue. An intense spot appears, indicating the position of the sun. The spot becomes a sliver, then a semicircle, and then a red disk. It climbs steadily, but we can only take quick, squinted glances.

ဆဆဆ Chapter Six

IT HAD BEEN three days since my binge at Darren's hotel, and I
was still unable to smile. Two consecutive days of almost uninter-
rupted sleep, hadn't restored me, and I was feverish and
thickheaded when I awoke. But then, comparing a cocaine hangover to
an alcohol hangover is like comparing a cat scratch to rabies.

After seeing billboards for several miles, advertising a truck stop
restaurant at one of the interchanges off I-75, I decided to eat, take a
room at Red Roof Inn, then get up early and drive the rest of the way
to New Harmony to spend a few days with Mother. I'd gone to Florida—and left without a tan—and my muscles ached as if I'd been
beaten with a two-by-four.

I watched Darren and Tulsa for hours that night. The three of us
did foot-long lines of cocaine every twenty minutes. Darren looked
pathetic with his face fastened on Tulsa's cock, and I joked at one point
that it would take a four-hour surgery to separate them. When I
opened the TV cabinet and discovered the VHS and porno, I got very
excited even though there was a live show before my eyes. Perhaps if
Tulsa had been paired with a smooth, muscled Brazilian, I wouldn't
have bothered with the pornography.

Darren had three newly purchased and unopened tapes, and I put
one into the machine. He came up only for air, and to do a line, and
paid no attention to the videos. I, however, watched the three tapes

over and over, holding the remote, controlling the action. In one of the films, a tall, sullen Latino dances for another boy, then they go into a park to have sex. I watched this film for hours, freeze-framing the action to capture the dancer's sneer.

Once the sun rose and invaded the room, I heard breakfast carts in the hall and people's voices as they stirred. I jumped after a particularly loud thump against the door, believing that housekeeping was about to enter the room, and got up to make sure that the *Do Not Disturb* sign hung on the outside knob. Where was the rain now that I needed it? Ultimately, I had to get out of this room and back to my own place in Miami Beach, but I dreaded the prospect of doing it alone. Tulsa hadn't done as much cocaine, and handled it the way I had when I first started doing it. He talked and laughed and still seemed to enjoy my company. When Darren arose from his position on the floor and staggered to the bathroom, his face was so contorted that I decided to leave before he came back out.

I gathered my scattered clothes (Tulsa had insisted that I undress) and announced my intention to leave, but when Darren emerged from the bathroom, I didn't look at him. If he had heard me, he didn't let on. He mumbled to Tulsa that he had a cock ring and some leather chaps and began to search through the bureau drawers. I took the opportunity to pull on my clothes, and then went into the bathroom. My hair was wet from sweat, my pupils were the size of nickels, and my heart thumped so loudly I imagined it could be heard outside my body.

I checked for my keys, and then remembered I didn't have my car. After saying "thanks," I went outside, first opening then closing the door as if I expected the Miami vice squad to be waiting in ambush. The hallway was empty. I started down the wrong way and had to turn around. I hurried past the rooms being cleaned, counting the flower repeats in the carpet so as not to face the maids, and made it to the bank of elevators without encountering anyone. I thought of Joey, I thought of my mother, and then I thought about Cynthia.

The *bong* of the arriving elevator startled me, and when the doors parted, I saw two stylish, older women inside, one dressed in peach and the other in lemon yellow. I smiled crookedly—the muscles in my face didn't behave any better than the rest of my body—and when the women moved back a few steps, I took a position in front of them convinced that they had immediately determined that I was high. My shirt collar was wet (I had combed my hair back with some of Darren's gel) but they probably thought I had the flu since the liquid was streaming down my temples.

Like at the end of *Death in Venice* where Aschenbach is sitting on the beach with black dye oozing out of his hair and onto his face. Suddenly it hit me that I might be coming down with Pneumocystis: I hadn't done a T-cell panel, despite Dr. Townsend's histrionics. For all I knew I might be getting sick at that minute. I should have asked Darren if he had Valium. I wouldn't sleep for hours. The women talked to each other on our descent; maybe Miamians were accustomed to being around drugs and simply didn't notice. It occurred to me that I didn't even know a hospital to go to. What if I didn't come down? What if I had to go to an emergency room? What if my heart pounded its way right through my chest? That's what finally got Daddy. The emphysema wore out his heart. I walked under the canopy to a waiting cab. There was not one cloud in the sky, not one chance of rain. Maybe I'd sweat out the drugs at the beach. A young couple in matching, turquoise blue and yellow outfits jogged past; I watched for a minute or so before I got in the taxi, then closed the door promising not to do cocaine again if God would let me get over this.

I wedged into the corner of the back seat—where the driver couldn't see me in his mirror—and announced my hotel. During the trip, I timed how long it took the traffic lights to change from red to green. Before I knew I was positive, I made it through periods of withdrawal with the understanding that, in a few days, I'd recover. I'd return to the gym; I'd get off the coke. It shocked me to realize that I had been doing drugs for the whole time since I arrived in Chicago. Ignoring the dangers. During the early years, the newspapers and television implied that it was chic to do blow. There were no pictures of addicted mothers then, or babies born addicted, or wasted people standing in doorways doing crack. Now that people were smarter, now that I knew the truth, how would I break a habit that had become a way of life?

At my hotel I groped in my pocket and pulled out a crumpled twenty for the driver, anxious to hide in my room. The desk clerk handed me the key and said: "Looks like somebody had a fabulous time." Then: "Are you okay?"

I threw open the bathroom door. I ran a hot bath and shivered as I undressed. I wrapped myself in the two worn, but clean towels the maid had left, thankful at least that I wouldn't have to contend with her. I needed rest, but my eyes were wide open and my body pulsed. Maybe the desk clerk knew where I could get tranquilizers.

I stepped into the tub of steaming water and sunk down so that only my nose and ears were above the surface. Then I slid lower and heard my heart's thrum, thrum, thrum. Almost at once I stood up out of the water, dried off, walked out to the bed, holding myself to keep warm, and pulled back the sheets. I went to the windows and closed the dusty Venetian blinds, though it did little to keep out the sun. I got into bed, and curled myself into a prenatal ball, and pulled the blanket over my head. In no time, the sheets were wet with my perspiration, and even though I'd put a hand towel on the pillow, it too was soaked. I trembled under the covers, trying to calculate how long I had. Cynthia had probably already left her house. Friday mornings she met Louie for breakfast. Joey would understand, but was never home.

I went from the bed to the tub and back again. I turned on the television; the Bulls were playing the Heat. I switched the channel and found an old movie. Nothing interested me. Nothing distracted me. Until I fantasized about a swaggering, muscular black man that I'd seen in Darren's porno. I imagined the man straddling my chest and slapping my face with his hard penis. Sexual fantasies dominated my thoughts for at least two more hours, and I still wasn't relaxed, let alone sleepy, so I reached for the telephone.

"Front desk," he lisped.

"It's Chris Hale," I said, my voice disconnected and hoarse. "In room 515." He didn't reply. He knew I was wasted.

"What is it, hon?" he asked at last.

"I'm sorry to bother you." I managed to stay composed. "I can't sleep. There was someone last night with…I ran into this person I know…I wondered if you—"

"Is it coke," he asked, "or Special K?"

"Only coke, thank God."

"I have Halcion. Will you be all right for a few minutes? I'll get Julio to watch the front."

"I appreciate it."

"Do you need to go to the emergency room, hon?"

"I'm mostly depressed," I said.

"I'll be up. Get into bed and think beautiful thoughts. Think about your favorite Lana Turner movie. *Madam X.* No, that's too sad."

My father died in bed. To the end I called him Daddy. How childlike. Dad is more grown up. Even the time he threw me over the footstool and thrashed me with the metal end of the fly swatter, I called him Daddy. I tried to talk about the beatings—to make him feel something—but he acted as if I'd imagined them. The second time Cynthia went home with me, I tried again. We sat on chairs next to his bed. He was propped up on pillows, pretty much confined by then. It's easy to identify a person with emphysema by the way their eyes mist and protrude from the sockets because they're working so hard to breathe. There's no elasticity in their lungs. They're suffocating, really. The tubes ran from the tall, oxygen containers lined up behind the headboard into his nostrils. Greenish-gray canisters, like military cylinders of poison gas. Cynthia patted his arm, and Daddy looked at her through filmy eyes. He said: "Chris tells everyone I used to beat him. And I'll admit," he gulped for air and his face reddened, "he got a spanking when he deserved it." Spanking he told her, as if changing the words could change the facts. I was embarrassed to tell people he beat me. Here I was—a grown man—saying: "My daddy used to spank me."

He made me plead; he made me beg for him to stop. I couldn't forgive him and yet I continued, the day after, the year after, and for as long as he lived, to call him Daddy. I should have called him the old son of a bitch, but instead kept right on calling him Daddy. Daddy.

There was a knock at the door, and I got out from under the covers and looked through the peephole. It was the front clerk, with a cart. I opened the door.

"Room service. Hot soup and orange juice. You need to replenish your body with vitamins."

He saved me that night. I needed to talk to someone; I needed to be nurtured; I needed a friend. I didn't even know his name, but he forced me to eat and stayed beside me. He listened to me groan and moan about how I couldn't stop doing coke. He gave me the Halcion, made me stay in bed, and remained with me until I fell asleep. He talked, he listened, and he massaged my face, and scratched my head. He had plucked eyebrows, and his cologne was overpowering, but I wouldn't have had any other person sitting beside me.

He took my keys and told me that he'd take care of my car. He'd had a drug problem himself at one time, he said. "You'll lick it," he said. "You wouldn't be going through all this guilt unless you were close to quitting."

The sign indicated that the Amoco truck stop was the next exit. I had driven without stopping into northern Georgia. I turned up my radio. A Chattanooga station. I'm not crazy about hard-core country and western, but the shit-on-me-baby-and-I'll-love-you-all-the-more theme of the songs was perfect for my mood of self-pity, and by the time I made it up the exit ramp and into the truck stop lot, I was crying so heavily I could barely see my way through the parked rigs.

ৡ•ৡ

Mother likes to sew, but she loves to quilt. She loves babies too and pressures Mae to get married. When Mae told her about the matchbooks and slips of paper with scrawled phone numbers that she found in Charlie's pants pockets, Mother didn't react. She wants grandchildren so badly that she's willing to risk her daughter's happiness. She aches to make baby blankets for her own grandchildren; she's tired, she says, of making quilted, wall hangings and blankets and comforters for everyone else's. She wouldn't face the truth about me either. She was going to hold out hope until the day she died—or until the day that I died—that I'd get married and give her grandchildren.

I was sorry Mother would live out her days with regret. Regret that her son died unmarried, that her son died childless, that her son died with AIDS. Mother is obsessive. She can't "forgive and forget." Daddy said that she "harped." But harps are pleasant, and there's nothing pleasant about Mother when she harps. She's scratchy and shrill and sometimes she makes me so sad that I want to run as far away as possible. Far away from her harping. When she gets something in her head, there's no amount of reason or logic in the world that can appease her.

One summer night after we got television I watched a variety show, the kind that was so popular in the sixties, while Mother and Daddy and Mae sat in the back yard. The house creaked with the heat of summer, but I stayed inside, my eyes fixed on the snowy, flickering screen, learning about New York and Hollywood. The show might have been Bob Hope or Garry Moore; I don't remember. The guest I remember: Jayne Mansfield. She wore a strapless, leopard-skin dress and had the most enormous breasts that I'd seen, although I thought even then that they were rather unnatural-looking. Of course I didn't care about her chest; I was interested in the pictures of musclemen in the back page ads of Daddy's hunting magazines. Mother came into the house to get a glass of iced tea, and peeked into the front room. One look at Jayne, in the dress, and Mother ran at the television and slammed the palm of her hand against the on-off switch. "What are you watching that disgusting woman for?" She spat out the words. These days Mother doesn't turn off the television or switch channels to another program; she watches as if mesmerized by a bloody accident. "Golden Girls" is one of her favorites shows and she sniffs with disapproval if the show is about anyone gay, but she doesn't stop watching.

Mother is talented. But she doesn't have the soul of an artist. She's a craftsman. She can cook with the best of them—and talk about a green thumb. Between her meals and her flowers, our house always smelled wonderful. No one makes better stewed chicken with homemade noodles and dressing. And her fruit pies have the flakiest, most perfect crusts. I always gain a few pounds when I go home and she never fails to make my favorite: apricot. There's an old tree in the back yard that bears a lot of fruit so she freezes the ones she can't use right away to make pies all year long. During the summer, her yard is beautiful with peonies, iris, and pots of geraniums and petunias. There are no fences, only shrubs, to indicate where one's property ends and another's begins. In the summer, people sit outside, on folding aluminum lawn chairs, and wave to one another. From Mother's I can look directly into Mrs. Epley's yard and at least seven others on down the street. Dogs roam freely and openly, and I think children would too, if there were any children left.

Humphrey's dog run is still there next to the back of the house, surrounded by lilac bushes now, and the garage is covered with morning glory instead of Mae's gourds. Every space inside the house has a plant too, and every window ledge holds several African violets. Mother can take a violet leaf, stick it in dirt, and make it grow. She is talented, but she's not an artist. She's too worried about what people think. She lacks the courage to be an individual. She's afraid of being excluded. The influence of a small town, I suppose.

"You would have left without a note?" Mother looked down into the pan of frying chicken and poked at a drumstick with her fork.

I sat on the chipped, red stool that had been a fixture in the kitchen since I was small. "You weren't expecting me, and I'm anxious to get home."

"I'll wager you could get your old job back," she said, still not looking up.

"Why does it matter so much where I work?"

"You had a prominent job. Why on earth would you want to fuss with flowers all day when you could be doing important things, things that matter?"

"What makes you think plumbing supplies and electrical parts are more important than gladioluses or roses? Nothing I ever did at Bradley mattered, Mother. Smelling a calla lily matters more. Why aren't you at the quilt club tonight?"

"We don't meet on Tuesdays anymore. Set the table, honey. Calla lilies don't smell."

"Narcissus, then. I'd rather smell a narcissus than prepare a report showing how dramatically sales of electric generators have increased." I got down the plates with the delicate red and yellow flowers that Mother had used for as long as I could remember. She purchased them, one plate at a time, from the Kroger food store in town. She was so excited collecting the dishes. I've seen the same dishes now in antique shops on Clark Street.

"I'm doing a lovely quilt. If you like it, you can have it. It's called the Rose of Sharon."

"Are you sure you want to give it away?"

"I've been making it for you—as a surprise. I didn't have it ready in time for Christmas. Wait till you see it. The colors are real nice." Mother put a pat of butter on the mashed potatoes and brought them to the table, then forked the chicken out of the skillet and put it on a paper towel lined plate.

"Smells delicious," I said.

"The green beans are canned from the garden last summer. I didn't put up many. Can't handle much of a garden anymore."

We ate silently. I hear people say they don't have much to talk about with their parents. Mostly gay. Married friends I had at Bradley said their parents didn't approve of the way they spoiled their kids, but at least raising children was something they had in common. My landlords, Angelo and Clinton, go every Sunday to Angelo's mom's house for dinner. Angelo's married sisters and brothers are there too, and Angelo and Clinton are treated no differently. They are loved and accepted in the family. When your parents don't know, or pretend they don't know, there's not much to talk about.

"This chicken is perfect, Mother," I said.

❧•❧

All those tiny, handmade stitches. She spread the quilt out across the living room carpet. It was beautiful; there was no denying it. All the repetition. How could she do it? And why? I asked her once if it was like some form of meditation, like saying a rosary, and her eyes widened as if I had accused her of practicing witchcraft or voodoo.

"Do you concentrate when you make these stitches?" I asked.

"Oh, I think about any number of things. It's plenty big enough for a queen-sized bed," she said. "Don't you think?"

My grandmother was a Quaker. There was an exhibit at the Gay and Lesbian Center in Chicago with a section dedicated to religion. An article on the board said the Quakers were the first religious group to declare homosexual love as morally equivalent to heterosexual love. I wanted to ask Mother if she knew that, but didn't. "Have you seen pictures of the AIDS quilt?" I said.

"There was a picture of it in *People*," she said. She began to fold up the quilt. She'd been making things for me and Mae since we were children. I wondered if she would make a patch for me when I died.

"It's so big now they have trouble exhibiting it," I said.

"It's disorganized-looking," she said.

"It's more like a crazy quilt," I said. She went to her room to put away my quilt. I used the lever on the side of the recliner to extend the footrest, and turned on the television with the remote. I could picture Art Linkletter in a chair like this, pressing buttons to slide it forward and backward. But it was comfortable; I was drowsy and it wasn't yet nine o'clock. She keeps the house at eighty in the wintertime and the carpeting is deep-pile polyester; after a day or two of sitting around and overeating, I feel as if I've been given too much Librium. I considered bringing up AIDS again—once Mother returned to the living room—and the next thing I knew she was tapping me on the shoulder.

"Go to bed if you're tired, honey," she said.

"I'm sorry. All the driving…maybe I will."

"Have you talked to Mae?" She sat in her chair and began to thumb through a magazine.

"Not since I left."

"She and Charlie are getting back together."

"For God's sake why?" I asked

"He told her he loved her," said Mother. Her eyes shone with excitement.

"I don't want to hear about it." I tried to sit forward in the recliner, but it wouldn't budge. I lay in the middle of the thing, helpless like a water bug on its back in the bottom of a tub. "I hate this damned chair," I said, and struggled out of it by climbing off one side, leaving it in its totally reclined position. "It's a lousy relationship. If he slaps her now, it'll only get worse." I went into the kitchen and opened the refrigerator door.

"He promised it wouldn't happen again," said Mother, from the living room.

I removed the cellophane from the dish of creamed coleslaw and took a tablespoon from the silverware drawer and stuck my head through the kitchen door. "You think she's doing the right thing?"

"It's not my business."

"You're so anxious to have grandchildren you don't care if she lives with a man who beats her?" I took a spoonful of slaw and swallowed it without chewing.

"He doesn't beat her. You're exaggerating just a little."

I came all the way into the room and stood over her, still holding the dish and spoon. "He slapped her, he's shoved her. He doesn't respect women. If Charlie strangles her someday don't come crying to me. I guess you'd feel differently if Daddy had slapped you around instead of taking out his frustrations on me and Mae."

"Chris, maybe now and then you and Mae deserved a spanking," said Mother.

IN REPOSE

It's an Indian summer night, and he doesn't want to run the air. We surrender to the heat, extinguish the lights, pile our clothes on the carpet. We're entwined in our under shorts on the living room floor, watching an Italian film; I sit close to the open window, propped against the sofa, and he's stretched out on his back with his head on my lap. The film proves hard to follow: subtitles compress at the bottom of the screen; key words are lost in the translation. Still, we understand everything. And I'm not really focused on the movie: it's enough to listen to the squeaky violin on the soundtrack and look down through the inconstant light at his face. His eyes are closed, his lips parted. His left hand rests on his stomach; his right arm is draped across my shins. I watch the movement of his chest as he breathes, taking this opportunity to study his body in repose. The flickering light transforms him: a bas-relief in blue and yellow and green until a shift on screen floods his body in crimson, accentuating the effects from an afternoon in the sun and revealing the patina of mist on his skin. There's roundness to his physique: the muscles curve into one another—there's spirit in his form. His neck, his shoulders, his chest, his stomach, his legs: I can't discriminate. I can't ignore his wrists because they're attached to his hands and I can't remember his feet because I'm looking at his knees. His boxers fit loosely at the waist, the white cotton clings and for a moment I consider arousing him, before deciding that the only proper thing to do is let him sleep to escape this heat.

ಜಜಜಜ Chapter Seven

I T WAS SUNNY and warm the morning that I decided to walk to work, but Chicago winters are tenacious; in April there's no guarantee that the snow and sleet won't return. I backed away from the curb as a passing car sent a spray of dirty water toward the sidewalk, and then stepped over the wedge of ice in the gutter to cross the street. The temperature, already in the high fifties and forecasted to reach seventy, would melt those final traces before the day ended, and at the end of the block, a forsythia bush was already in full yellow bloom. I broke off a stem before rounding the corner onto Halsted. White, round clouds, lazy and unthreatening, hung in a brilliant sky. Definitely, the worst was over.

I inched my way up the street, stopping occasionally to check out a store window for inspiration. A guy came out of one of the upstairs apartments and checked a mailbox. I didn't pay any further attention until he said: "Hello, Chris." I looked at him.

"Hello," I said, staring into his face.

"How are you Chris?" he said.

The hollows of his eyes were dark and deep, making his cheekbones too prominent, too angular. He had a jacket on, open at the throat, and under that a sweater, but his frame was considerably lighter. It was his voice, strong and clear, that I recognized. "Mark," I said, "It's nice to see you. Which way are you walking?"

"I'm getting a cab; I've been in the hospital," he said. "I came down with pneumonia." I stood, silent, counting on my fingertips the months and weeks since Ron's New Year's Eve party. Mark continued: "The doctor says I did really well. I'm already getting my strength back. I've already started working out again."

His appearance, so drastically different, raised so many questions: How did you know? What were the symptoms? Did you have any warning? Did you have a cough or a temperature? Did it sneak up on you, or did you collapse suddenly in the middle of a strenuous set at the health club? Instead I asked: "How long were you in the hospital?"

"Fourteen days," he replied. "My parents came down from Wisconsin and stayed at my apartment to take care of my plants and my cat."

"That's good. At least you didn't have to worry about things—the little things I mean."

"I'd been seeing someone—for a couple of months—but he split," said Mark. "My parents wanted me to come home so they could take care of me, but I'll be around to bury them." I took a step backwards, as if he had jabbed at me with his fist, and then he delivered the knockout. "Eddie died. Eddie Fineman, from Equinox. He gave me my first job in Chicago. Services are Thursday in Skokie." I said that I'd heard he was sick, but that I hadn't known him personally. "He got down to a hundred pounds and went blind," said Mark, and then in the next breath, added: "Let's go out for coffee sometime. Just to talk, you know. No strings. Just for the company. Still have my number?"

The air gusted, sending a chill through my neck and shoulders, but I stood in the middle of the sidewalk as his taxi pulled away from the curb and merged into traffic. Because of his bulk, bulk I now attributed to weights, I'd always thought of Mark as a relatively big guy, but seeing him that morning was, in a sense, like seeing him for the first time. Mark was slight and small. And then there was age. Even though I knew Mark was at least thirty, he'd always looked like a boy. He had good skin, a spiky haircut, he dressed young—usually in jeans, sneakers, and a tee shirt—and had the carefree attitude of a boy in his twenties. But the person who stepped in front of me on the walk was forty-five at least. In three and a half months, Mark had covered a span of twenty years. I'd never thought of him as thirty and suddenly I could see him as fifty—even sixty. How awkward when he furnished the details about Eddie. The irony of hearing someone so withered, speak of someone else's demise in such an offhand manner, was eerie. And I'd started the day practically celebrating that I hadn't done coke since Miami. Two whole months. And it hadn't been easy. I stayed home a lot.

After Dr. Townsend gave me my results, I never went back. I convinced myself that I wouldn't get sick; I rationalized that I'd take care of myself, eat right, and stop drinking. Since I couldn't be cured, I figured that it was the best thing for me.

When I came to Equinox, I stopped, pressed my face against the glass, cupping my hands around my eyes to block out the sun, and looked inside. It had closed in March, and stacked bar stools lined the edges of the room. The double doors leading to the dance floor were shut, so I couldn't see in there, but rumor was the place would reopen as a straight club, under a new name. Eddie divided his time between this front room, where he rushed forward to drool on the regular patrons who spent big money, and his private office where he drooled and snorted coke with the beauties. Looking at the soiled carpet, I could almost smell the stale cigarette smoke and sour, spilled alcohol. Haunted. The place looked haunted. Haunted by Eddie's shrunken, shriveled, drooling ghost. I checked the pulse in my neck with my middle finger, and felt my forehead with the back of my hand to see if I had a temperature, almost as if I thought I might come down with pneumonia before I got to work. I continued on up the street and stopped in Walgreen's to buy a thermometer.

At the shop, Joey was filling orders and Norberto was taking them to the truck. "Man," said Norberto, when he saw me, "who punished you? You look like you seen a ghost."

"I just saw Mark—I don't know his last name—he used to tend bar at the Loading Zone and before that he was bar back at Equinox." I looked at Joey to see if he knew who I meant.

"I thought you were coming in late today," said Joey. You said you had errands. We've got *beaucoup* orders for Eddie Fineman's service. Are you all right? You are pale."

"Mark was in the hospital. He had pneumonia," I said.

"Pneumocystis? No excuse for that," said Joey. He fussed with several stems of white glads and began snipping off the tips of the buds that hadn't come out yet. I taught him to do it—to reveal more of the color and make the arrangement more appealing.

"What do you mean, 'no excuse'?" I said.

"Obviously, he never got tested," said Joey. "If he'd been tested he could have prevented the pneumonia."

I picked up the stack of orders and glanced through them. "Maybe he didn't want to get tested because he didn't think there was anything he could do," I said.

"That was fine a couple of years ago," said Joey.

I had resisted getting tested myself. I knew that if I were positive, I'd worry myself to death. But I was worrying myself to death anyway. As they say: The suspense was killing me. I hoped I was negative—that's why I finally decided to find out—but it was a gamble that hadn't paid off.

"They can prevent the pneumonia with drugs now," said Joey. "PCP was killing everybody and most people don't have to get it anymore." I nudged Joey away from his position behind the counter and started to remove some of the baby's breath from his arrangement of two-dozen red roses. Then I looked more closely at the roses and tossed three brown-edged ones into the trashcan and replaced them with fuller, healthier flowers. Joey seemed well informed; was he positive too? "AIDS is like cancer," he said. "If you catch it early, you have a better chance."

"Are you going to Eddie Fineman's funeral?" I said.

"Don't be severe," said Joey. "I couldn't stand him. I'm sorry he had to suffer, but death doesn't redeem him in my eyes, doll."

∾•∾

The waiter put me in a corner booth and drew the drapes. "Mark's a regular," he said, and assured me that when Mark came in he'd send him over. It was still a few minutes till seven, so I ordered a beer. I'd walked past this restaurant for ages, but had never been interested enough to go inside. My booth, paneled in dark, barn-like wood, had chocolate-colored drapes across the doorway. The waiter—his nametag said Randy—had darting, gray eyes. He made two trips to the booth, first to bring water and bread, and then to demonstrate how I could summon him by flipping a switch on the wall behind me. There was a similar switch on the opposite side for the overhead light, except that it had a dimmer. The sign outside indicated that the Kasbah had won Chicago's Most Romantic Restaurant Award, but it didn't say who had sponsored the competition.

Mostly I got junk mail. As I went through it one night after work, tossing out the credit card mailers and sale announcements, I was surprised to find an invitation to my high school reunion—and a card from Mark saying how much he had enjoyed running into me. I felt guilty for having never called him, since he really was a nice guy and kind of humorous, so the next day after receiving his note, I called and suggested dinner. He said: "The Kasbah. It's too, too much."

My watch was a little fast, but Mark was ten minutes late, and just as I decided that he might not show, the curtains flew back and he appeared in the arched doorway. "Good evening and welcome to the Kasbah," he said. He looked improved and seemed more spirited. It was less than two weeks since I'd seen him, but he looked like he'd gained back several pounds.

"I thought you weren't coming." I said.

"You're the one who forgets his promises," he said. "I told you this place was a hoot."

"How's the food?" I asked.

"You don't come here for the food. You come here because it's so bizarre. They've even got straight waiters. Can you imagine?" He sat sideways, drew his right leg up, and put his foot on the seat. In the process of adjusting himself he sat on the edge of the drapes, and with a tearing sound, one side toppled down from the rod. "Now what will we do for privacy?" He wadded the material in a ball, shoved it in the corner on the bench, and laughed. He asked me how my week was going, and I told him that since the weather had improved, we were busy. He laughed, a mischievous giggle, as if I'd made a witty remark. Until that moment, I hadn't identified his tendency to laugh suddenly at serious comments and then remain stone-faced at jokes.

"How's Joey to work for?" he said.

"You know him?" I said.

"I always thought he was a spoiled, rich brat. The shop's a hobby, right?"

Randy appeared with two menus. "What happened to the drapes?" he said.

"We had an accident," said Mark. "I'm afraid I'm a clumsy cow."

"No problem," said Randy. He put down the menus, pulled over a chair from a nearby table, and stood up on it. "Hand me the curtain." Mark looked at me and smiled and handed the material to Randy. "See, they're fastened with Velcro," said Randy.

"How ingenious," said Mark.

"And ingenuous," I added, getting into the spirit.

"What do you recommend this evening, Randy?" said Mark, winking at me.

"My favorite is steak and lobster," said Randy. He finished repairing the drapes and got down from the chair. He opened a menu and pointed it out to Mark. The steak is a twelve-ounce choice filet mignon, and the lobster's frozen, but it's real good."

"Why do you like it so much?" asked Mark.

"Because you get meat and seafood," said Randy.

"You convinced me," said Mark, closing his menu. He rested his chin in his palm and peered expectantly at me.

"How's the Chicken Valencia?" I said.

"It's fine, Consuelo," said Mark. "Why do you ask?" I groaned, and Randy looked confounded.

"I'll have the Chicken Valencia," I said.

"Salads?" said Randy.

"Whatever you think. Surprise us," said Mark. "Bring us a bottle of chardonnay too." Randy left, and Mark smiled again. "I told you this place was a hoot. There's a girl that works here who's a singer, but she's off tonight. I came in here with a priest friend of mine, and he'd come straight from church so he had his collar on, and she sang 'Yes, Jesus Loves Me' to him right here at the table. He didn't know what to do."

"You must come here a lot," I said.

"I can't believe we finally got together," said Mark. "In a civilized manner, that is."

"I'm glad," I said. Something about Mark's behavior seemed vaguely flirtatious. I tore off a piece of bread. "You look like you're feeling better. I was a little worried about you when I saw you a couple of weeks ago."

"I'm excellent," said Mark. "I quit AZT."

"How long were you on it?" I said.

"Seven days. Long enough."

Randy brought our wine and showed the label to Mark. "Umm," he said. "A Michigan wine. Sensational choice, Randy."

"It's California," said Randy.

"I'm kidding, Randy." Mark smiled and scrunched his shoulders at me as if to say again: Isn't this place a hoot? Randy splashed a taste of the chardonnay into Mark's glass. "I'm sure it's heavenly. Go ahead and pour."

"You think a week is long enough?" I said. Mark frowned. "Do you think a week is long enough to try AZT?"

"Chris, AZT is a failed cancer drug. It was supposed to be a pill form of chemotherapy. Not everyone tolerates chemo. No offense, but do we have to talk about this? I'm excellent. Okay? Lighten up."

I took a long, slow drink of wine. "It's just that I don't know very much about all of this and I'm tired of seeing everybody sick," I said. "I mean had you been tested when you came down with pneumonia?"

"Chris, you're starting to get on my nerves. No, I hadn't been tested. Now can we talk about something else? After, let's go to Scream for a drink. They've got a new bartender. Hot, hot, hot."

He meant the new video bar. I'd been tempted for the past several weekends to go. I didn't bring up anything to do with AIDS again, and a short time later Randy brought our food. I looked at mine in disbelief and asked Mark to turn up the lights. "There's a hair on top of my chicken," I said. "A long, black, curly hair." I twisted toward my switch to call Randy. "Gee, Mark," I said, "such discerning taste in restaurants."

"Let me handle this," said Mark. He stretched across the table and moved the call button rapidly up and down several times, and minutes later Randy came to our booth. "Randy," Mark cooed. "Could we please have another bottle of the Michigan chardonnay and a hair net for his chicken?"

I couldn't bring myself to even take a bite of salad. Needless to say, on two bottles of wine and an empty stomach I was rather drunk by the time we crowded through the front door at Scream.

᪰•ᪿ

Why are doctors' offices so chilly, and why do they have you strip to your under shorts and sit on a cold metal chair to wait? After five minutes, I had memorized the contents of the room: jars with cotton swabs, stainless steel tools, an examination table covered in waxed paper, magazines from the 1970's. I heard someone take the patient record and clip board out of the holder on the other side of the door. There wasn't anything on my chart; this was my first visit to Dr. Jacoby. I decided to see him on Joey's recommendation.

"How are you today, Chris?"

"I don't know, Doctor. That's why I'm here."

"Peter. Call me Peter."

It's my upbringing. My parents were so in awe of doctors that they would drink paint thinner if one told them to. It never occurred to them that physicians are as human as anyone else—and that they make mistakes. Big mistakes. My mother never questions anyone of such authority.

I'd known Dr. Jacoby—Pete—for at least five years. He used to go to Equinox. I didn't really know him though, other than to see him and say *hello* quickly, then fight my way on through the crowd. Still, it put me at ease that he preferred for me to call him Pete even though I'd never been to a dinner party at his house or seen him at any social gathering other than the bar. There are three gay medical practices in town that I know of; thank God I had a choice and didn't have to go back to Dr. Townsend. Joey said he was sick—and very bitter. Joey said the *sleaze-bag* was exploiting the gay community, getting rich off H.I.V. They only offered the antibody test for free to get new patients. Joey said Townsend had a new Rolls Royce and had built a huge house on the lakefront. I don't know about any of that, but looking back, I know that Townsend's attitude was the reason I never returned: I couldn't put my trust in such a cold man.

Peter has kind eyes and seems like a normal person; he doesn't go around with his nose in the air as if to say: *Kiss my ring; I'm a healer.* I gave him my theory about clean living as the most sensible thing I could do to fight AIDS. "How you live is important," he agreed. "Taking care of yourself is important," he repeated, "but we can do more. There are options." I told him I'd heard the side effects of AZT were worse than the disease, and he told me not to speculate until we knew more about my condition. Then he said: "I don't want you to walk out of here and forget what I'm telling you."

"Not likely," I said. "If I believe what I hear on television, I'm not likely to forget."

That's when he explained the T-cells, how they could determine whether, or how much, a person's immune system had been compromised. When he mentioned AZT as a possibility, I told him that I'd heard it was hard on the liver and that it made a person pretty sick. He put his hand on my shoulder and told me to relax; he told me that we were going to take things one step at a time and that the first step was to do blood work. Then he pressed his frost-covered stethoscope against my back and began to listen to different areas.

"How are you otherwise?" he said.

"You mean physically?" I said.

"And psychologically?" he said.

I told him that I was depressed a lot, and he asked me if I was still doing drugs. I said that I wasn't, really.

"That's good," he said. "You should stop completely, Chris. Drugs includes alcohol too. Drink in moderation, and if you can't, don't drink at all." Peter examined my ears, then my mouth.

"I don't care that much about drinking," I said.

Then he asked about the spots in my mouth. He wanted to know if they were sore, and when I admitted how painful and irritating they were and said that during the last year I seemed always to have one and that they even made it hard for me to chew my food and that sometimes it felt like they went down my throat and into my ears, he wrote me a prescription for some specially-formulated mouthwash to use. He told me that I looked healthy otherwise; he hadn't found any swollen glands or detected any rashes.

"Any problems with diarrhea?" he asked.

"No."

"Night sweats?"

"No."

"Fatigue"

"No"

He scratched the prescription. "You're right, you know. The main thing is to take good care of yourself and relax." I nodded. "Kenny will draw some blood." Peter looked at me, intensely and without speaking for a few seconds, then said: "I want you to come in for the results so we can discuss things in more detail. Have Judy set up an appointment." He stood and put his hand on my shoulder. "Try not to worry. You can put your clothes back on. Just roll up your sleeve for Kenny."

Kenny is a sweet, hillbilly boy with freckles. His hands are rather small—I would describe them as delicate if it weren't for the fact that he chews the nails to the quick. When he first came in I was staring out the window at the dark clouds. He smiled and told me he recognized me from Equinox. He told me to make a fist as he swabbed the crook of my arm with alcohol. The sky grew darker, violent-looking. The clouds swirled and seemed almost to fold into one another. The first drops of rain splashed hard against the glass. The weather report called for *falling temperatures and late-afternoon thunderstorms—with the possibility of snow*. Too turbulent to be classified as an April shower. Kenny cupped his left hand under my elbow. He told me that he wouldn't have any trouble finding a vein, because I was muscular.

FLAVORS

We listen to Mendelssohn on the radio while we scrub potatoes and peel shrimp. After years of neglect my kitchen is alive: limp celery and darkening lettuce have been replaced by red peppers, crushed garlic, and nosegays of parsley. Each pan knows its place; every glass is clean; the refrigerator has a new sense of purpose with its organized shelves of brown eggs and yellow apples and smooth young cucumbers. There are bananas and oranges in a bowl on the table, baskets of potatoes and onions on the counter, a vase of blue asters on the oak-grained table; the cupboards contain bay leaves, coriander, cumin, and peppercorns. He needs the cider vinegar, so I break the seal, twist the top, and take a whiff before handing it over. Portuguese cooking is his specialty; tonight it's Pescada Asada: white hake, cooked in the fish-shaped, earthenware casserole which he purchased when I wasn't looking. As the nights grow longer and cooler, I plan life around these evening meals: the warmth of this space with its rising steam and chirring appliances and the brittle ticking of the hot oven are a sanctuary from what lies beyond. Different times, other spaces are irrelevant. After all the ingredients have been combined, when the pots are on the burners and the dishes are in the oven, we sit at the table and talk about passion till it's time to eat. I chew precisely to memorize the flavors, and when we're finished, we clear the table and stand side-by-side to wash the dishes. Then once everything has been put away, after the counter is clean and the table polished, we turn off the lights and leave. Some nights we stay in the kitchen so long that there is nothing left to do but go straight to bed.

ఞఞఞ Chapter Eight

"**M**AYBE I SHOULD keep on driving," I said, "all the way to St. Louis." The dash lights illuminated Cynthia's face.

"Better decide; our exit's only two miles," she said. "I'm still not sure why we are going."

I hadn't seen Stanley since I quit. I'd turned down two chances for dinner, two invitations to parties, and found excuses not to have lunch four different times. I took my eyes off the road to look at her again and said: "I always think if I socialize with him once in a while, he'll be happy."

"And he asks you more often. He adores you, Chris."

"That's a little strong. I made him look good, that's all. He said I was the company's best report writer."

"It's more than work. You're what he'd like to be: young, handsome, in great shape."

"And?"

"That's all I can think of. And I exaggerated about being handsome."

"You're funny," I said. "If Stanley would join a gym or start jogging…he spends weekends on a golf cart and wonders why he's fat. What did you finally tell Louie?"

"I told him I had a baby shower. Remember the shoes Stanley wore last time?"

"If you make me start laughing in front of them, I'll kill you," I said.

"You could see the outline of his toes. The leather was like flesh," said Cynthia.

We were laughing as I coasted onto the Bolingbrook exit and turned onto Route 53. Every possible fast-food restaurant exists within a two-mile stretch of this road, and as we passed the White Castle, I remembered the time I stopped to get coffee and ended up eating an entire stack of the square, onion-soaked sliders before continuing on to Stanley and Beth's for dinner.

When we pulled into the driveway, I saw Emma jump up on the couch in the front window. Beth and Stanley don't have children, but Stanley talks about Emma as if she were a child—I'd actually seen new employees at Bradley assume that Emma was his daughter. Emma is a Standard Poodle—not a toy poodle with ribbons and bows—but a big, hunting dog. Beth talks baby talk and lets the mutt lick her in the face. I offered my arm to Cynthia, and we started up the sidewalk. "Act like you're crazy about me," I whispered. "Maybe this will be our last performance."

Stanley opened the door, drink in hand, and Emma rushed out to greet me. She jumped up, paws on my trousers, barking in sharp, staccato bursts that rattled my eardrums.

"That's right. That's Chris. Emma remembers Chris, don't you girl?" said Stanley. "Say hi to Cynthia, Emma. Good girl. Now go fetch the martinis." He glanced at me and shook in silent laughter.

I waited for Cynthia to go in, then wiped my feet on the mat and stepped inside onto the white, sculpted carpeting. Their house, a split-level contemporary, is furnished in French provincial. There are white chairs accented in gold, dozens of mirrors, oversized table lamps, chandeliers, and paintings of Paris street scenes framed in gilded, ornate frames. The centerpiece of their living room is a white grand piano—with candelabra.

When I go to someone's house for dinner, I guess what's cooking. Usually, Beth and Stanley's house didn't reveal clues. Tonight was different; I smelled butter, garlic, and what I was believed was pork. Stanley took Cynthia's coat and went to the bedroom, and Beth came out of the kitchen wearing a frilly apron and a chef's cap. It almost looked as if she knew what she was doing; it almost inspired confidence. But I was skeptical. Actually I liked Beth. I thought she was a sweet lady—even if she was incompetent with the Cuisinart.

Beth is tall with long arms and legs and a truncated upper body. She wears her brown hair short and straight with bangs and, if one looks only at her face, it's possible to visualize her as a child. "Cynthia, you look so pretty," she said. "But then you always do. If I only had your figure. Sit you two; I'll get the munchies."

We sat on the couch, and Stanley came back in from the bedroom and went directly to the service bar on the dining room buffet. Emma plopped down at my feet, and I rubbed her head. Without asking, Stanley brought in two martinis; Beth followed close behind with a tray of hors d'oeuvres. "Toast points with caviar," she announced. After holding the snacks out to us, she took one and fed it to Emma, who sat up when Beth came into the room. All of them—Beth and Stanley and Emma—appeared to have gained weight.

I was feeling a little ashamed that I hadn't come sooner: Beth and Stanley were obviously trying to make the evening special. Surely he wouldn't try to get me to take back my old job; it had been six months since I left.

Beth excused herself to tend to dinner, and Stanley took the overstuffed chair next to us and started to talk about the office. He said that Bradley's son was having an affair with Donna—a defiant blond whose long, red fingernails prevented her from typing properly—and that Marty, the older guy who had replaced me, couldn't write reports for shit. But, Stanley allowed, he did try. Then, Stanley talked about his golf game until Beth announced dinner.

Stanley held the chair for Cynthia, and Beth brought in a beautiful roast. I was pretty sure she couldn't ruin pork, as long as she hadn't under-cooked it. "We're going to eat the salad last," she said. "Like they do in France."

"Beth's been taking cooking classes," said Stanley. "We're all guinea pigs. That's what you said, wasn't it, pumpkin? Or did you say you were going to serve guinea pig?" He laughed hard. Stanley has such a strange laugh. He doesn't make much noise; he mostly exhales his breath and bounces up and down.

"You're real funny, Stanley," said Beth. "Pour the wine and shut up." She looked at me ironically and gestured toward him with her thumb. "Ten thousand comedians out of work," she said, then in an official tone: "Tonight we're having pork, roasted in Sauterne wine and Juniper berries."

"Umm," Cynthia and I said in unison.

Cynthia asked Beth about the cooking classes while Stanley loaded his plate with au gratin potatoes. The food was unquestionably the best I'd eaten at their house, and I complimented Beth several times.

"I guess I didn't cook too well before," she said, in a good-natured tone. When a person compliments someone too much, they look at the other side.

"Who teaches the cooking class?" asked Cynthia.

"He's a big fag," said Stanley. "When I picked Beth up, he practically kissed me when she introduced us."

Beth tightened her mouth. "He's a very talented man," she said.

Stanley put a forkful of pork in his mouth and continued talking while he chewed. "He plays opera on the stereo while they cook. I'd keep my hands in my pockets around that sucker." Stanley started exhaling again and bouncing up and down. I looked at Cynthia out of the corners of my eyes. In almost the next breath, Stanley brought up the flower shop. "I'm going to come up that way some day and pay you a visit," he said. I couldn't imagine what he would think if he met Joey or what he really thought about me working there.

That was when Stanley speared a piece of meat, peered intensely into my eyes and, stabbing the air with his fork, said: "Are you going to tell us the truth tonight?" I almost dropped my own fork; Cynthia jabbed me with her knee.

Beth said: "Stanley, don't pry."

"No," said Stanley, "Chris and I've been friends too long. I want to know. I don't see why I shouldn't know."

I think for one instant my heart actually stopped beating. I know my mouth dropped open. I would have given anything to be at Oak Street Beach in the sunshine, or riding a bicycle through Lincoln Park, or driving through the country on a Saturday afternoon. I imagined I could hear Cynthia's rhythmic breathing, the sound of Beth's gullet opening and closing as she took a drink of water, and Stanley's steady chewing while he waited for my response.

"You got a piece of the shop didn't you?" he continued. "My guess is that with the money you took out of the company savings plan you could get about a fifty percent interest." He put another forkful of meat in his mouth, looked up at me once more, and resumed chewing.

I almost laughed aloud. I took a deliberate sip of wine and said: "You didn't think an astute businessman like me would be satisfied with less than controlling interest, did you?"

"You son of a bitch. I told you, didn't I?" Stanley looked at Beth. "I knew he had something up his sleeve. Why else would he quit the company?"

Cynthia jabbed me again with her knee, and I said: "When an opportunity comes along, you've got to take it."

"You'd better be careful with all those queers in Newtown. You're liable to get AIDS." Stanley exhaled another laugh, then reached for the bottle of wine and poured a glassful.

"Stanley, I don't think that remark is appropriate. It's not a laughing matter," said Beth.

"Come on, pumpkin, I'm not serious. They know that."

Cynthia drove on the way home, because she'd only had one martini and a glass of wine, and after Stanley's remark about AIDS, I got smashed. He wanted us to spend the night instead of driving back into the city. "We'll take a hot tub; we'll sleep like babies," he said.

I kept my window open, and by the time we pulled up in front of Cynthia's building, I had sobered somewhat. She wanted to know if I was all right to drive to my place.

"I'll drive through the park," I said.

"You're sure?" she said.

"I'm on AZT," I said.

The doorman came out to see if we needed help. Cynthia leaned across me and waved through the passenger window. "It's me, Cletus," she said. "Can I pull up there for a few minutes?" She pointed to a vacant spot just off the tarmac, and Cletus nodded. "It's late; we ain't busy," he said and directed her into the space. Cynthia shut off the engine and turned to face me.

"I ran into a bartender friend a few weeks back," I said. "He looked terrible. He'd come down with pneumonia. It scared me, so I made an appointment and had my T-cells done. Don't tell anyone what I'm telling you. It's between us. Right?"

"Chris, you know I won't say anything," said Cynthia.

"You told Louie I'm gay," I said.

"I thought he would understand. Anyway this is different. It's no one's business," she said.

"I only have three hundred and sixty T-cells," I said. "Normal's a thousand or more."

"I thought AZT was for people with AIDS," said Cynthia. She looked panicked, so I told her how they were using it now for anyone whose T-cells were in the 400 to 500 range and under. I told her that it made me nauseous from time to time, but that I was one of the lucky ones because some weren't able to tolerate the drug at all. I didn't tell her about the Pentamadine to prevent pneumonia, that I had to go in and use an inhaler once a month.

Cynthia wiped a tear away from her cheek with the back of her hand. How can women cry so easily? I hadn't cried since Georgia, and that was the first time in years.

�•�

For almost the entire month of May, I was to be responsible for the flower shop. Joey had gone back east to visit his older brother, a partner in a Wall Street firm, and immediately afterwards planned to leave for a ten-day cruise in the Caribbean. I didn't need him anymore. Joey lacks imagination. Until I came to work, the shop had mostly common flowers: carnations, gladiolus, and daisies. Gradually, though, I'd convinced him to diversify into more exotic varieties and house-plants. We now had delphinium hybrids, orchids, parrot tulips, cyclamen, gloxinia, hydrangeas, and cornflowers. I took control of inventory. When ordering, I paid attention to color, of course, but I also considered the shape, the texture, and the patterns of the plants. I mixed bold, lacy, rounded, arching, spiky, and sculptural shapes. I chose rough textures, feathery textures, and waxy surfaces. I purchased a mix of striped, spotted, and variegated leaves. We offered clay pots, ceramic pots, and realistic plastic alternatives. I bought humidifiers to make the plants happy during the dry months, and I must say that the shop looked very inviting from the outside. We had Boston ferns hanging from the ceiling of the shop, and in the bay window I did a display of potted flowers each week. What made the display different was my practice of keeping it simple: I limited it to one color at a time. One week, everything would be white: Flowering dogwood, gardenias, Shasta daisies, and Easter lilies. The next week I'd make it all red: Geraniums, roses, and amaryllis. Then I'd go to blue, then orange, then purple, then yellow, then white again. I even bought several books on ikebana, so I could advise people on flower arranging. I learned the names of the parts of the blossom: the petals, the filament, the stamen and the pistil. I knew the plants that preferred filtered light and those that thrived in the direct sun; I knew the plants that needed to be drenched and those that liked having "muddy feet." I had learned how and when, and with what food, to feed the plants, and I cautioned our customers to be good to their new plants, but stopped short of suggesting that they sing to or play music for them.

We had new customers who lived in the high-rises on Lake Shore Drive and Sheridan Road—a more discerning clientele to go with the regulars who came in to get daily bouquets or weekly arrangements—but no matter how much we grew, the big money wasn't in our immediate neighborhood of restaurants and gay bars. So I suggested opening a second store, downtown in one of the new buildings on Michigan Avenue. Dinner at Stanley and Beth's gave me the idea of investing my profit sharing money from Bradley. When I suggested that we go fifty-fifty in the new store, Joey made reservations to go home to get his brother to back him.

Joey had hired an elderly man with a German accent and body odor, Walter, to make deliveries; he replaced Norberto, who stayed inside now. These days Norberto looked great. He got weekly manicures and monthly haircuts, he went to the gym six days a week, he had several pairs of shoes and boots, a closet full of silk shirts, and during April, he got his teeth fixed. Joey sent him to the best dentist in the city. Nothing should stop Norberto now in his desire to become a model, though Joey had recently shown some concern that Norberto might be able to become one without his help. He came back from errands one day and found Norberto talking with Cal Durocher, a fashion photographer. At forty-one, Cal was already a *dirty old man*. He didn't take many pictures of girls, and the ones he took of boys were nudes.

I'd seen Norberto talking to him twice, but this was the first time Joey had seen him. Norberto told me that Cal wanted to do body shots some weekend and he asked me what I thought. I told Norberto there were better photographers in town, and in my opinion, there were. He wasn't interested in helping Norberto—though for that matter neither was Joey. Cal was interested in a few voyeuristic thrills. I hadn't mentioned to Joey that Norberto and Cal talked, but after the time he saw Norberto standing close to him, in the back of the store behind the fishtail palms, there was tension between them. Joey never said so, but I believe the incident was the reason he didn't take Norberto on the cruise: to teach him a lesson.

One night while Joey was away, and after Walter had gone home for the night, Norberto and I were alone in the shop. We had just about finished cleaning up when he asked me if I wanted to come to his house to eat. His girlfriend, he said, had made rice and beans.

As I drove past Clemente High School on Western Avenue, Norberto told me that he'd played outfield on the baseball team. "You want to see the Cubs sometime?" he said. I made the turns, as he directed, and pulled into an empty space in front of a four-story, brick building. Norberto lives in a rowdy neighborhood; the streets were filled with waterlogged paper trash, and my tires crunched over broken glass as I inched to the curb. His was the only building left on this particular block, and six or seven teenaged boys stood around smoking and drinking in the empty lot next door.

The building's security system, a rusted panel of tiny black buttons, preprinted numbers, and names written in pencil, was broken, and he didn't use the buzzer or intercom to gain entry; he simply pushed open the door and motioned me inside. Norberto and his girlfriend lived in a front unit on the uppermost floor, and when we got to the top of the stairs I saw that his apartment door was ajar as well. The smell of cooking onions in the hall made me hungry.

Lydia met us at the door. She's small, nineteen or twenty I think, and very pretty in a natural way. She doesn't wear make-up, except for lipstick. She has long eyelashes, full lips, thick eyebrows, and a beauty mark on her cheek, close to her mouth. She came into the shop once to see Norberto and wasn't wearing make-up then either. She works in an office downtown as a receptionist; Norberto said she took college classes for a while.

"Chris, come see my daughter," said Norberto. He directed me to a crib over by a space heater in the corner. The apartment was sparsely furnished, but neat and homey. Lydia stood in front of the TV for minute watching "Wheel of Fortune" and when the buzzer indicated that there was no *C* she looked up from the set and said: "That woman whose teeth stick out, she's stupid. They already asked for a *C*. You two want beers?"

"Yeah, get us some beers, baby," Norberto said. He lifted his daughter from the crib and she smiled as if she recognized him, although it seemed she was barely old enough. "Celia, say hi to my buddy, Chris." He started to hand her to me.

"No," I said. "She's too small."

"You won't drop her." He pushed her at me, and I reluctantly took the beautiful, brown girl bundled in pink. Both ears were pierced and she had gold posts. She smiled at me too, but I thought I detected a slight difference now that I held her. She looked puzzled, wrinkling her forehead into a frown. "Sit in this chair." Norberto patted the arm of the worn, upholstered lounger that matched the sofa.

I sat, rigid and not relaxed, holding Celia. "Who takes care of her during the day?" I asked.

"Lydia's mother," said Norberto.

"She seems like a good baby," I said.

"She's been quiet-like ever since she was born," said Norberto. I wondered if they always kept the apartment so hot. It was relatively warm outside, maybe fifty-five or so, but it had to be eighty-five or ninety here in the living room next to the space heater. First I noticed how close the crib was to the heater and then I saw that the vent pipe, leading from the stove and into the flue next to the ceiling, gaped open at the right angle elbow where it connected into the chimney. I told Norberto that the gap was probably letting fumes into the room, and suggested he ought to get it fixed. I told him it wasn't healthy. "I never noticed it," said Norberto.

Lydia came in and asked if we wanted to eat in the living room, so we could watch television. "Did you call about the water heater?" said Norberto.

"I called him; he said he'd check it out as soon as he could," said Lydia.

"Have him check out that pipe too," said Norberto, pointing to the elbow.

"You can make a call too, you know, Norberto. You got fingers," said Lydia. "Set up the trays, okay?"

Norberto got two trays from the closet and unfolded them. He put one in front of the couch and one in front of me. Celia seemed quite comfortable in my arms. As a rule, when I hold a baby, it starts to squirm.

"Back to bed, baby," said Norberto. He took her from me and returned her to the crib.

Lydia asked if I wanted another beer as she put the plate of rice, beans, and shredded meat in front of me. "Carñitas," she said. "My mama made a big, pork roast last Sunday. You're not Jewish or nothing?" My plate was piled high, with enough food for three people.

"I love pork," I said. "Aren't you eating?"

"I ate when Mama was here," she said. "I never know when Norberto is coming home, so I eat." If this bothered her, nothing in her voice gave her away. She seemed so accommodating. I wondered if she ever mentioned marriage. I told her that the carñitas were delicious and thanked her for having me. "I like Norberto's friends to come over," she said. "Especially the polite ones like you." She smiled. Did this include Joey? "I got flan," said Lydia. She went to the crib and picked up Celia, though the baby had yet to make a sound.

After supper, Norberto wanted to take me to a bar called *Agua Caliente* where some friends played in a band on Wednesday nights. And Lydia hadn't flinched; she smiled and thanked me for the fifth time for coming.

"My buddies from high school," said Norberto, as he indicated a parking spot on Damen Avenue. "We used to gang-bang together."

"Were you a Latin King?"

"I wasn't in no gang. We were hanging at my bro's crib and got shot at. In the middle of the day these dudes are shooting at us. I knew I didn't want to be no King." I asked him what he meant exactly by gang-banging. "Hang out with your friends," said Norberto. I said that I always thought that meant when a bunch of guys screwed the same girl. "Yeah? That right?" he said, as if he thought I was having fun with him.

I locked the car and stepped onto the curb. "I have to open tomorrow. I can't stay late; it's already ten-thirty."

"After you meet my buddies, we can watch the tube at your place," he said. Before I could say more, he opened the door to the bar.

It was nearly empty inside; at the back of the room, a few guys were up on a makeshift stage talking and laughing. The bar looked like a pool hall with the tables removed. "Come on." Norberto tugged at my arm. He led me down an aisle through two rows of Formica-covered tables to the boys. There were five members in the group and, as Norberto introduced them, each told me what instrument he played. One, a small boy not much more five feet tall, the drummer, nudged Norberto. "You going to sing a couple numbers, Norberto?" he said.

"Not me. I ain't working tonight. Me and Chris are chilling. Right, Chris?"

"Man, you got to sing 'Perico'," the boy said.

"Yeah, Norberto. Sing one song," another insisted.

"'Perico.'"

"Yeah, 'Perico'."

"We got to leave," said Norberto.

"Let's do a warm-up," the drummer suggested.

"Cool, man," the others said.

"Yeah, that's cool," another agreed. "Sing 'Perico' for Chris."

Norberto smiled. "'Perico'." And that's it."

The drummer smiled too and motioned me to the first table. I sat down and a girl came over with a tray of beers. She popped her gum and smiled at me, then placed one bottle in front of me and left another for Norberto. The band, which now included him, huddled and tuned-up.

When I try to recall the exact hour after Norberto and the band performed *Perico* for me and I sat like royalty at a command performance—I can't. What I know is that I somehow became complicit in the plan to get cocaine. I never studied Spanish, and even if I had, I probably would have translated perico in the traditional way.

"Cocaine, baby," Norberto said to me. "A *perico* is a little bird. A parakeet. A parakeet that moves *muy rapido*. Like a person on cocaine." He scooped up a pile on the corner of my credit card. "Open your mouth, baby." He blew the powder into my mouth and throat and I washed it down with my saliva. It's amazing how disgusting I used to think coke tasted. It tasted pretty good, sitting across from a beauty like Norberto.

My apartment felt chilly—maybe it was the coke—so I got up to adjust the heat. It seemed stupid to hear a grown, straight man like Norberto call me baby. Latins were like that often. I wasn't sure what that was all about or why it secretly pleased me and made me feel warm. It was touching—this kind of affection. It wasn't sexual. It was the way a man talks to a little boy.

I didn't plan to have sex with Norberto. It just happened. I knew I'd feel guilty the next morning. I knew it was wrong, but I felt so connected at that moment that I didn't care about anything or anyone else. Not Joey. I was filling my own needs—whatever they were.

∽•∾

The girl with the gym shoes and brief case came in at her usual time for flowers. Seven-thirty. She'd been coming in every weekday morning for six months and we'd become conversational. The difference in Annette occurred over time as I improved the store. One morning about a month ago, she'd stuck out her hand, introduced herself, and said: "I think what you've done here is exquisite." On this morning she chose a simple, elegant arrangement of Dutch irises and golden marguerites.

I tried to make intelligent conversation, but I was slow-witted from the coke and relieved when she left. A night without sleep couldn't have helped me, but I took comfort in the fact that I'd been safe with Norberto. I didn't want to weigh down my conscience with guilt over having exposed someone to my condition. He wanted to screw me, but I had talked him into oral sex. From all I had heard or read, he couldn't catch the virus if he penetrated me—only if penetrated. That wasn't going to happen. Somehow in the Puerto Rican culture—at least those I'd known in the States—screwing a man was acceptable masculine behavior. As long as he was the aggressor, he wouldn't be considered gay.

Norberto swore that he'd never had any sexual contact with Joey or done drugs around him, and was concerned that I would mention that we had. I had no intention of talking about what we'd done. Norberto didn't seem tired or depressed; he whistled as he prepared Walter's morning deliveries, and every time he walked past he touched my ass—as if to remind me of his promise to get what he wanted sooner or later. At one point, when Walter walked in from the back, I'm sure he saw Norberto grab me.

At exactly eight o'clock, nine o'clock New York time, Joey called, just as he had every morning. "Is everything all right?" he asked.

"Yes."

"You sound funny. Are you catching cold?"

"It's the flowers. Sometimes I get clogged. Did you talk to your brother?"

"I'm waiting for the right time, Doll. When she's in the right mood. She's under a lot of pressure because it's a bear market. All he does is talk about the market, how the current surge doesn't mean it's a bull market, how it's just a temporary lull in an otherwise bad market. He bores me to tears, but I'm putting on an Academy Award-winning performance. I sit on the edge of my chair, hanging on every word. What an ego. Sarah and I give each other looks behind his back."

"Aren't you leaving on the cruise Monday?"

"I'll ask him Saturday. After he's had a few martinis in the afternoon. Is Norberto there?"

I called for Norberto and handed him the phone. I went into the cooler and rearranged the cut tulips. When I came out I heard Norberto say: "I don't have no cold. It's the pollution or something like that."

All morning I wanted to sit without moving. But all three telephone lines stayed lit. Cynthia called, and Mae, then the dentist's office—to confirm my one-thirty appointment. It was while I sat in the waiting room that I started sweating. Whenever I drank too much coffee I perspired, but coffee was the only thing keeping me going. Paranoia began to set in. Should I have left the shop with Norberto in charge? If Joey called again he'd be upset that I had. He was wildly attracted to Norberto, but no longer trusted him. Trust wasn't an important consideration for their relationship.

The mirrored glass slid back. "Dr. Reynolds is ready for you now." The receptionist was an older woman who treated the doctor with obsequious respect. I'd seen her arrive for work, maneuvering an enormous, battered Cadillac into one of the compact parking spaces next to the office. She buzzed the door open and directed me to the second room on the left.

The assistant, Terri, fastened the smock around my neck. "Just wash your hair?"

"I think I might be coming down with the flu," I said.

"You should be in bed," she said. "You shouldn't be up. You'll expose other people."

"Hi, Chris." Dr. Reynolds held my chart and offered his right hand.

Terri said: "Chris has a fever I think. He says he feels like he's getting the flu."

Dr. Reynolds swung the light down toward my face and turned it on. He examined the inside of my mouth and turned off the light. Then he told Terri to check the schedule to see what time the next patient was due. After she closed the door behind her, Dr. Reynolds said: "Chris, have you been tested?"

"I'm planning to," I said.

"There's something going on in your mouth," he said. "Who's your doctor?" I told him, and he suggested I see him right away. "Call him from the front desk; tell him it's important. If there's a problem getting in, let me know. We'll re-schedule you for next week; there's no point being here when you don't feel well."

The waiting room at Dr. Jacoby's was full of patients. One boy was accompanied by a woman, probably his mother judging from the resemblance. He couldn't stop coughing, and when he got up to get a drink from the bottled water dispenser in the corner, he moved like an old man whose clothes no longer fit. The others in the room looked healthy; a few I recognized from the bars, though no one said hello or nodded an acknowledgment.

Peter wanted to do another P-24 antigen test, to see if the virus was active, and gave me a prescription for the fungus in my mouth. My temperature, he said, was elevated somewhat, but he attributed that to the fact that I had done cocaine. He was irritated, but understanding. He suggested, strongly, that I try an AA meeting. I asked him if I wouldn't be better off at a Cocaine Anonymous meeting.

"If you've seen one twelve-step program," he said, "you've seen them all."

COMING ATTRACTIONS

The wind has picked up and snow is swirling on the sidewalk, so I'm waiting in the lobby of the theater, just beyond the ropes, holding our tickets. I think we should live together. I'm hoping to catch a glimpse of him outside through the glass double doors; I'm anxious to buy popcorn and settle down next to him in the warm darkness. I'm falling in love with him. I like to sit in front—and on the aisle so I can stretch out to watch the movie. In the meantime I'm watching the people in line. A girl with sphinx-shaped, black hair looks up and leans into her friend as he bends to kiss her. I want to marry him. A blonde woman wearing a raccoon coat smiles at her companion, but when he turns away and stoops over to speak through the cut out circle in the glass, her smile fades and she looks down at his feet: he's wearing galoshes like I wore as a boy—the type that fasten with metal buckles. I'm not sure how I feel about him. A corpulent man rushes in out of the cold, shouts to get the attention of a woman he calls *Helen*. He wants to know if she has tickets and she nods and frowns and gestures with her hand as if to tell him to hurry if he wants to get a good seat. I want to spend the rest of my life with you. My friend had a late afternoon interview; we haven't spoken since morning. I want to exchange rings and have a ceremony. If he doesn't show up, I can always sell the extra ticket, then go inside and watch the previews of coming attractions.

༺༺༺ Chapter Nine

CYNTHIA PROPOSED GOING with me to my reunion. "You know you want to go," she said. But there was no way that I would—alone. Being unmarried and childless didn't mean I needed to answer everyone's questions as to why I had never married. When I went home, it was to visit Mother, then leave. "We'll stay overnight; it's still two weeks till the wedding; we'll have fun," insisted Cynthia.

She wanted to do this for me, and I did appreciate it. I did want to go. I'd been a loser in high school. I was skinny and had big hips. I didn't play sports, I wasn't in the class plays, and I didn't belong to a social club. My only extracurricular activity was the scholarship society. Now, after years of working out, I looked better and wanted to show off. Not that appearance should be so important, but I didn't have children to brag about and I wanted to see how my classmates had aged. And, on the morbid side, I didn't know if I'd be around the next time they decided to have a reunion.

A dinner and dance were being held at the New Harmony Country Club located about five miles from town. The list of class names and addresses had been mailed out over two months ago; judging from it, most of the alums still lived in or around Ohio, and all of the class officers still called New Harmony home. Our school can't claim any famous graduates. No one has risen through the ranks to become chairman of a large, multinational corporation. No one has been elected to the state legislature or Congress. No one has become a world-renown fashion designer or artist. No one has become a concert pianist or member of a rock band. Keitha Overholser, from the class, is a disk jockey on a Los Angeles radio station, though; Mother showed me an article with picture from the *Daily Call* while we waited for Cynthia to get ready. Unlike me, Keitha had been an outstanding athlete. Senior year there were rumors that the girls' physical education teacher, Miss Batson, and Keitha had a friendship outside of school activities. I thought Keitha might show up, but Miss Batson had left New Harmony long ago for butcher pastures.

"Do you expect Colleen Dimitrius to be there?" said Cynthia, as she came into the living room. She had chosen a black, tailored suit with chiffon sleeves and looked sophisticated and chic.

"Mercy, you are beautiful," Mother said. "I like your hair longer, too."

"I hope Colleen will be there," I said. Privately, I suspected that of all the people in my class she would be the one to figure me out—and not care. "She went to college back east, and I haven't seen her since," I said.

"She married an older man from Paris, France," said Mother. Don't ask me how she knew Colleen's husband was older, and French, but that's the kind of information my mother always seems to have.

As we drove up the cedar-lined driveway to the club, I wasn't sure that coming had been a good idea. The parking lot was full of people and cars; it promised to be a big crowd, by New Harmony standards. We waited for a woman to pass in front of our car, before pulling into a space, and I started to make a flippant remark about her dyed-blue carnation corsage, when I remembered Cynthia's orchids.

"I almost forgot. Your flowers. They're in the back seat," I said.

"What kind of florist are you?" said Cynthia.

"Wilted."

"Chris, this is going to be fun. Calm down."

We walked through the parking lot and onto the sidewalk to the front of the club. The original part of the building is an old Victorian farmhouse with gingerbread trim, and the year 1890 is carved in the cornice just beneath the third-floor gable. A porch runs the width of the front, wraps around the corner, and continues down the east side, and the side portion is screened and has tables for outside summer dining. I gripped Cynthia's hand tightly as we climbed the front steps and crossed the threshold into the vestibule. There's a reunion every year, but because our school was small, all the classes meet on the same date. A sign, at the foot of the circular, cherry staircase, read: *Welcome New Harmony Alumni.*

"Well look who actually decided to show up. How the hell are you, Chris?"

We shook hands. "How are you, Steve?" I said.

"Perfect; I'm perfect," he said, smiling at Cynthia.

I introduced them, and his smile blossomed—full, open-mouthed, and toothy. He was at ease and confident. When a person grows up popular and good-looking, that's the way they stay. I nodded my head toward him as if to say to Cynthia: This is the guy. Steve is still attractive: he's grown a bit of a belly, his hair is thinning on top, and he wears his sideburns a little too bushy, but his face is lean and unwrinkled. "Look who it is, Pam," he yelled.

She ran over and hugged me, and when I introduced Cynthia to her, Pam immediately commented on her dress. In school Pam complained about being tall and flat-chested, but no one in the entire class had more stylish clothes or looked as cosmopolitan. After three children, Pam was no longer flat-chested, but she was slender as ever and had resisted the local practice of using black eyeliner, blue or green eye shadow, and perming her hair. Pam and Steve married after college. In high school, she was a cheerleader, on Student Council, and a class officer. She wasn't popular because she was fast or wild or hung out with hoods. Senior year, her locker was next to mine.

"You never come to see us," said Pam. You know your mom's in the quilting club with my mom; I've told her so many times to tell you to come and see us. Didn't you get the message?"

"I don't stay long when I do get home—"

"You're here now, pal," said Steve. "Pam's chairman of the reunion committee; you're sitting with us. It's good to have influence. I was freaked when she told me you mailed the postcard back. Hey, what are you a bodybuilder now?"

Steve led us into the front parlor that connected with the dining room. In junior high he brought me to the club to go swimming and a few times I'd come here with him and his parents for dinner. I always thought that my invitations made Mother a little jealous. In the corner of the dining room, a pianist was singing to accompany himself. As we passed, he ended his current selection and, pausing only to change key and raise his voice an octave, plunged into: "Why Oh, Why Oh, Why Oh? Why Did I Ever Leave Ohio?"

"Did you see the tent out back?" said Pam. "We got a combo; there's dancing after dinner."

We entered the new dining room and sat down at our table, and Steve said: "So you're a big executive in Chicago."

"Not anymore," I said. "I invested in a flower shop."

"Your own business, eh? That's great. Dad retired so I'm running our store now. Did your mom tell you?" Of course she had; Mother kept me thoroughly informed on newsworthy developments in town. Schroeder's has always been the only place in town that has decent furniture. "I'm changing things," said Steve. "Our new name is Schroeder's Interiors. Not a major change from Schroeder's Furniture, but an important one, I think. We're moving away from Early American to Scandinavian. Now that the kids are older, Pam helps out and comes up with concepts for a whole room—or even the entire house if the customer wants it. Without design consultation, we can't compete with stores in Cincinnati. You need a drink. What are you drinking?"

"Soda water with lime. I'm trying to lose some weight," I said.

Steve got up to get the drinks, and Pam took my hand. "Why don't you ever come and see us?" she said. I repeated my earlier remark, about not getting back often, and she turned to Cynthia. "Chris was always a loner. One time in first grade his mother made him a mouse costume for Halloween and he took it off before he got to school, then hid under the fire escape during recess."

"You sound like the school psychologist, Pam. I never liked dressing up."

Steve came back, handed me the glass of soda water, and sat down. "We used to try to get him to play baseball too, but he stayed inside reading and drawing."

"I didn't know you liked to draw," said Cynthia.

"I wanted to be a cartoonist. I sent my drawings to Walt Disney, but he never wrote back."

Pam shrieked. "Remember your caricatures of Mr. Elliot?"

He was bald on top, with tufts of hair on the sides—and wore braces. All the pretty girls in his Economics class got an *A*. Pam and I enjoyed making fun of him because he used to drive his favorites to the out-of-town basketball and football games. He was thirty-some years old and hung out with high school girls.

Steve explained who Elliot was to Cynthia and laughed. "Chris drew his head in a martini glass like an olive."

"And rolling down a bowling alley with pins scattering every-where," said Pam.

"He had a perfectly round head," I explained.

"Chris did one of Elliot in a ballerina's tutu, and we passed it around in fifth-period Econ class," said Steve.

"And somebody signed my name to it and threw it on the floor and Elliot found it afterwards. I felt so stupid when Mr. Summers—our principal—came into my next class and said he needed to see me after school. He was upset, mainly because Elliot was furious. I told him it wasn't my writing and he said, 'Yes, but it's your drawing.' He could hardly keep from laughing himself when he looked at the draw-ing." I laughed now. How could I help, seeing how cracked-up Cynthia, Steve, and Pam were?

I never did know who signed my name. A month afterwards someone wrote Chris Hale sucks cock in one of the stalls in the bath-room. I'd never had sex with any boy in high school. Really I'd never had sex with anyone unless trying to make out with Colleen counts. And I was a virgin in college too until senior year. Steve's the one who told me about the writing in the bathroom and he helped me erase it that evening after school. Steve said he knew it wasn't true. I didn't speak about it after we scrubbed off the ink. I didn't tell Steve that I believed Mr. Elliot wrote it. Mr. Elliot was a small town fag. I could see it in his eyes. Who would have believed me? Accusing a teacher of being that evil, that full of hate to do such a thing to a kid? People might have said: "It takes one to know one." Maybe Mr. Elliot was fighting back the only way he knew.

Cynthia and Pam were fast friends. They talked and talked and talked, but by the end of dinner, Steve and I'd run out of things to discuss. Pam said that, from our graduating class of fifty students, twenty-six responded and planned to attend. Most of them lived in or around New Harmony. Before dinner several of our classmates stopped at our table to say hello to Pam and Steve. Most of them didn't recognize me but pretended to after Steve prodded: "You remember Chris, don't you?" As in high school, I was a non-person. A shadow in the hallway. Steve's shadow.

I drank soda water until after dinner, and then Steve talked me into having a vodka tonic. I was halfway through my third when he looked down at the table and cleared his throat. "Jesus, this is only the second time we've seen each other since we graduated—and that was at your dad's funeral." He almost swallowed the word funeral and made as if something had caught in his throat.

"I figured you and Pam had your hands full with your family. I didn't think it made much difference whether you saw me or not. You could have called too."

"I know your mom told you. I called. Every holiday, every Christmas, every time I thought you'd come home, I called. Never once did you call back."

"I guess I wanted to forget about New Harmony."

"And that includes me?"

"I said I was sorry. I'll stay in touch better."

Pam interrupted her conversation with Cynthia. "What are you two so serious about?"

"I was giving him a hard time about not coming to see us." Steve had started to slur, but poured himself the last of the dinner wine, then looked at me again. "Jesus, you've never even seen our new house."

"The English Tudor, out on Vaughn Road, right? Mother showed me. It's great."

After dinner everyone went outside to the tent. They had a photographer; people from different years were introduced; there were announcements and awards; Steve kept drinking—and so did I. Cynthia and I danced twice, although I absolutely hate to dance when I'm sober. It was a couple of hours later, Steve had taken off his sport coat and loosened his tie and I was relaxed myself, when he told the girls he needed to talk to me privately. "Don't you ladies have to powder your noses?" He took me by the arm and led me from the tent.

"Where are we going?" I asked.

"By the tennis courts," he said.

As we walked onto the lawn, the music faded. It was an ideal evening: too early for insects, and warm without the humidity. We walked past the first tee. I also used to refuse to play golf with Steve. As far as the grounds were concerned—the layout of the golf course, the location of the tennis courts, and the landscaping around the swimming pool—nothing really has changed that much. The sky was clear and the moon was three quarters full that night, but I couldn't see Steve's face when he asked me.

"Chris, are you gay?"

ENERGY

He turns away from me to scrape chipped paint off the windowsill. I watch his triceps muscle flex. I walk up behind, put my arms around him, cup his pectorals in my hands. He leans back, twists his head to kiss me at the side of my mouth. I nibble at his neck. He turns back and looks at me. Just when I think I know his face completely, I see it from a different angle or in a new light and I have to take a deep breath to keep from gasping aloud. His lips are full and soft as he kisses me, and I want to touch them with my fingers and rub my cheeks against them and feel them on my chest and on my arms and on my neck and thighs. I want to feel his breath on me everywhere. He clutches at the buttons on my shirt, and I struggle with the zipper to his chinos. We fall down onto the unfolded drop cloth. If he didn't plan to stay, I'm sure he wouldn't be expending all this energy.

ಖಿಖಿಖಿ Chapter Ten

OVER THE YEARS, I've arranged to meet people under one of the clocks at Marshall Field's. The ornate, brass clocks suspended high above the sidewalk, remind me that I'm part of a great city. Meeting at Field's, to go shopping or have lunch in the Walnut Room, meant that I liked someone. Things had progressed beyond at least two sexual encounters. Maybe. Many times it meant that I had given in and accepted an invitation, coercion, to have lunch. Of course, I would only do this after having made sure there was nothing obvious about him. Funny, outrageous types were fine in the privacy of a dark bar or at a gay party, but I didn't want to run into someone from work and have to be embarrassed by a boy who stood with his feet too close together or with his hands folded in front of his chest.

Mae said she'd meet me at one-thirty to shop and have lunch. We planned to get a wedding gift for Cynthia and a birthday present for Mother. I checked my watch and stood back to peer up at the clock. Cynthia was registered—we could point to a soup tureen or a place setting or some silverware and have it shipped—but Mother presented a challenge. I didn't have any ideas, and Mae wanted to go in together on something special.

I usually selected an electric can opener or a blender, because women's clothes were not something I understood. And it had to be clothes. Mae insisted. "More personal," she said, reminding me that

Mother loved having new things to wear to quilt club meetings and church.

"Been waiting long?" said Mae. She has a strong accent though she's been in Chicago nearly as long as I have. She sounds like Mother and looks more like her every day.

"Do you have any ideas?" I said.

"I got here as soon as I could," said Mae.

We went through the revolving doors and were assaulted by a heavily made-up girl armed with a perfume atomizer. Her black hair spiked into the shape of a tiara. "Would you care to try some *Obsession*?" she asked. Mae smiled and declined, calling the girl, "honey," but I asked if she had *Evening on the Wabash*. She gave me an immediate smile and told me to try Wal-Mart.

We passed Cosmetics and stepped on the escalator, and Mae said, "Remember how embarrassed Mother would get when Daddy flirted with the cashiers at Woolworth's?"

"I think you should be friendly to people, who have dreary jobs," I said.

"You're just like Daddy," said Mae.

We spent about twenty minutes agonizing over cashmere sweaters and skirts with a saleswoman, and I was ready to go along with any choice Mae made, but she couldn't make up her mind. "Mother would look good in red," I said.

"She doesn't like red. Too noticeable," said Mae.

"She always wears dark colors," I said.

"This forest-green is tasteful. And I think she'd wear it," said Mae.

"Where do you want to eat?" I said.

"I don't think she has shoes that would go. Can we afford to get her shoes?"

"This is getting complicated," I said. "Get the green and let's go eat. We'll worry about shoes later."

The saleswoman wore her hair in an Imelda Marcos bun, pulled back so tightly that I wondered if she were in pain. She anticipated the sale. "The green is really splendid," she coaxed, batting heavy, black lashes.

In the Walnut Room, we waited for our food. We had waited in a long line before being seated too, and I was now quite hungry and irritable. "Nothing ever changes when we talk about Charlie, so why do you bother asking what I think? He's a jerk. He'll always be a jerk," I said. A comment about Cynthia's impending marriage had led Mae to bring up Charlie. She tightened her mouth and looked down at her place mat. I softened my tone. "Daddy never hit Mother. Ever. He may have beat the tar out of us, but he never hit Mother," I said. Beat the tar was one of Daddy's favorite expressions. "There's something wrong wanting to be with a man who hits you."

"There are all kinds of self-destructive behavior," said Mae.

"Now what could you possibly mean by that remark?" I said. "I'm trying to quit; I haven't done any for three weeks. Joey says I'm not an addict. I'm compulsive."

"I worry about you," said Mae. "You look so tired and your face seems swollen."

"It's stress. I was on AZT, but my T-cells still went down. If I keep losing them at this rate, I'll be able to name the ones I have left: Moe, Larry, and Curly."

"You feel all right, don't you?"

"I feel okay. I'm combining AZT and ddC. Dr. Jacoby tried to put me on a drug called Bactrim, to prevent pneumonia, but I only took it for a week cause I was allergic. It's a sulfa drug. One night my temperature went up to 102, and I started shaking all over and sweating and throwing up—it even blurred my vision and I thought for a while that I might go blind. So I'm still doing Pentamadine. They wanted me to try a drug called Dapsone, but after the Bactrim I was afraid. Don't discuss this with Charlie. I don't want him to know anything about my medical situation."

Mae had put her hand up to her mouth and was looking at me wide-eyed. "Why didn't you tell me? Why didn't you call?" she said.

"I didn't tell anybody. Except for Dr. Jacoby. You don't discuss me with Charlie, do you?" Something about her expression made me wonder. A slight narrowing around the eyes, a failure to hold my gaze, the way she swallowed instead of answering.

"Doing coke and drinking can't be good for you when you're already taking all these strong things. I read an article—"

"Mae, the thing about my behavior is that I'm my own victim. What if you get pregnant? Then you won't be the only victim."

The waitress brought our salads, and Mae adjusted her napkin, and then kept her eyes trained on the girl as she walked back toward the kitchen. "You never told me about the reunion," said Mae, as soon as the girl was out of view.

I told Mae that I was surprised by what a good time I had. She wanted to know who was there from her class, and I told her that Sally Hardenbrook said, "Tell Mae I had twins." Mae wanted to know if I'd seen Steve and Pam, and when I nodded, she asked if Steve was still handsome.

"He's losing his hair," I said, "but Cynthia said he was adorable."

"When he came over to the house, I had the biggest crush on him," said Mae.

"I told him I was gay." Mae was in the middle of a sip of iced tea and pulled the glass abruptly from her lips. "He said it didn't make any difference—that it didn't change anything. We were pretty drunk. Maybe he'll change his mind after he thinks about it awhile."

"Yes," said Mae, "but I don't think so."

Mae didn't understand. I don't understand about girls growing up either. When Steve and I were kids, in the sixth and seventh grades, we played in his basement. He had his train set, an erector set, and a chemistry set down there. There was also a cot and a rollaway bed. We spent a lot of time pretending we were scientists in a laboratory doing important research. We also spent time lying together on the cot with our arms around each other. We used to strip down to our under shorts, rub against each other, and get erections. We never screwed or gave each other blowjobs—I've heard gay guys tell of experiences like that with their straight friends when they were adolescents, but Steve and I never got that heavy. We eventually did work our way up to taking off all our clothes and rubbing against each other until we had orgasms, and in all the times we did that in his basement his mother never once came downstairs to interrupt. Steve insisted it was his playroom. His mother felt it was important, he said, that children have their privacy. She called me Steve's "intellectual friend." Steve invited me to sleep over, but Mother would never allow it even though she liked Steve because he was so good at sports and because his parents owned the furniture store. To Mother, the Schroeder's were rich and Steve had been a star since the first year of Little League. I think that Mother wouldn't let me sleep over because she feared for what I might do. The only time we messed around at my house was the last time. It was the summer between the seventh and eighth grades. Mother had gone shopping, and Mae had gone to Patty's house. Steve always got everything he wanted when we were kids, and that summer he took riding lessons from a man named Merriweather who kept horses outside New Harmony. Steve had a cowboy fantasy. His mother dropped him off at my house one afternoon, in his cowboy clothes, after she'd picked him up from his lesson.

In the front part of our garage, which was located in a separate building in the back yard, Daddy had opened up a small appliance repair shop to occupy his spare time. It was one of his many money-making schemes, but the work at the brick factory left him too tired to work in the evenings and on weekends, and after a month or two he abandoned the idea just as he had all the others. The remnants of the repair shop were still there in the small front room of the garage: the work bench along the east wall, an old plaid couch, an upholstered chair, and a table-model refrigerator where he kept beers and soft drinks for the customers. After Steve showed me his outfit, complete with boots, silver spurs, and chaps, he wanted to go inside to see if there were any beers in the refrigerator. It was too hot to play outside, but our garage had a second story attic, shaded by a tall elm, and was covered with the gourd vines that Mae had planted from seeds in the early spring. We went inside. We found a six-pack plus two singles, but I feared Daddy would notice if any were missing. Steve promised to sneak some out of his father's bar later, claiming that he wouldn't know the difference, and so we each opened a beer. I was spinning after one and wondered how I would hide it from Mother and Daddy. Steve pushed back his cowboy hat and said he had a surprise, and then reached in his hip pocket to pull out a pack of Lucky Strikes.

"Where did you get those?" I asked.

"I found them in Merriweather's barn," he said. "Get matches." I looked around on the workbench and, when I didn't find any, ran to the house. I came back and Steve had taken off his shirt. We sat at opposite ends of the couch puffing on our filter-less cigarettes. I didn't inhale, but still felt dizzy. Steve liked to appear worldlier, and the truth of the matter is, he was. He went on vacations to Lake Erie, to Florida, and had even been to New York. Our family never went on vacations. When it came time for Daddy's vacation he went fishing or hunting, and never took any of us with him. Steve was an athlete; he took riding lessons; he belonged to the country club; he played baseball. But I was smarter. That was our relationship. I understood it, and he understood it. I got the A's and Steve hit the home runs.

He glanced at me. "I reckon I got myself a greenhorn here," he said. He'd been talking like a cowboy since starting the riding lessons; his version of their dialogue was based on the TV westerns that ran on Saturdays and Sundays. He shoved me on the shoulder. This was how he usually started. Even drunk I was too self-effacing to pretend to be a stupid cowboy. Steve tossed his cigarette on the concrete floor and crushed it under his boot. Then with no further signal he jumped on me and wrestled me off of the couch and onto the floor. The first time that this happened, Steve was surprised at how strong I was. But I lacked stamina. He always wore me down. I put up a fight, because it would have been a sissy move to give up right away. Steve had strength from football practice, plus endurance from basketball and track. I felt his bare chest against my face as he held me down. I grabbed his arms around the biceps, trying to push him off. My strength was already gone. He slid down, his cheek against my cheek. I could smell the beer. "I got you," he said. I made a sudden thrust upwards. "Not yet, you don't," I grunted. We wrestled around for a few more minutes. Steve never relinquished his position on top. Eventually I was too out of breath to continue the struggle, but I was afraid Steve would make some comment about my hard-on. He sat back once he was sure I had quit struggling. He straddled my chest; his knees pressed down on my shoulders. He had a bemused expression, and his eyes drooped with drunkenness. He unbuttoned his jeans and began playing with his penis. He gave me a crooked smile. "Take yours out," he said.

"After all, you two were best friends." Mae smiled knowingly.

She didn't understand. Teenage boys fool around. It's a stage for most, but it was never a stage for me. I knew every time that Steve and I wrestled that he would have preferred being with a girl. I was a substitute. I didn't want to be with a girl. I wanted to be with Steve. I was in love with Steve, but I never told him.

"What's wrong?" said Mae.

"I was remembering the time in Daddy's workshop. That's what you mean, isn't it?"

"It was a heck of a shock for a little girl."

"You never told Mother, did you?"

"I never told anyone."

"I thought you were at Patty's."

"Obviously."

The waitress brought our sandwiches, and we finished our lunch in silence.

ॐ•ॐ

During the remaining weeks of June, there was one crisis after another. Cynthia married Louie. Mae and Charlie eloped. Joey said his brother wouldn't loan him any money to open a second store. I got a sinus infection and then a fungus under my toenails. I probably got the fungus at the gym.

When I went into Dr. Jacoby's office, Kenny told me that Mark had refused to do prophylaxis and ended up back in the hospital, with a second bout of pneumonia. And as I was leaving, I ran into Arvo. He'd lost weight and had purplish splotches around his neck, close to his collar. Arvo had always made a point of telling me that he was H.I.V.–negative, and I now supposed he'd been lying—though lately people had been saying Kaposi's Sarcoma was caused by an entirely different virus altogether. Arvo acted the same; he slipped me his new number in case I needed anything. I took it, but told him I'd been laying off. Later back at the shop, Joey said that Arvo had lesions almost entirely covering his legs. Joey didn't cite any sources, or tell me how he knew, but it was typical for him to have detailed information of this kind about others.

He was agitated on Saturday. Norberto hadn't come to work, and Lydia didn't know where he was. Joey went out the front door, looked up and down the sidewalk, then came inside and hurried through the store to the back. I heard the screen door slam as he checked the alley. Lately, Norberto had become unreliable. I knew he wasn't to be trusted, based on my own experiences, and I could have told Joey not to count on him, but for selfish reasons I said nothing. Joey, as they say, had created his own monster. The shop had its share of queens coming in to look at Norberto. They'd stand around, as if trying to make a decision about flowers, whispering, giggling, and rolling their eyes. One afternoon I walked among them, and they scattered like doves.

Norberto hadn't showed up at all on Friday, and when by Saturday afternoon there was still no sign of him, Joey insisted that Lydia call the hospitals. He didn't mention which ones to call, or make any effort to do it himself, because I'm sure he had done this for Lydia's sake—or for dramatic effect. I think he feared the worst: Norberto was with another man. Had Norberto been with a woman, it would only have increased his appeal.

Even though we were so busy we couldn't keep up with customers, Joey announced—in the middle of a surge—that he had to leave. He didn't say he was going to look for Norberto, but I knew that in his neurotic state it was exactly what he had in mind. I didn't argue. I would handle the store as best I could. If he wanted to neglect the business, it was his decision. If he wasn't going to be conscientious, I wasn't going to exert myself taking care of things for him. I couldn't imagine where he planned to look. He rammed his shoulder against the back room doorjamb on the way to his car and yelled out in pain. Joey never drank, but behaved as if intoxicated.

"Will you be back?" I said.

"If I'm not, lock up," he shouted. I heard his engine, then his car door. I almost applauded when Norberto came in the shop ten minutes later, as if he'd been watching for Joey to leave.

"Where's Joey, man?" He was casual. Perhaps I expected him to behave like a teenager whose allowance was in jeopardy.

"He's looking for you," I said.

Norberto didn't react. He helped with the customers. For the next hour there was a steady flow and not much time to talk, but while I was wrapping an arrangement of bird-of-paradise and banana leaves, he came up to ask me the price of the elephant-foot tree, then gave me a particularly elated smile and said: "You ever been to LA, man?"

What was up? Norberto was acting like he did right after he started hanging around with Joey. Ever since Joey returned from his cruise, Norberto had been openly abusive to him—and on one occasion even referred to him as *La Gorda* in front of a client. This mistreatment, I think, was responsible for Joey's renewed interest. When a hillbilly kid, new in town, came in one day to apply for work, Joey initially wanted to hire him. As he shook hands with the boy, he commented on his firm grip, and the boy told us that he was raised on a dairy farm and knew how to work. He had wheat-colored hair, a thick neck, pronounced traps—which I decided came from adolescence spent lugging around milk cans—and playful, gray eyes. He seemed the mature type, so I gave him paperwork to fill out. We needed the help now that Norberto had gotten flaky. The very next day, I had to let him go because Joey changed his mind. After I implored, he admitted that Norberto had objected; he didn't want anyone new around.

"Where have you been?" I asked Norberto, when the last customer left the shop. "Joey's a wreck."

"I met a movie producer, baby." Norberto leaned in close. "Don't say nothing to Joey. I'm not telling him nothing."

"You met a movie producer in Chicago?"

"He's visiting. He lives in LA, and I'm going back on his private plane. Man, he's got a big old jet plane." Norberto pressed me against the cash register. "I need your help, baby."

"If you can meet a movie producer in Chicago, you don't need my help," I said.

"Explain things to Lydia."

"Explain what things? I don't know anything. You're going home first, aren't you? You have to pack, don't you?"

"No time. We're leaving at seven." Norberto grabbed me and gave me an energetic hug. "This is wild shit, man. I can't believe it's happening to me."

"What's this producer's name?" I said.

"Corey something."

"He must be handsome."

Norberto tilted his head back and to the side. "He's okay. He's real short."

I interrogated, worrying the entire time about what to tell Lydia and how to keep her from talking to Joey. I didn't like the idea of lying for Norberto, but I didn't refuse. I decided to say that Norberto had unexpectedly gone to Los Angeles for a job interview and that was why she couldn't tell Joey if he called. As far as Joey was concerned, I'd convince him to hire someone else. It was time to employ someone qualified who took his job seriously—like the farm boy. I'd tell him: hiring on the basis of sex appeal is poor management.

I told Lydia that I didn't know when Norberto was coming back. I didn't know where to reach him or when he would call. I didn't know much. I did know that rich, older gays often bought plane tickets for boys, and I tried to tell Norberto that he was the one being used, that he was the one being taken advantage of, even implying that it might be a dangerous situation. He didn't know what Corey, the producer, might be into. Norberto didn't scare easily. He didn't convince easily. He put his arms around my waist and pulled me into the back room and convinced me that what he was doing was right. When we finished, I felt like a hypocrite.

ରେଓଓ Part II ଶୁଶୁଶୁ

ಒಬಒಬ Chapter Eleven

W HEN CLINTON CAUGHT ME in the entryway one evening after work, he invited me down for dinner. I made the mistake of saying I was a little depressed, then quickly tried to blame it on the July humidity.

Norberto hadn't been back in town, and Joey was so bored with the shop that he decided to open an Argentinean restaurant. He approached me to see if I'd be willing to manage it if he found a space and got the backing; he claimed to be holding talks with potential investors. Except when he popped in to have me write a thousand dollar advance check, only to vault out the back door without explanation, I didn't see him. When he showed up, late one Friday, driving a new, red Eldorado, I wouldn't let him leave until he gave me a twenty percent salary increase and named me manager. After that, I relaxed.

Restaurants don't interest me, though it amuses me the way owners become celebrities. That's what Joey was after. He'd never shown the slightest interest in food preparation, and if his lack of creativity with flowers was any indication, any bistro he opened would have zero ambience.

Annette came in faithfully each morning for an arrangement, and after I increased Walter's hours and still couldn't keep up without working eleven hours a day, I asked her to help out in the store—on a part-time basis. I didn't need any Puerto Rican distraction now that I was responsible for operations. When she said "How soon can I start?"

and we worked out her schedule, the idea of buying the shop occurred to me, but then I thought about the financial risk—and my status—and dropped the notion.

A couple of weeks earlier, Dr. Jacoby had done blood work again. My hemoglobin was fine; I wasn't anemic. But my T-Cells dipped—to under 300. I didn't take the news well: for the next two Saturday nights, I did cocaine. When I went to Arvo's apartment to pick up the stuff, he insisted that I sit down and have a glass of wine, and that's when I learned Darren had died, of a heart attack.

I hadn't seen Darren since my aborted vacation in Florida, but his removal from the gay scene hit me hard—as if he'd been a close friend. I suppose it was a combination of events that led me to ask Angelo and Clinton to take me to an AA meeting—my first. We went one Saturday night, and I hated it. This chapter, made up of gays, met at Northside Hospital on Wednesdays and Saturdays. The humorous stories I'd heard about people drinking gallons of coffee and smoking cartons of cigarettes turned out to be accurate. The meeting room was set up with tan, metal chairs, and the floor was covered in acrylic tile squares that made sound reverberate. Latecomers slammed the door, dropped keys, then kicked chairs in their rush to join the others, who lit cigarettes and smoked them down to the filter before stubbing them out in metal ashtrays. There was a constant flow of people to and from the coffee pot and their slurping noises at times nearly succeeded in drowning out the whirr of the air conditioning system.

An angular man with oily hair spoke first. He told a rambling story of his ordeal with cocaine and had a tendency to mumble until he related a particular incident, at which point, he began to bellow in a mournful tone. He stood at the front of the room—he'd been one of the first to arrive—and said, in a voice cracked with emotion: "You're my family. When I laid in bed with my eyes glued open, I didn't have no family. I did so much blow one time that my eyes swelled like golf balls and I couldn't shut them because my lids wouldn't close." I considered interrupting to ask: Tru-Flite or Spalding? Could you feel the dimples on the outside? "My cats sensed something was improper," he said. "They'd come into my bedroom and jump up on the edge of my bed and stare at me like I was a side show. They made a bawling yell that I never heard any other time. I'd get myself out of bed and give them one of their favorite foods, but it didn't make no difference. They'd be back in five minutes up on my bed. Like Satan was talking to me through them. I'd lock them out of the room, but they clawed at the door and bawled." At this point the man himself began to bawl. Clinton said that the man told this story quite frequently.

The Wednesday after, I was supposed to go to Angelo and Clinton's for dinner. We planned to eat, and then go to the meeting. In all the time I'd lived above, I'd never eaten with them, but Clinton claimed to be a fabulous cook. Sometimes he brought up a batch of cookies or some homemade brownies, but what if he served venison or lamb or something else I didn't eat? The real problem was, I had decided that I couldn't go to the meeting. There was no way I could listen to those horrible stories. When I went downstairs at six-thirty, it smelled appetizing. Clinton was in the kitchen at the back of the apartment, and Angelo came into the front room to greet me. "Clinton's making one of his specialties: Daisy's Braised Beef. It's from his Scottish cookbook," he said. I'd never associated the Scots with fine cuisine.

Angelo offered me a choice of Diet Coke or Evian water, and I handed him the bouquet of yellow tulips. He removed the cellophane and commented on the beautiful, pale shade and gave me an appreciative peck on the cheek. Then he went to the kitchen to put them in water.

I sat down on an ottoman, propped myself against an oversized throw pillow, and peered through the French doors into the dining room. The table was set with white china, crystal goblets, and porcelain candlesticks on a white linen tablecloth. I wasn't sure how I was going to get out of going to the meeting.

Daisy's Braised Beef turned out to be beef stew, and tasted excellent. Clinton served it with a green salad and an orange dish, which he called Carrot Puff—a soufflé that seemed strangely appropriate to his Scottish meal.

The three of us don't have much in common. It was a strain to keep up my end of the conversation—though I didn't really have to say much with Clinton talking about Lalique, Steuben, and Baccarat crystal all during dinner. After Angelo cleared the plates—Royal Doulton, he informed—I said that I didn't think I was going to be able to go to the meeting. "You're going," said Clinton, "and it's all right to feel apprehensive."

"It's my sinuses. I've got this headache all around my temples," I said.

"We've got Tylenol for sinus. No more excuses, please," said Clinton.

The meeting started as we arrived. There were still about ten people crowded around the coffee pot, and the room was covered with a canopy of blue smoke. At my first meeting, I had surveyed the crowd, without finding anyone interesting. The same situation existed that night. Until the leader called the group to order, that is. There were two entrances to the room, and when the front door opened and two well-built boys—one dark and the other blond—came in, I felt a rush of adrenaline. The first one—the tall, Italian-looking boy with the chiseled features and thick neck—bothered me so much that I couldn't concentrate on the meeting. He and his friend sat about five rows in front of us on the right side of the room, close to the door, and I was unable to see him unless I sat forward on my chair to peek between two balding heads. Every once in awhile, the dark boy would lean over and say something to his companion. I decided that they were lovers.

My attitude has always been that there are plenty of sexy men to go around and that was all the reason I needed to keep away from lovers. Many gays enjoy the challenge of coming between lovers or men who have started dating, but I could never understand why someone would get their thrills from home wrecking. So, knowing that this sublime creature, a mere five rows in front of me, had a lover, made me anxious in much the same way that I was anxious coming down from coke. I couldn't sit in the meeting any longer and whispered to Clinton, who sat beside me, that I would wait in the hallway. Then I moved as quietly as possible to the back of the room. I knew heads would turn to see who was leaving as soon as the noisy door clicked open and I didn't look up because I didn't want to meet eyes with anyone. I decided to walk home and was halfway down the hall, when Clinton called to me.

"Is your headache worse?" he asked. I turned and went back to meet him.

"Did you see those two boys that came in last?" I said. "The blond and the incredible Italian?" Clinton shook his head. "Sitting about five rows in front of us on the right," I said. "Both are tall, both have on Levis and white tee shirts."

"Chris, half the men in there have on Levis and white tee shirts."

I wanted to ask if he'd ever seen them at a meeting before. Since I'd never seen them at the bars, I figured they must not go out—and that proved they were lovers. I told Clinton I couldn't stay. I told him my sinuses were throbbing. I thanked him for dinner and said I'd see him and Angelo at home. I'm sure he thought that my behavior was weird, but I couldn't help that.

I walked north on Lincoln Avenue. It was a good sign, I told myself. There were two sexy men at an AA meeting. I should have been elated that it was possible to meet someone interesting in a place other than the bars. So why did I want to cry?

മ•ഏ

I made a tuna salad sandwich and tried first to read, then to get interested in television, but it was no use. Saturday nights were the worst. I'd decided never to go to another AA meeting. Once, I picked up the phone to call Arvo, then focused on how I would feel on Sunday if I gave in to my urge, and hung up. I'd have the whole next day to recover, because Annette worked the flower shop on Sundays, but knew I'd feel achy and grouchy until at least Wednesday. Boredom was what this was really about. If only I could go out for a drink or two, then go home like normal people did. But in the past that had never worked, and I knew it was a dangerous idea. I vacuumed my apartment, mopped the kitchen floor, and considered cleaning the oven. I checked the newspaper to see what movies were playing, and had started downstairs to visit Clinton and Angelo when I remembered they went to the meeting.

My telephone rang as I came back through the door. It was Mae. "Guess what," she said in a high, playful voice, "I'm going to have a baby." It was interesting that she said I am going to have a baby, not Charlie and I or we. Until now I had assumed they eloped because Mother didn't have the money for a big wedding. I stared at the mouthpiece till I could think of something to say, and then tried to sound enthusiastic.

"Great. When?"

"February fifteenth."

"You've known for quite a while," I said.

"We didn't want to tell anyone until we were sure everything was okay."

"Have you told Mother?"

"She's real excited."

"When did you tell her?"

"A few weeks ago. I haven't told them at work yet. I'm going to work as long as I can."

"I see."

"You don't sound very excited to be an uncle."

"Don't be silly. I'm jubilant." I had to grit my teeth to keep from saying something like: Charlie will make a great father; he knows how to use his hands.

I was on my way out the door when the phone rang again. This time I let the machine pick up. "Isn't it great news about the baby?" said Mother. "I'm making a quilt." There was a long pause; I stood quietly as if she could detect any motion at the other end. "Call me," she said, apparently satisfied that I wasn't home. "Will you?"

By the time I headed down Clark Street to Arvo's house, I had erased Sunday from my thoughts. I surrendered to thrill, to pleasure, to the sensual relief the cocaine would bring. I couldn't wait to get some up my nostrils. One gram. That's all I'd get. I'd go out for an hour or so. There was too much pressure in my life; the pressure would kill me. I deserved a break from the pressure. I'd sleep all day Sunday. I could miss work on Monday if I had to. After all, it was still Joey's business. He didn't take it seriously. Why should I? I wouldn't disappoint anyone. No one would have to know. I'd do some tonight and make sure it was two months before I did it again. What was the point in quitting cold turkey? I'd wean my self, the way I had quit smoking.

I should have taken a cab instead of driving. Arvo lived in a basement apartment underneath a beauty shop, a block off Rush Street, and there was never any parking without going into a city garage. A taxi would have been cheaper and would have kept me from driving while high. I worried increasingly about such logistics these days.

I pressed the buzzer without a name. The intercom crackled. I didn't hear a response, so I identified myself, and the front door clicked open. Arvo's unit was the first on the left. I stood in front of the viewhole while he checked my identity, but it was Tim who stood inside when the door opened. He ducked his head, and we exchanged timid greetings—though he could barely form words because he was grinding his teeth so intensely. I took two steps inside the dimly lit, one-room apartment. The odor of permanent wave solution instantly cleared my sinuses. Arvo's king-sized bed was at the front end, close to the street, and he was in it; the noise of Saturday night traffic was only slightly muffled through the ground-level windows.

"I've got the flu," he said. "Tim's handling business." I remembered the flu shot notice sent by Dr. Jacoby's office. I hadn't gotten mine. Then I reassured myself that Arvo had a bigger problem than the flu. "How much do you need?" he said.

The end table next to his bed had several remote video controls, and a lamp gave off a feeble, yellow light. Arvo took a control and put *The Sound of Music* on hold. Liesl von Trapp would stay sixteen, going on seventeen. Except for the large-screen television, a video recorder, and a camera on tripod, plus lots of stereo equipment, Arvo had few pieces of furniture. A glass-topped table, encircled by overstuffed chairs and a couple of floor lamps, held the centerpiece: a soup bowl of cocaine. The exposed-brick wall behind the table was hung with twenty, maybe twenty-five, pictures of young boys—most of who looked like hustlers—that Arvo had taken. A person could write his obituary by studying this room: Arvo Balsavia was a self-made businessman. He collected video and audio system components and enjoyed portrait photography. He was survived by his friend and business associate, Tim Zolinsky.

My father's life had been little better. He was selfish and incapable of expressing emotion—except for anger and disgust. There wasn't an introspective molecule in his body. How had I come from so different a man? Still, to see him gasp for breath with those tanks of oxygen behind the headboard…

Tim went to the bureau and withdrew a fistful of snow seal packets. He was so wired I wondered if he would be able to come down. He couldn't control the muscles in his face—only one side of his mouth moved; the other stayed stationary—and he didn't attempt to speak. And Arvo was dying. Abruptly, I turned to face him. "I don't need any," I said. "I just stopped to see how you were doing."

"Suit yourself," he said.

I left quietly. My skin tingled, pleading: it's not too late to get a half. I didn't turn back. I was right where I started. How would I get through the night? I paid the parking attendant, drove up Clark Street, and headed over to Halsted. I'd stop at Scream, have a soda water, and go home. I'd go to the gym on Sunday and lift.

I seldom hung out at video bars; the crowd was too bizarre. Scream is one long room with a dozen video screens suspended from the ceiling. Boys crowd together so closely that it's a struggle to push through to the bar. A mass of young heads, mostly with geometric haircuts, stood gazing up at the nearest monitor; occasionally one would glance down to see who had entered or passed by. People are distracted in video bars. In the beginning, with coke, I approached even the most beautiful: the bigger the arms, the smaller the waist, the better. As the years passed, I found it more appealing to go home, do my drugs alone, and watch porno.

The bartender that Mark had called *hot* was working. He had a shaved head, never wore a shirt, and had barbed wire tattooed on his right arm around his biceps. He also had a pig-like nose, which enabled me to look straight into the nostrils. I'd have overlooked the nose if I'd been high. I took my change and left a dollar tip and glanced down the length of the bar to the largest screen, which hung in the corner. They were showing "The Price Is Right"—the one where the black woman in a tube top runs down front after Bob Barker yells her name. She's halfway down the aisle, jumping and screaming, when her breasts pop out. People are hysterical, though they've been showing this one forever. I'm smiling and when I look down to the end of the bar I see him. The one from the AA meeting. It's difficult to describe what I felt when I saw him leaning on the bar, looking up at the screen, and laughing. I wanted to know him. Knowing him would help me to see his flaws. Seeing his flaws would help me to relax.

His profile was classic, but maybe he had a high voice or effeminate mannerisms or a nervous tic. Something. Maybe his eyes rolled back exposing the whites when he talked. He wore a black, leather jacket, open at the neck, and under that a red T-shirt. I fought the urge to get a beer. I peeked at him occasionally, carefully, so as not to be caught. I was no longer interested in meeting anyone else in the bar, but I lacked the courage to approach him. I ordered another soda water and glanced down the bar. He looked at me and smiled. It was a friendly *how-are-you-doing grin*. I smiled back, inhaled a deep breath, and took a casual swallow of my water before glancing at the screen. I straightened my shoulders and pulled in my stomach—though it was hidden below the bar—and looked again. He was gone. I surveyed the crowd. I was surrounded by geeks. I could go back to Arvo's and get some stuff or stay here with the geeks or go home. I checked to see if he had returned. I couldn't see into the crowd; I saw only the first row lining the bar. An Annie Lennox video came on. I thought about taking a walk to the other end of the room, but worried about running into him, if he hadn't left, and I didn't want him to think I was following him. Then I felt a nudge at my elbow.

"My name's Dean," he said. "I saw you at a meeting a few weeks ago."

"But you were sitting in front of me," I said.

"You knocked the coffee pot over when you left," he said. He held up his hand, chest-high with the palm facing out, and I clasped it in mine. I asked if he was from Chicago, said I'd never seen him around.

"Boston," he said. "I moved here a month ago."

"You're really handsome," I said, surprised by my candor.

"I think you're handsome," he said. "But you don't think so, do you?"

"I'm average." I glanced at the monitor.

"You're more than average," he said, "and I like your modesty."

"May I buy you a drink?" I said.

"I was thinking of leaving, but I'll have a beer. It won't bother you if I have a beer?"

"No," I said, "but I did see you at an AA meeting."

"I go because Bob asks me to go with him. He doesn't know many people in Chicago."

"The blond with you at the meeting?"

"We moved out here together."

"You're lovers?"

"Friends—since high school."

"You're not lovers, but you moved out together?"

Dean explained how, when Bob got transferred, he decided to move too since he'd spent his entire life in the east and figured he was due for a change. That way, he said, they'd each have at least one friend in town. He smiled without parting his lips, and small dimples appeared at the corners of his mouth.

I ordered one soda water and one beer. "Saturday nights are tough for me," I said. "With everyone doing drugs and drinking."

"I was never into it that much. I'm lucky, I guess; at least Bob tells me I am. After I have one or two drinks, I get a buzz and don't want any more."

"What about cocaine? Did you ever do blow?"

"It didn't do much for me."

"Maybe it wasn't good shit." I shook my head. "Listen to me. I sound like a junkie."

Someone in the crowd fell, or was shoved, against my back, and I turned around. "Well," he said, "aren't you the handsome couple. Are you an item?" It was Lenny. "I recognize you," he said. He held a drink in his right hand and uncoiled the index finger to poke me between the pectorals. "We were supposed to get married and you never showed up at the church." I hadn't seen him since Ron's party when he had taken me to the bathroom. He didn't seem to be handling his drugs very well this evening. He'd changed his hair to Andy-Warhol-white and wore tight-fitting Capri pants.

"This is my friend, Dean," I said, when I saw Lenny salivating.

He changed his glass to his left hand and extended his right in a manner suggesting he wished to have it kissed. "Leonard," he said. "It's a pleasure to see two gorgeous men with such healthy, thick hair in a place where everyone else either looks like a convict or Sinead O'Connor. Desert Storm was a disaster for men's hair styles." Dean smiled and winked at me. "And you." Lenny turned back to me. "How could you have left me at the altar?"

"He was saving himself for me," said Dean.

Dean's remark pleased me enormously, but before I had a chance to worry about his sincerity or decide that I'd read too much into it, someone in the crowd yelled for Lenny. "I guess we're leaving," he said. A boy, dressed in black, now waited at his elbow.

"Let's leave," the boy commanded.

"Okay. Okay. Okay." While still looking at Dean, and me Lenny fluttered his hand as if to say *hold on* to his friend. "We're off to Styx. Why don't you come with us? I've got ecstasy."

"No, thanks," said Dean.

"Now, Lenny," said the boy.

Lenny puffed out his cheeks. "Straight boys are so droll." I watched his white head above the crowd as he and the boy weaved their way to the door. Lenny shrieked repeatedly, goosing a path through the people. Half his victims laughed and the other half looked annoyed.

"What a character," said Dean.

"An original," I said. Really, I thought he had become something of a cliché.

"If you're not busy we could work out tomorrow, then go to brunch?"

"No," I said. "I mean, no, I'm not busy. I'd like that."

"I'd like that too. Give me your number and I'll call." He took a piece of notepaper from the bar and motioned for the pig-nosed bartender. "We need a pencil," he yelled.

"I have one in my car," I said. "If you're leaving, I'm leaving."

HUMAN IMMUNODEFICIENCY VIRUS

I sit up in bed with foreboding. My imagination betrays me; I struggle with issues inhabiting the black, cold space between the planets. A pressing tightness pinches my head as if with a phrenologist's forceps; wetness surrounds my feverish form on all sides; clean, smooth sheets which welcomed me warmly cling to me now, soaked and soggy like a nutrition-less slice of white bread, bloated and peculiar in the bottom of an unscoured sink. My shoulders slump, recollecting the nightmare, replaying the diagnosis: seropositive reactive. I cough up the disorders, pneumocystis, toxoplasmosis, Kaposi's sarcoma, and lymphoma like phlegm and lie down beside him on the saturated mattress one more time.

౭౬౭౬ Chapter Twelve

W HEN DEAN PLACED HIS TOWEL on the hook, I glanced at his ass, but I made sure I was looking into his eyes when he turned around in the shower spray. He had an archetypical physique—complete with rounded pecs and a washboard stomach—and his manner told me he'd never felt self-conscious about nudity. We had walked into the vacant showers through a practically empty locker room. "I've never really worked out in the morning," I said. "It's harder, but it's great to be up early—on a Sunday."

Dean tilted his head under the stream of water until his hair was completely wet. "The people most likely to keep on jogging, run in the morning." He poured a dab of shampoo into his palm and began to wash his hair. "You're strong," he said.

I checked out his body again, while he had his eyes closed. He had the exact kind of build that I admired. V-shaped. Small waist. Muscular ass. He had a long, thick, nicely shaped penis too—that stuck out a little and didn't just hang limp. I started to get aroused so I turned, closed my eyes, and held my head under the hot water. "I haven't been working out very seriously for a while," I said. "I've lost strength."

"We could train together if you want," said Dean. He rinsed out all the lather and massaged his scalp with his fingertips. "I get better workouts with a partner." Initially his suggestion thrilled me, and then I wondered if he only wanted friendship. "You've got a nice shape," he said.

"I've always had this belly," I said.

"I think it's sexy," said Dean.

❧ • ❧

The restaurant showed slides of artwork accompanied by classical music, and that prompted Dean to ask if I ever went to the symphony.

"I've been to concerts in Grant Park," I said.

"Bob and I went to the Pops," he said. I added this bit of information to the friendship column. "There's a Grant Park concert on Wednesday. Want to go?" I nodded, but didn't actually say yes. "We could go see the Chicago Symphony too," he said. "I want to see Orchestra Hall."

"That won't be until fall," I said. "How do you know we'll still be friends?"

"I'm a great judge of character." Dean smiled.

There were few times, if any, when I'd been as sexually attracted to someone. It wasn't an easy feeling to deal with either, because I couldn't believe that Dean felt as strongly about me. He seemed so composed, so at ease, while I had difficulty not worrying about where this would all lead. I can't honestly say that I'd thought that seriously about having a lover, but I was already fantasizing about Dean in a way that made me fearful. I didn't know his last name; I didn't know what he did for a living; I didn't know what his relationship with Bob had been; I didn't know if he'd ever had a lover. What I didn't know added to the excitement of being with him, for sure, but I'd never been good at taking emotional chances. During the promiscuous early eighties, gays jumped easily from one long-term relationship to another, but that seemed unnatural to me. I knew one fellow who wouldn't break up with a lover until he was sure he had a replacement. Cold-hearted behavior. In spite of all the things I thought were wrong about my parents' marriage, it had at least lasted, and I am relatively sure that my father had been monogamous. Marriage to me means for keeps—and that goes for gay marriages as well.

These thoughts were foolish. At least I was up early, I wasn't strung out on cocaine, and I had already been to the health club. Why not enjoy the moment? No one, not even I, could say this temperate man sitting beside me wasn't a good thing—at least for now. I took a drink of coffee and put my hand in my lap to straighten my napkin. That's when Dean reached under the table, took my hand, and held it; he didn't let go either—even when the waitress came with our breakfasts. "I'm glad we met," he said.

After brunch we walked through Lincoln Park, then along the lakefront. It was cool, almost fall-like, for early August, and the air smelled of new-mown grass. Autumn is my favorite season in Chicago, as spring is usually a disappointment around the Great Lakes—since the bleakness of winter is most often replaced without pause by oppressive, summer humidity. I couldn't help thinking how satisfying it would be to spend September watching the leaves turn to red and gold and yellow—with a friend.

"Do you like baseball?" said Dean.

"I'm not a great athlete," I said.

"I meant do you like the Cubs or the White Sox?"

"I grew up in Ohio. I like the Reds. I like going out to eat and seeing a movie."

"Let's go to Wrigley Field this week," said Dean. "They should never have gotten lights."

"Traditionalist," I said.

"I'm from New England," he laughed.

"What kind of name is Azevedo?"

"Portuguese. I grew up in New Bedford."

"Call me Ishmael," I said.

Dean smiled again and nodded. "Our claim to fame," he said. "My grandparents came from Porto—in northern Portugal—but they weren't fishermen."

I had, of course, assumed Dean was Italian, but this new, correct information only heightened his appeal, and when we stopped at Diversey Harbor by the boats, I glanced once again at his face before looking out over the moorings. "Let's get a sailboat and go around the world," I said. "Just the two of us." The sun reflected off the water, and a sudden gust of cooler air dimpled the surface, giving it the appearance of polished pewter.

"The Windy City," said Dean.

"Actually, it's because of the politics," I said, "not the wind. Don't you like the idea of sailing around the world with me?"

"I'd go anywhere with you." He smiled and leaned against me at the shoulder. "Let me cook dinner for you tonight. I'll make Portuguese, if we can find all the ingredients." Apparently he didn't want the date to end. "There's one catch," he said. "We have to mess up your kitchen—so we can be alone."

He and Bob had a place together. Dean talked a lot about him, just as I talked about Cynthia. Was Bob the jealous type? Was Bob in love with Dean? Would he resent me? I was getting ahead of myself. I'd only known Dean for a day.

While he prepared dinner, I started a conversation about lovers. Dean said he'd always had a one: he didn't enjoy being alone and wasn't willing to spend an inordinate amount of time in bars. He seemed incredulous that I'd never had a lover. His first relationship, he said, had involved an older man; they were together for three years. They met during Dean's first year at design school and there'd been a twenty-year age difference between them. When I asked him if he had left the man for someone else, he told me that the man, Reese, left him. "I got too old," Dean laughed. "You don't have many pots and pans," he said.

The first thing he had done, after we came back with the bags of groceries, was clean out my refrigerator. I stood silently while he tossed things in the empty grocery bag, as if I had no idea how the green bread, fuzzy mayonnaise, and black cheese had gotten there in the first place. He even threw out the half dozen remaining eggs though I protested that they weren't that old. "Dinner smells good," I said.

"Really? I think it's the worst part of *Caldeirada*. Some seafood doesn't smell so great while it's cooking," he said.

"It feels homey having a meal prepared in my kitchen. I eat a lot of tuna fish."

He finished poking in the pot of seafood, went to the sink, and put down the long-handled fork, then turned to face me. He leaned back against the countertop, resting the heels of his hands on the edge. "Come here," he said. I took a step toward him. "All the way," he said, reaching out. I moved into his arms. "Hungry?" he said.

"For dinner?" I kissed him, and then rested my chin on his shoulder. His neck felt warm and smooth, and an image of Steve Schroeder came unexpectedly to mind.

We stood there in front of the sink, leaning into each other, making out; there was no groping—I was content to feel his lats and to have my arms around his waist—but there was no hiding my excitement. I was happy to discover that Dean was just as excited; that did wonders for my confidence. I thought maybe after dinner we'd have sex, and I felt a little uneasy about the prospect. Even before AIDS, sex for the first time with a person could be an unsettling experience. Some would only get screwed, others would never get screwed, some only wanted to have oral sex, some only wanted masturbation, and some got kinky the first time. Others defied categorization.

I once brought a college hockey player home one night, after we'd gotten loaded in a bar. He was home for semester break from Minnesota. He had curly, brown hair and the most innocent, cherubic face. We sat on the edge of my bed for hours talking and laughing, and I became progressively more impassioned. He was excited too; he kept rubbing the top of my foot with his foot. We'd both taken off our shoes, but he'd left his thick, white socks on. Ever so often I suggested that we get undressed down to our underwear, but he kept prolonging our foreplay. He was stocky, but well built, and I was dying to roll around with him in bed. Finally, he asked me to turn the lights completely off—I'd already dimmed them leaving enough light to see his face—and I stood up to comply. I heard the rustle of his Levis as he pulled them off, then the sheets as he stripped them back, and the creaking of the mattress when he got into bed, and I practically tore off my own clothes to get in beside him. He had covered himself with the top sheet, so I got underneath as well. He snuggled up against me and we began to kiss. I felt his smooth bare back and arms, then gradually reached down to feel his ass. He was wearing something, but it wasn't soft or cottony. I explored the waistband with my fingers, then moved my hand down to his thighs. They were covered with the same stiff, satiny material. I reached lower, felt his calves and feet. Here the texture of the fabric was different, almost lacy. I felt his thighs again and detected a ribbon-like basting. I began to see with my hands. I rolled over and turned the light on by the bed to confirm what I had discovered. He smiled, guiltily, and I pulled back the sheet. Leggings. He wore powder blue leggings. Like the kind a ballerina wears under her tutu.

Dean prepared the most delicious dinner: clams, white fish, huge chunks of squid, shrimp—cooked in tomatoes, olive oil, and wine, and seasoned with peppercorns, onions, and garlic. We sat across the table from one another talking between the bites and eating until both of us were stuffed. It was an entirely wonderful evening and although I never actually ask him to spend the night, he stayed over; it was the first time I could remember willingly having an overnight guest, because I simply preferred sleeping alone. There had been times when a trick drank too much and passed out in my bedroom, and there'd been times when I couldn't persuade someone to leave, but I'd never in recent memory been so willing to have company in my bed.

Dean and I walked into the bedroom. He turned the lamp on next to the bed and took off his tee shirt. Then he sat down in the chair and pulled off his gym shoes and socks. He stood up again and unbuttoned his fly. He pushed his jeans down off his hips, and then hesitated. "Aren't you going to get undressed?" he asked, standing there in the sexiest pair of white boxer shorts that I've ever seen.

❧•❧

He stayed every night for the next two weeks. And every evening I worried that this would be the night when he told me he couldn't sleep over. We had breakfast every morning at the Golden Nugget, close to my apartment, and then he came to the shop at noon so we could have lunch. One day I bent to smell a pot of yellow jonquils and looked up as he came through the door with his design portfolio; he was dressed in a plum-colored polo shirt, crisply-pressed khakis, and cowboy boots, and my hands and fingers tingled and my knees and legs shook so that I sat down on my stool to calm myself.

When Joey first met Dean, he described him as breathtaking, but he called later and cautioned me to watch out. I attributed his warning to jealousy, but I didn't relax each evening until after Dean and I'd had sex—which I'm pleased to say was tender, affectionate, and safe.

Mae and Cynthia were busy with their new lives, and I saw less of them, but in a way, especially where Cynthia was concerned, their absence left the opening that Dean now filled. I called Mae. She responded to my comments about Dean with: "That's nice; that sounds like fun." Then she continued with her pregnancy update and that turned to complaints about Charlie's refusal to go to Lamaze classes.

Cynthia and I had two lengthy telephone conversations about Dean when she called the shop. "I love you, Chris," she said, "and don't want to see you get hurt."

I was surrounded by negativism, and as much as I wanted to ignore anything negative, I became obsessed that he would suddenly tire of me one evening or morning and leave. He wouldn't deliberately hurt me. He'd simply get bored and go. Dean was confident and aggressive and went after what he wanted—and he could replace me in an instant.

My pragmatic side insisted: I couldn't lose. I was seeing the hottest man in Chicago. No one disagreed on this point. Joey, Annette, all the gays who happened to be in the shop when he came to get me for lunch, and Cynthia. She had taken the day off to run errands and select things for hers and Louie's new apartment, and stopped in at lunchtime, so I asked her to join us.

We ordered three soup and sandwich specials and handed our menus to the waiter. Conversation between Cynthia and Dean was relaxed and easy, and it pleased me to see them get on so well. Dean presented his background, recounting how we'd met with elaborate detail, and I began to appreciate the things one learned when a third person enters the equation. Apparently he had found no need to say such reassuring things to my face. Dean had overlooked, or underestimated, the depth of my insecurity. He leaned closer and put his hand on my leg and gave it a squeeze.

"The smile was the clincher for me," said Dean.

"And his eyes," said Cynthia. "They sparkle when he's happy." She reached across the table and held my hand.

"Do you suppose the three of us could have lunch together every day?" I said.

Back in the store, Dean hugged me, kissed Cynthia and left for his afternoon interview. He waved to us through the window and disappeared from view. Cynthia said that he looked like Clark Gable. I'd never seen Rhett Butler in his face, but I agreed that he was distinguished-looking.

That night she called while Dean and I were eating dinner. I couldn't talk freely with him sitting across the table, but I wanted to say: *Why the sudden interest after two months?* I answered her inquiries with *uh huh, no, yes,* and *huh?* Her most pointed question had to do with whether or not I'd told Dean about my H.I.V. status. She was tactful, if indeed it's possible to be tactful where a terminal illness is concerned, but I found her inquiry a little insulting. I'd never questioned her about her sex life. Louis struck me as the unfaithful sort—he may have even been with prostitutes—but I would never have asked if she and Louie had been tested, or if they'd discussed the results. And my sex life was none of her business either. It was my own fault for being so honest with her in the past, but I made up my mind that when she called next time, I'd tell her.

I hadn't yet broached the subject of my status. It was selfish. But I didn't want to scare him away. He was, no doubt, positive too. We were safe; there was no real threat to him as long as we masturbated each other and were careful not to exchange fluids. We kissed, but people didn't get AIDS by kissing. I made sure I didn't have any canker sores—I had my special mouthwash with tetracycline—and I resisted deep-tongue French-kissing. Infection wasn't the real problem; Dr. Jacoby said it was a difficult disease to contract. The ramifications, if one did get the disease, however, were terrifying. That was the problem. How could I let a person get involved with me when I might die in a few years? I tried not to think that way. I hated the newspapers and television for talking about AIDS as if it were a death sentence, but I assumed I wouldn't outlive Mother. Each time I did something, I found myself wondering if I would do it again. The second Sunday that Dean and I spent together, we went to the Lincoln Park zoo and while I was watching a particularly beautiful Bengal tiger, my eyes misted. I thought it might be the last time that I'd ever see a Bengal tiger. I told Dean that I wanted to come back to the zoo the very next Sunday, but I didn't tell him why.

There's no winning a game like that. Whatever I do, whatever any of us does, the possibility looms that we'll never see or do the exact thing again. It's always possible that each sunrise, each sunset, will be our last. My health hadn't deteriorated. I felt fine. But meeting Dean at such a time in my life troubled me.

Dr. Jacoby's office gives each patient a suggested prophylaxis for H.I.V.–positive people. At 500 T-cells, a person should go on AZT or ddI or ddC. At 200 a person should be taking preventive measures for pneumonia. At 100 a person should take a drug to ward off toxoplasmosis—a brain infection. Below 50 something called cyrptosporidium can occur and intestinal protozoa can cause diarrhea and gallbladder disease. Cytomegalovirus becomes common only in people with fewer that 50 T-cells. CMV, as it's known, causes esophagitis, colitis, and blindness. And then there's Mycobacterium Avium Complex: high fevers, anemia, weight loss, diarrhea. In a life that had been plagued with irrational, illogical behavior, here was perhaps my most irrational and illogical act. Allowing myself to form an attachment with someone. Allowing myself to think of another man as my lover.

છ•ઙ

"This is a strange restaurant," said Dean.

"A friend brought me here once, sort of on a date; he thought it was a hoot."

"Is the food eatable?"

"The booths are private, and we have to talk. I'll need humor to get through this."

"What? Are you dumping me?" Dean smiled at me.

"You may dump me," I said. "We're not ready to order, Randy; give us a few minutes."

"You think we should slow down? I know I'm obsessive when I meet someone, but—"

"It's just that you've had so many relationships and I haven't really ever had one. I feel like this, us, is not that big a deal to you. It's life as usual and when you get bored with me, you'll be gone." I felt like the breath had been knocked out of me, but I had to go through with this.

"That's pretty insulting. What have I done to make you think I'm such a jerk?"

"I'm crazy about you—"

"It sounds like you're attracted to me physically, but not in any other way. If you have that low of an opinion of me—"

"How can you expect me to really know you after only one month? I'm getting too used to you; I'm don't want to get hurt. You've had five lovers for Christ's sake. You practically belong to the Lover of the Month Club."

"Don't turn this into one of your jokes."

"At least you're smiling."

"You're upsetting me."

"It's not just physical. If it were, I'd be over you. I know. But I have to make sure this is not just another affair for you. I'm not like you. I didn't love my father, I barely get along with my mother, I always had to do drugs just to have sex, and I don't like to be touched that much. But I haven't been able to push you away."

"Keep trying. You know what a self-fulfilling prophecy is? If you surround us with all this negative energy, if you keep thinking something bad is going to happen—"

"See. You're already getting pissed off."

"I'm not pissed. I love you and I don't want our relationship to be quite so difficult."

"We're still not ready, Randy, unless…Do you know what you want, Dean? We'd better order or we'll keep getting interrupted."

"I don't feel like eating—"

"Bring two of the steak and lobster combinations with baked potatoes—no butter or sour cream. Do you have Dijon mustard? Medium-well on the steaks.

"Do you like it when I order for you? Cynthia used to work in a restaurant, and one time these two dykes came in, and after she took the first girl's order, she turned to the second to ask her what she wanted, but before she could say a word, the first girl yelled: 'I'll order for her'."

"Stick to the bad news."

"Remember in the kitchen about three weeks ago, when we talked about being tested? And I avoided the issue. I said I was fine. Well, I am. I mean, my health is fine, but—"

"Please—"

"I'm positive. I'm sorry I didn't tell you sooner; it's not an easy thing for me to discuss, but I've never really had to before."

"How long have you known?"

"Almost a year."

"Do you have any idea when you were infected?"

"I've been careful for at least three years, but before then it could have been lots of people. There's such a long incubation period that some people don't show any symptoms for up to eight years."

"I know. I'm lucky to be negative. I have so many friends who aren't. Give me your hand, because I have a confession."

"You met someone else. I knew it—"

"Shut up and listen. I've seen your medicine under the bathroom sink and I've seen you taking your pills. If you didn't want me to know, you'd have done a hell of a lot better job of hiding it. You can trust me, Chris."

"There was this time when I got really loaded at home. I'd done about three grams of coke and I was sitting on the floor watching porno and drinking vodka—right out of the bottle. I started blacking out at home at some point and decided to go out to a bookstore on Broadway. I have flashes of memory where I'm walking up the stairs and past the counter—and I remember seeing a guy with curly hair standing in a patch of light in the back room. The next thing I remember is being on my knees and looking up at him in a booth. When I'm sober, I don't care for bookstores that much: they're too dark and they smell like locker rooms. We must have decided to go back to my place, because I remember crossing Clark Street together and I remember having a conversation. I remember not being affected by the cold even though it was really windy. I don't actually recall getting to my apartment or climbing into bed, but I have images of us kissing. That's all. Next afternoon—Sunday—I woke up at three o'clock and felt like I'd been ridden in the Kentucky Derby. My mouth was dry and sour, and I had a headache. I went into the kitchen—at first I forgot that I'd had someone there—but slowly I began to remember the fragments that I'm telling you. Then, in the kitchen, I saw a note on the table: *I didn't want to wake you. I borrowed a soda. Hope you don't mind. Mike.*

"I never did hear from anyone named Mike. I panicked. I didn't have any idea what I'd done. I've heard lots of people talking about blacking out. In college, friends laughed about it happening to them. I went back into my bedroom and looked at the sheets. They were stained, and I remembered that he'd been on top.

"I'm a mess; I'm sorry to put you through this," I said.

"No you're not a mess. You're sensitive and you're lonely. I'm not going to leave you. I hate to see you cry."

"I feel stupid."

"Give me a kiss and wipe your eyes before Randy comes back. You've told me. Now stop worrying and try to enjoy us being together. We haven't even begun to have fun."

"It's not fair to you to get involved with someone who might not see 1990."

"I think you're getting a little ahead of yourself. The whole idea now is to treat AIDS like a chronic disease, you know, prevent the diseases that result from infection to buy some time till there's a cure. I wish I could say you were the first person I'd met that was positive, but you're not. I know lots of people in Boston on AZT."

"They're not even sure now that AZT does any good. I read that one research study showed that it only masked the symptoms while the person's immune system continued to deteriorate. There have been so many false leads; I'm afraid time's going to run out."

"Have you always been so negative about things?"

"No pun intended? I think it's better to expect the worst and be pleasantly surprised than the other way around. Thanks, Randy."

"Can I get you gentlemen anything else?"

"Dean?

"No, I'm fine."

"I'll come back when you're ready for coffee and dessert," said Randy. "Save some room; we have a killer cheesecake. You guys didn't eat your kiwi. Don't you want your kiwi?"

DREAMS

I stand at the top of an outdoor stairway. The steep steps hug the building's exterior, and then turn at a sharp angle to span the flat roof. This stairway wobbles; it's wooden and worn, without a trace of paint, and there is darkness of the early morning or late night variety all around. My back is turned on sin, spreading like ink. It's enveloping me, surrounding me, like exhaust from cars as I peddle through traffic. I've been dreaming a lot lately. Dreaming of high limbs and forgotten wars and iron lungs with rear view mirrors. Last night I dreamed I awoke to find two of my teeth on the floor, then a gold filling as long as a tooth pick came out in my mouth while I chewed on wet grass. I tried to slip it back into its slot—past the roof of my mouth, into my sinuses, close to my brain. The night before I dreamed I sat in a restaurant in my underwear and the night before that I dreamed about poverty and the night before that I dreamed about death. This dream must be about love, because suddenly there's no railing; the staircase is floating, no longer anchored to the roof. I fall to my knees and use my hands to find my way in darkness to the treads. When I get to the edge where the first riser begins, the wooden surface falls out beneath me, or do I simply float above it? There's blackness now all around me, and the air is hot. Now that everything has gone wrong, I question why I came up these steps in the first place. Did I see him? Was I following him? Did he ask me to come up here with him? And where is he now that I've made the climb, now that I've gone out on this limb missing two of my teeth and one gold filling?

సుసుసు Chapter Thirteen

E VERY FRIDAY AFTERNOON, precisely at four, Joey stopped
in to pester me about buying the flower shop: purchasing the
receivables and the delivery truck and taking over the lease.
With Thanksgiving less than two months away, it sounded like a reasonable idea, and since Dean hadn't found a design job, I wondered if
he'd consider going into partnership with me. I still had almost $20,000
left of my profit sharing money from Bradley, invested in a low-rate
CD, and during the nine weeks that Dean and I'd been together my
money had gone a lot further. And for the first time I allowed myself
to think about the money I'd wasted on cocaine: over $4,000 since I
had resigned. No question, I was frightened by the responsibilities of
owning a business—for obvious reasons—but I also fantasized that this
shop might merely be the first step and that soon I could have an entire chain of outlets. I suppose I envisioned myself as some sort of
Mildred Pierce of the flower business. But, I also worried that getting
involved with Dean in this way wasn't good judgment. After Norberto
left, I had resolved to keep work and romance separate.

But Dean had saved my life—or extended it—for we had settled
into an agreeable, healthy routine. We were in bed immediately following the ten o'clock news, we ate three nutritious meals a day—broiled
filet of sole, steamed broccoli, and brown rice was typical—we lifted
every morning before I went to work, and we spent our Sundays visiting museums or watching football or driving to the Northshore to see

the mansions along the lakefront. I was up each morning at 6 A.M., rested and optimistic, and amazed that I'd ever stayed up all night without sleep. I seldom drank alcohol, and didn't miss it, but attended AA meetings with Dean and Bob. Dean wanted to continue going until Bob made friends—since he'd already deserted him to some extent. I didn't like AA any more than before, but went without complaint so as not to be the source of jealousy. One evening when we stopped to pick up Bob, we heard rhythmic, driving music coming from inside the apartment, and we opened the door and found him wearing a shoulder-length, red wig and black leotards and dancing around the living room in an impression of a maniacal aerobics instructor. He jerked his head—and hair—from left to right and rotated his shoulders in an up and down circular motion. "Hi, I'm Mitzi," he said, in a doll-like squeal. His movements were so ridiculous that Dean and I burst into laughter. I got the feeling that since Dean had chosen me, Bob had automatically approved, but I still believed that he was in love with Dean. Dean laughed. "Not possible," he said. "We've been friends too long." Still, I sensed something unusual about their relationship. I sensed resentment on Bob's part. Even though Dean had most of his clothes at Bob's apartment, he stayed at mine. Lately, to my discomfort, Dean had been including him in our Sunday plans, because he didn't want him to be lonely. I told myself that his concern was noble, but I had to fight off feelings of jealousy when Dean asked if I'd mind Bob going with us to Lake Geneva to see the fall colors on Sunday. On that trip late in September, after Dean went inside an ice cream shop to get us sundaes, Bob pinched my nipple and said, "You better be good to me or Dean will drop you."

That entire day in Lake Geneva, Bob brought up events from Dean's past: What was that French boy's name from New York? And: Marco was crazy for Dean! And: Dean and Robert disappeared for a whole month. Bob left the impression that Dean had had hundreds of boyfriends. Initially I convinced myself that Bob didn't resent me, and then gradually I began to resent him. But I didn't show it. I can thank my father for my ability to conceal anguish and embarrassment.

Shortly before we left Lake Geneva, at dusk, Bob said, "We're going home to Massachusetts for Thanksgiving." Dean was in a store, looking at slacks, while Bob and I waited on the sidewalk, and the news unnerved me so that I took hold of a parking meter to steady myself and changed the subject before he could see that I was upset. I'd had no inkling of this trip; Dean hadn't hinted of plans to go east. First I tried to infer how long he'd be gone, and then I began to worry that he'd go back for Christmas too and decide to stay over for New Year's as well because Bob had already related how he and Dean had gone to New York City for New Year's Eve on several occasions in the past. By this point I had concluded that I'd be alone for the holidays. What would I do? Cynthia had only told me that they were going to spend the holiday with Louie's parents in Melrose Park. Mae had plans too. I could go home to see Mother for Thanksgiving, but knew I'd be miserable. I'd spent every single day and night with Dean since we met, and the prospect of being without him was more than I could bear.

We'd taken my car, and Dean had promised to drive on the way home, but I said it wasn't necessary. I gripped the steering wheel tensely and barely spoke as we turned south on Route 52. The two of them did the talking: Dean said that Wisconsin reminded him of Vermont; Bob said the Green Mountains were more dramatic, but admitted that Dairyland was prettier than he had expected.

After about an hour Dean noticed that I responded to his questions with *yes, no,* or *I'm not sure,* and when he also got quiet, Bob fell asleep in the back seat so that the final hour of the trip was spent in utter silence. I hated not being able to control my emotions. As a child I'd gone for days not talking to Daddy, but he didn't notice. He didn't have anything to say to me anyway. Mother, on the other hand, would know at once that I wasn't talking and would reprimand me, warning that I'd better start acting civil or she'd tell Daddy. Until I was a teenager she'd slap me for ignoring her, but after I grabbed her hands in midair one time and held them so she couldn't, she limited herself to a warning that Daddy would punish me when he came home. What usually happened was that he would come home, tell me to sprawl over a footstool, and then take off his belt. After he had thrashed me for about five minutes, Mother would scream, "Dale, that's enough. Stop it. Stop it." But for him these beatings turned into something like a 1960's version of an aerobic workout. He worked up a sweat, his feet raised off the floor as if he were dancing, and he made grunting noises when he landed especially vigorous blows.

On one occasion, when I was fourteen, he came home, and Mother reported my sins. He looked at her briefly, sighed, slumped into his chair, and started to cry. He looked so pathetic that I'd have preferred a beating. He leaned forward, holding his head in his hands, and wept without stopping. Mucus hung in strands from his nose, and he didn't look up. I went over, sat on the edge of his chair, and put my arm over his shoulder and tried to comfort him. "It's not so bad, Daddy," I said. "I'm sorry."

I merged the car into the *Incorrect Change* lane. It was dark, and I hadn't been able to see Dean's face. We pulled up next to the tollbooth, and as I reached into the ashtray for a dollar bill, I caught his expression. He looked sad and confused. I took my change, the light changed to green, and I accelerated onto the Tri-State and headed toward Chicago. Dean reached over and put his hand on mine. "Is everything all right?" he asked.

Even if Bob hadn't been in the back seat snoring, I couldn't have talked to Dean, because I felt too alone and isolated. We drove the whole distance down the Tri-State, onto the Kennedy, and into the city, and bypassed the Fullerton exit before Dean tried again.

"You're taking Bob home, right?"

"I'm taking both of you home."

"Why? What's wrong?"

"I need to be alone."

We drove the remaining blocks to Bob's apartment in more silence. Bob stirred, then stretched. When we pulled into the driveway of his apartment, he sat forward. "We're here already? That was fast." The doorman came to the car and opened Dean's door. "I'm not getting out," said Dean. "I'll call you tomorrow, Bob."

Bob got out of the car. "Thanks for driving, Chris. I had a great time. And thanks for letting me tag along." I managed to say *goodnight.*

"Can we go somewhere for coffee?" said Dean.

"I'm tired," I said, "but if I have coffee, I won't sleep."

"Have decaf. Chris, I'm not letting you drive off without talking. This doesn't feel right; if I did something wrong, we should talk. Let's go to Periwinkle's."

"I don't think I can."

"I don't understand. Please tell me what's wrong."

"Can't we talk tomorrow? I can't go into a crowded restaurant and talk."

"Let's go to the lake."

There's a stretch of terraced rocks to the north, frequented by lovers late in the evening, where Dean and I'd been before. It overlooks Lake Michigan on a jutting strip of land where it's possible to see the center of the city to the south. We came here one morning before sunrise; I'd never before felt so connected to another person. That morning represented a new high in human relationships—and I wasn't on coke, or alcohol, or pot. And yet I felt exhilaration. A part of me now said I was pushing our relationship to an end. It was no big deal that Dean was planning to go home for Thanksgiving; I was only jealous that he would be with Bob instead of me. I was feeling sorry for myself. I would be alone, but I'd spent thirty-one years alone and gotten by. And I'd get over Dean. In time, I'd be back to normal. The other part of me couldn't ignore what normal had been. If Dean could go to Massachusetts without me, then that was all the proof necessary: Dean wasn't as in love with me as I was with him. There was no way I could spend a weekend with my mother and leave Dean behind in Chicago. It was the beginning of the end, and I didn't see any sense letting our affair die a slow, painful death. I pulled into a spot, far away from the three other parked cars. Despite that it was early October, that it was nearly midnight, balmy air wafted off the lake; it was the quintessential Indian Summer night. I shut off the engine and looked straight ahead.

"I'm better off alone," I said.

"You're breaking up with me?"

"Don't worry; you'll have someone else in no time."

"I don't want someone else. I don't even know what's wrong and you're accusing me of starting with someone new."

"Can you honestly say you wouldn't have a new lover if you weren't with me? You can't stand being by yourself."

"I like sharing experiences; that doesn't make me bad. You're the one with a problem. You're the one afraid of emotional commitment. I'd like to know what brought this on because I think it's an excuse to break up so you can get back out in the bars. Would you please look at me?"

"Oh, I have a problem? That's it? I have a problem? Don't try to pretend that you and Bob won't hit the bars in Boston and maybe that'll be such a kick you'll go on to New York for the weekend. When were you going to break the news about your trip? Were you going to call from the airport?"

Dean looked away, exhaled and slumped back against his seat. Then in a low, deliberate voice said: "I'm not planning to go out while I'm home unless you want to see the bars. And I'm not even going home unless you go with me—and who said anything about New York?"

"Bob. He gave me all the delicious details of what riotous fun you two always have in the Big Apple. According to him you've had boy-friends from every country in Europe except Liechtenstein. Maybe you'll get lucky this year and complete the set. And you don't have to pretend you were going to ask me to come along because my feelings are hurt."

"Call United Airlines right now, Chris. You'll find reservations for both of us. And if you talk to Annette, you'll see I've already made sure that you can get away from the shop for a four-day weekend."

What could I say? I felt stupid. I felt relieved. I am afraid of inti-macy. I have a right to be. I felt stupid when I was growing up. I'm smart enough to understand that my parents didn't know any other way, that they weren't happy with their lives, and that I didn't turn out the way either of them had intended—but that's a boring subject.

Whatever the reasons for their behavior, I'm the one who has to live with the results. I had a breakthrough with Dean. I was beginning to know real love. Or was it the slant of his eyes, the crimson of his lips, the curve of his shoulders, the olive smoothness of his skin? It didn't matter. No one had been able to hold my interest, my concern, my desire, for this long. I was compelled to be with him. Since I'd met him I'd been on a high, and the idea of him leaving me behind, the thought of him going off to Boston, had dropped me as low as when I was coming down from a night of drugs. The physical symptoms weren't there—I wasn't tired and headachy—but my state of mind was the same.

We stayed awake for hours talking. He had wanted to surprise me; that's why he hadn't said anything about Boston. And he admitted, after I coaxed, that he was worried too: Bob was jealous. Now that I was the clear winner, I was able to feel sympathetic toward Bob. He depended on Dean and didn't want to lose his friendship. But Dean wasn't in love with Bob—and had never been in love with him. Dean confessed that Bob had been in love with him at one time, but wouldn't admit that he was still in love with him. I knew he was, and believe it troubled Dean not to respond in kind to his friend's affection. He prayed that Bob would meet someone, he said. He hoped Bob would fall madly, head-over-heels, so to speak, in love.

❧ • ❧

"These floors are oak," said Dean, after having ripped the corner of the carpeting back in the living room. We'd just finished moving all my bedroom furniture out of this room and into the den—the room that was supposed to be the bedroom—so we could paint. "I'll be right back," he said. I stood as if in an eddy, as he whooshed past me to the door. I listened as he descended the steps, three at a time, and unbolted the door at the foot of the stairs. I heard him in the entryway when he knocked at Clinton and Angelo's door, then muffled voices as he and—Was it Angelo?—exchanged greetings. Gradually, the voices died down and I heard their door close, and when the silence held, I knew Dean had gone inside.

I smiled to myself, holding the new paintbrush at my side, and surveyed the walls. He was right: the room was dark and dreary, but I'd argued, long after realizing he was correct, that if we were going to paint, we should choose a color—like Confederate Blue. Dean said since all the rooms were small, it would only complicate our redecorating if we tried to work with color. This way we could get by with the pieces of furniture that I had and use the Rose of Sharon quilt that Mother sent to me in the spring. Dean had discovered it on the shelf in my closet when we were making room for his clothes, and raved about it. He marveled at how meticulously the stitches had been made and said it was hard to believe that it was all handwork.

I heard the downstairs door squeak open and Dean's footsteps as he ran back up the stairs, three at a time.

"We're going to refinish the floors," he said. "Clinton will pay for the materials and equipment rental, and we'll supply the labor."

"I don't know, Dean. What if we ruin them?"

"Chris, look at this carpeting; it's rust-colored shag."

"So rip it out, and we'll polish the wood. I think those sanders are kind of tricky; it's easy to grind ruts in the wood, isn't it?"

"Not if you don't let the machine idle in one spot while it's rotating. I've done floors hundreds of times in my dad's apartments. That's how I earned extra money in the summer. Chris, these floors will look fabulous. Look." He dashed to the corner and pulled the carpeting all the way back into the center of the room, sending up a dust cloud.

Sometimes I'm overwhelmed by his enthusiasm. And evidently it shows, because Dean almost immediately says something persuasive to defuse my hesitance to see things his way.

"Imagine how great those Chinese egg pots you found for the shop will look on bleached oak floors with lush, sexy palms in them," said Dean. He unfolded his arms to indicate how big the palms should be.

"Bleached?" I said.

Dean turned around and scraped a little bit of the finish off the windowsill. "And we'll paint the woodwork glossy white. It's only maple and it doesn't have much grain."

I watched his triceps flex as he chipped at the window and I felt the familiar twinge in my groin. I walked up behind him and put my arms around him, cupping his pectorals in my hands. He leaned back into me and twisted his head to kiss me at the side of my mouth. I nibbled at his neck.

"You're putting a lot of sweat into this place," I said. "You must be planning on staying. I might just have to have my way with you, right here in the middle of the floor."

"No. Please." He dropped his scraper and turned to face me.

Usually Dean combs his hair back off his forehead. The effect is handsome because he has such a nicely shaped face and such a masculine, straight nose. That night though, his thick hair had fallen down over his forehead giving him a different, more boyish look. It was a sensation I'd never experienced before Dean with any other man; it was as if I were seeing him for the first time. It happens even now. Just when I think I know his face completely, I see it from a different angle or in a different light and I have to take a deep breath to keep from gasping. His lips were full and soft as he kissed me then, and I wanted to touch them with my fingers too, and rub my cheek against them, and feel them on my chest, and on my arms, and on my neck and thighs. I wanted to feel his warm breath on me everywhere, all over my body. Dean clutched at the buttons to my shirt and I struggled with the zipper to his chinos and we fell down and onto the unfolded drop cloth.

I told Bob that what scared me the most was the number of lovers that Dean had had.

"Don't worry about Dean," said Bob. "He's as loyal as they come."

We walked under one of the lions, turned to climb the wide expanse of stairs leading to the entrance, and steered through the crowd clustered at the admission desk. Dean had decided that Bob and I should spend some time together, to talk, and Bob suggested that we go to the Art Institute. "They have an entire wall of Haystack paintings," he'd said, referring to the museum's collection of Monets.

We gave our receipts to the uniformed man and stepped past. Bob went to the main stairway, turned and leaned back against the banister to consult the pamphlet with the diagram of museum exhibits. "And I'm no threat to you," he said. "Where do you want to go first?"

"You like the Impressionists," I said.

Bob consulted the pamphlet again, glanced up at the stairway, and gave me a nod. "Upstairs," he said.

We went upstairs and through the double doors into the first exhibit room. I was thinking of Bob's remark about not being a threat. He had a habit of making quick comments and then changing the subject before I could reply. He looked at me during these remarks, then immediately averted his eyes. That was what he had done the day we went to Lake Geneva. He fluttered like a moth, talking about any number of things as pleasantly as possible, and then at the opportune moment, changed direction, hovered at my ear, made a clipped statement, and floated off. I don't know why I hadn't realized it before: he didn't want to have a conversation or engage in a dialogue; he wanted to deliver his information and get away before I could respond. This time it wouldn't work. In front of the Van Gogh self-portrait, in the exact spot where Dean and I stood on one of our first dates, I took hold of his elbow.

"If you think you're going to bring me to a museum just to make your little comments and dart away before I can answer, you've got another think coming," I said. "Because I'll leave right now." Bob looked at me startled—I guess my voice was kind of loud—and an old man and woman standing next to us began to stare. They were so old they'd given up being discreet. "Talking to you is like boxing. You jab with your left, then with your right, and then you dance around the ring away from me, hoping I'll get tired or bored and forget to keep my guard up."

I was angry, but felt rather smug about my boxing analogy, because I am no boxer. When my dad was in the Navy, though, he was a boxer. He had blown-up, brown and white photos of himself where he was posing for the camera in his boxing gloves and shorts, and he used to show them to me when I was young. Grade school age. He'd tell me who he boxed and how many victories he'd had. I remember him watching television when there was a big match on too. He looked so young in the Navy pictures; his skin was tight, unwrinkled, and his nose was pointed. I used to look at his nose and try to compare it with the one in the pictures, but they were so different. His smile was different too. He never looked as happy as the man in those pictures. Being a champion in the Navy was his fifteen minutes of fame.

Along about fourth or fifth grade he started making me and Mae put on gloves. He kept them in a box in our garage. Even though Mae is almost two years younger, she was heavier and rather aggressive where I was concerned. I landed ten times the punches, but Daddy celebrated each of hers by slapping his leg and yelling: "Whooee!" Mother didn't like him having us box, but he'd use his nastiest tone to say something like, "For Christ's sake look how padded they are; they're for sparring," and then he'd shake a glove at her.

One summer evening between my sixth and seventh grades, Mae and I were playing tag in the back yard. We ran around, ducking behind trees and bushes, having the best time. Daddy and Mother were sitting on our dented, metal lawn chairs next to the house, and I suddenly became aware of Daddy watching. Something about the way I played must have hit a nerve; I was an effeminate child—I imagine I screamed too loudly or ran with my arms held too high. I stopped for a minute and confirmed that he was staring.

"Chris, get the gloves," he said.

"Dale, not tonight," Mother said. "Leave them alone; they're having fun." This time he didn't even bother to look at her, let alone answer.

Usually he'd have Mae and me spar for a while, until after she got in two or three blows, then he'd let us stop. I didn't enjoy punching my sister and hated getting hit in the face—even with those big padded gloves. I hated having my nose mashed flat. I hated the feeling of numbness. It all seemed so unnecessary. He'd say, keep your guard up, jab with your left, punch with your right. I'd say something about how my nose felt, and he'd answer by saying if I kept up my guard I wouldn't get hit in the face. I came back from the garage with the gloves, walking really slow, and threw the box down on the ground. "Pick a pair," he said. I took out two gloves, slowly untied the laces, and put the right one on, then clumsily put my left fist in the other. Then I held out the gloves, palms up, for him to lace. I used exaggerated, deliberate movements, showing no sign of enthusiasm. As a matter of fact, I acted bored, like: Okay, I'll do this, but it's really a stupid idea.

Mae had picked her gloves and was doing the same, but after he finished lacing me up, a little more aggressively than usual (I could feel his tension) he took them off her and threw them back in the box. He rooted around for another pair, and to my surprise, put them on himself and held his fists out to Mother. "Lace them tight," he said.

His first punch took me by surprise; he hit me squarely in the face, and I landed on my back in the yard. "Get up," he said. I got to my feet very slowly and stood facing him with my gloved hands at my sides. He punched me again in the face and this time I flew backwards a few feet. He was gritting his teeth, and as he punched, Mother and Mae both screamed. I rolled over on my stomach in the grass and curled myself into a ball. I suppose he thought he would get me so angry that I'd defend myself, but I hated him so much I didn't even want to look at him. The second time he hit me, it hadn't scared me as much as it made me angry. If it had been a boxing lesson, I might have tried for a while, but this was clearly not a lesson, and if it wasn't a lesson I knew it was simply an excuse for his humiliation. Since there was no way I could win a fight with him, I decided not to give him the satisfaction. That's when he kicked me in the ribs. The kick took away my breath, and did scare me, because I wasn't sure what it meant. He'd never kicked me; I'd never even see him kick Humphrey. I felt something hit my back—so I opened my left eye very carefully and saw one of the gloves on the grass next to my head. I wondered if he was going to keep on kicking or if he was going to start using his fists, and I clamped my eyes shut once more and got ready to take it. When nothing further happened, and Mae and Mother stopped yelling, I opened my eyes and saw him go around the corner of the garage to the driveway—past Mr. and Mrs. Epley who stood at the edge of their yard. Seconds later I heard him start the car and drive away.

"What did I do?" said Bob.

I motioned with a nod of my head for him to follow. The old couple watched us leave. I led him out of the room and onto the mezzanine next to the stairway. We walked over to the wall of architectural ironwork and I stopped next to a gate designed by Daniel Burnham.

"You say you're no threat, but all you do is say things to hurt my feelings," I said. Bob opened his mouth, but I put the palm of my hand out as if to say *stop* and continued. "All day long in Lake Geneva you mentioned boys Dean went with, boys Dean tricked with, boys who were crazy for Dean, boys, boys, boys. You may not be in love with Dean, but you sure as hell don't want me around, do you?"

"It's not like that," said Bob. "I like you, but—"

He looked embarrassed. "I know," I said. "I think we get along great and it's probably hard not to be able to spend the time with him you did before, but—"

"Let me finish," said Bob.

"No let me finish," I said. There were dozens of people going up and down the staircase beside us and their noise allowed us to stay inconspicuous as long as we didn't yell, but I had gotten loud again and Bob was starting to wave his hands, and I suddenly realized that the two of us were in a heated argument in the middle of the Art Institute.

"Let's get out of here," said Bob. This time he looked at me in a way that made me realize he was asking a question and waiting for an agreement; he wasn't making a closed statement or giving an order. I felt relieved because I had been on the verge of suggesting that we leave.

I smiled, and made a gesture toward the stairway. "Lead the way."

It was warm in the sun and I proposed walking over to the park to find a bench. We headed up Michigan Avenue silently and it was several minutes before either of us tried to resume the conversation. Bob finally spoke.

"I feel lost," he said. "What you say is true. But, I know the closer you two get, the less time I'll spend with Dean. And that freaks me out."

"You're great-looking, don't you think you might meet someone?" I said.

"There's a little problem," said Bob.

I had been so involved with my new relationship, and I'd been so jealous of Dean's friendship that I hadn't even considered Bob's status. Looking back I don't know why I didn't, since it's a game everyone seems to play. You meet a person and immediately wonder if they're positive. You talk to an acquaintance and listen while he speculates on someone else's status. Everybody is always whispering about everybody else. I've heard gays are more open with each other in San Francisco and New York, but here they're not. Bob didn't have to say another word because his frightened eyes said it all. So I told him I was positive too.

"I was pretty sure," said Bob.

"Dean didn't tell you?" I said.

"I asked him if he was having safe sex. And I asked him if you were all right. Dean's real honest. Something about the way he reacted told me you probably were. With Dean if you ask the question the right way…"

That night while we were fixing supper, Dean said he didn't have the right to tell me that Bob was positive. He said he didn't believe in discussing other people's status, but he thought I should know. He said he wanted to tell Bob and he wanted to tell me; he felt that we should talk about it with each other, that we might be able to give each other a strength that he himself couldn't. It was up to us, he said, but it could be good.

Dean took the marinated tuna steaks from the fridge—he'd prepared them the night before—and asked me to pass the olive oil. About once a week, he prepared tuna steaks by marinating them in garlic, mint, salt and pepper, lemon juice, and white wine. Then he sautéed them in olive oil over a high heat. It was one of his healthy meals, and one of my favorites, even though I made him groan with my comment: *Gays who sauté together stay together.* I removed the boiling potatoes from the stove, and wiped my hands on the dishtowel.

"How would you like to be part owner in a flower shop?" I asked.

CENOTAPH

Each of us takes a brochure as we enter the chapel. Initially I am more interested in the architecture of the interior: I study the pulpit, then the gallery upstairs with its wooden pews, trying to imagine Melville seated in the front row leaning forward in his seat to fix details in place. Then I walk along reading the plaques on the walls of the bethel. Perhaps at first I thought that all of my journal entries would be full of whispers and heat, or perhaps I thought that as with all journeys mine would come to an end and, being unsure of the destination, wanted evidence for later when I sat down alone in my kitchen on a squalling Saturday night. This bound leather book with its cream-colored pages and blue scripted passages would stand as a memorial to someone who was a part of my life before leaving to die in another place. A cenotaph—like the marble tablets lining the walls of this whaleman's chapel on Johnny Cake Hill. These pages: a testament to his touch, the smell of his hair, his warm breath, the sound of his shoes on the hardwood floors. Maybe I'll line the walls of my apartment with these framed pages, print brochures, and invite people up to examine a piece of history.

ಜಜಜ Chapter Fourteen

I'D ALWAYS EXCUSED my parent's parochialism by rationalizing that they were blue-collar, but I could no longer do that after meeting the Azevedos. The most impressive thing about our trip to New Bedford was Dean's family. He had three brothers and two sisters, his mother was a housewife—who had never had a job outside the home—and his father owned an Amoco service station. Dean's parents had known that he was gay since first year of college, and he said it never made any difference. His mother wrapped her fleshy arms around me the minute we walked through the door. She squeezed hard, then with her hands resting on my shoulders, stepped back, looked up at me, and said: "My, you are handsome." His father, a quiet man who seems always ready to smile, hugged me just as enthusiastically. My father and I never embraced.

Early Thanksgiving morning, Dean's father came into the kitchen and announced: "I'm taking Chris to see the station. Dino, are you coming—or are you going to stay in the house all day?" Dean wanted to stay behind, because his mother needed help getting table leaves and extra chairs down from the attic, so his father and I got our coats and started for the door. But first, Dean's father kissed him, then Mrs. Azevedo on the check and, wagging a finger, told them: "Do good work."

At the sound of the truck doors, and its engine, Tina came racing around the corner of the house and jumped in the truck on my side. Based on her size, about sixty pounds, and her black, curly coat, I had assumed that Tina was some type of standard poodle, clipped naturally. She sat between us on the way, looking ahead as if to help Dean's father navigate through traffic.

Mr. Azevedo pointed out where Dean had gone to grade school and junior high and he talked about his other children as if I'd known them all forever. Occasionally, I glanced at Tina, impressed by her behavior. One of her paws was white, and she had a pattern of white on her chest in the shape of a cross. "She's a Portuguese water dog," said Dean's father. Then, excited, he began to tell me about the breed. He said they were nearly extinct until efforts to save them increased their total number to about five hundred and that the fishermen used them for all kinds of jobs like bringing in lines and retrieving nets. He said they also used them to carry messages back and forth from the boats and shore. He patted Tina's head, and she licked his hand and resumed her watch. I told Dean's father that I thought working dogs were the amazing animals and that they made the best pets. "You're a hundred percent correct about that," he said.

When I had ridden with Daddy there was tension. He was angry at the wheel: he gripped the gearshift tightly and braked too hard. Some people communicate without speaking, but Daddy and I had nothing to say. One Saturday he and I drove to Dayton to shop for a power lawn mower, and as we crossed the river at the edge of New Harmony, he commented on the high water and laughed about the idiots in the bottoms who got flooded out every spring; he knocked on his head with a knuckled fist as he described how they moved back in and shoveled the mud out of their house, only to repeat the sequence a year later when the rains came. I couldn't answer. The further we drove, the more obvious I thought my inability to speak, but to this day I'm not so sure he noticed, because he didn't ask any questions and didn't have to wait for a reply. After his comment about the yearly floods, he didn't talk either. We rode the entire twenty-nine miles to Dayton and the entire twenty-nine miles home in utter silence. I focused on the emerging landscape—the maples beginning to leaf and the tulips in bloom—but when Daddy shut off the engine in our driveway, I hopped from the car and ran to my room, thinking that I was constitutionally inadequate for the world into which I'd been born.

At twelve-years-old, I worried that I might be crazy. When I chose to stay in my room, reading *The Red Pony*, and declined Steve's invitation to go swimming, Mother said, "I don't think you're all there," and after I forgot to close the gate in Humphrey's dog run and he roamed town for several hours one afternoon, Daddy called me a "stupid idiot." Years later, after I went away to college, I didn't really want to go back home. Gradually, I understood that I wasn't really an idiot or stupid, but I never really believed that I was intelligent—in spite of my A's in English. Considering that I survived the solitude of my childhood makes me proud now, when I think about it. I know I'm pretty tough, pretty resilient.

Dean's father reached over and turned off the radio, and I patted Tina's head. The silence in the truck, and not the chill, made me shiver. And just when I feared he was poised with questions about Dean and me, he asked how I liked New England. I replied that I found it interesting, especially because I had always loved history, and I addressed him as *Mr. Azevedo*. "Call me *Frank*," he said. "You're part of the family now." It may sound like a simple thing, but my eyes watered and I had to look out my side window.

Frank Azevedo cited figures about how many gallons a month his station pumped—figures which meant nothing—and pointed out that there were never fewer than seven or eight cars at the islands getting gas. He took me into the office and introduced me to his son-in-law, the station manager. "Dino's buddy from Chicago," he said. Frank's attention flattered me, and Dean told me later that his father called me "a gentleman, every bit as likable as he'd been told."

I saw that Dean's father looked out for him and protected him, but that morning Mr. Azevedo didn't ask embarrassing questions and didn't seem to expect a certain kind of behavior. I was at ease, even when he draped his arm over my shoulder and stood close, though I still tried to ascertain his interests and then make them the focus of conversation—as I did with all straight men.

With Stanley I asked about his new putter, or the Mexican family who had moved into his neighborhood; I wanted job security, and that kept the spotlight off me. Until I grew older, I'd done that with Daddy. After I left home and didn't need anything from him, I stopped, but once he was confined to bed, I felt pity for him and returned to the practice: Was Cassius Clay as strong as Joe Lewis? Were coonhounds really as smart as golden retrievers? I had developed the ability to become a chameleon around men—and women for that matter—at an early age. But with Frank Azevedo I talked with a man, very nearly my father's age, without pretending to be straight. I told him that I respected and admired Dean for his warmth and honesty and admitted that I'd never had a long-term relationship and even acknowledged that I found it difficult to trust that it was really happening. "Sometimes, I don't know what he sees in me," I said.

During the high school years, when I lay in bed trying to fantasize about Colleen, only to end up masturbating over my friend Steve, I spent many afternoons at the public library—in the psychology section on the second floor. The New Harmony Public Library is located in an old mansion, just off the courthouse square. I went after school let out, and still get anxious when I think about how I slipped by Miss Engel at the checkout desk on the main floor and sneaked up the stairs to the deserted, reference section. The shelves with the books on homosexuality were at the very end of the room in the rear of the building, and I always sat on the floor between the stacks, never at the table in the open, to pull the dusty books out—one at a time. Sometimes I crouched in a state of nervous agitation reading for hours. The fluorescent light was never bright enough, and the room was either too hot and stuffy or too cold and drafty, but adrenaline kept me reading. My survival was the issue there in the stacks. The texts were outdated, but I read everything in the section, all the time listening for Miss Engel's footsteps on the creaky stairs.

Now days a teenager trying to come to terms with being gay gets better information by watching talk shows, but I'm referring to a time before such subjects were mentioned in the media. In the library I read that overly protective mothers caused their sons to be gay. It didn't explain how one boy in a family might be gay while all his brothers were straight, or how with twin boys one could be gay and the other be straight. (My friend Paul Peyton had a straight twin.) I also read that a woman—if she had the horrible misfortune of marrying a homosexual—could tell he was gay if he treated her coldly after sexual relations. The author explained: *The homosexual male resents having to play a masculine role during the sex act and therefore treats the woman with hostility afterwards.* I also read articles claiming that homosexuality was caused by abusive, absent, or negligent fathers. Wouldn't that mean that an abusive, absent, or negligent mother would cause the same son to be attracted to women? How about someone with an abusive, absent, and negligent mother and father? Would they be bisexual? What if a father abused his son for the first nine years of his life, then suddenly repented, suddenly changed his ways? Would the boy likewise change direction in midair? If behavior had determined my preference, couldn't behavior also alter it?

I believed, or tried to believe, what I'd read in spite of the inconsistencies. After all, who was I to question something found in the public library? I went home at night after these afternoons of research in such a state of depression that I could not join in the conversation at the dinner table and was barely able to comply when Daddy said, "Pass the potatoes." I'd sneak looks, first at him: he was abusive. And then at Mother: she was hardly overprotective. Long before Daddy was abusive or absent, from at least the age of four, I was drawn to males: discovering the blond boy on his tricycle down the block—Mrs. Gable's visiting grandson—had disquieted me, and I couldn't change that.

Not long ago, I read a theory that made sense. Sexual orientation is established at birth. In heterosexual children, infants are erotically attracted to parents of the opposite sex. Boys are interested in their mothers and girls are interested in their fathers. In a homosexual, though, this attraction is reversed. The small boy is interested in his father and this causes the father, who picks up on the attraction, to distance himself. From this comes the estrangement between father and son. Perhaps, in the case of Dean and his father, affection was such a normal part of their family that there was no reaction. Perhaps it's a Latin or Portuguese characteristic. Whatever the case, Dean's sexuality didn't seem to be an issue. His father mussed his hair, tugged at his ear, squeezed his neck, and kissed him. To me, that explained a lot.

On the way home, Frank stopped in his favorite diner and we had coffee. He knew the waitress, the fry cook, and the cashier, and it was obvious how much they liked him. And again he introduced me as Dino's "buddy."

I've never experienced anything quite like Thanksgiving at Dean's house. I don't know a thing about my father's parents, my mother's father died before I was born, and as I said my grandmother died before I was six. Daddy had two brothers, but never talked about them, and Mother hadn't gotten along with her sister for years. When we sat down for holiday meals, there were only four people at the table, and we ate with a somberness reserved for families whose number has been diminished by estrangement or disease or accident. Every unhappy family is unhappy in its own way. (Tolstoy said that.) But it was like a church dinner at Dean's: two brothers and their wives and babies, his sisters and their boyfriends, his grandmother and grandfather, two uncles, one aunt, and neighbors were there. I've never seen so many leaves in a table and they had to borrow chairs so everyone could sit down. In all, twenty adults and three children crowded around the table when the turkeys were served. (They had two smaller turkeys rather than one because Dean's mother did one bird and his grandmother, Eugenia, did the other in a traditional way by rubbing more than two pounds of salt on the skin to seal in the juices.) There were other traditional Portuguese dishes too, which his grandmother and mother prepared. Things like *caldo verde* to start (a soup made from green cabbage though Eugenia complained it wasn't green enough), a casserole of salt cod, potatoes and onions (delicious), bay-scented potatoes (very subtle), yeast-raised corn bread called *broa*, flan and a variety of sweets.

After the wines were poured, we had a red and a white, Dean's father made a toast: "To our family, our neighbors, and our friends—

especially Chris—our new friend from Chicago." Dean raised his glass and beamed. Then, he squeezed my neck with his free hand and said: "To many more holidays together." Everyone at the table, it seemed, let out a yell of approval, and Tina, who sat beside my chair, barked as if in agreement.

☙•❧

I started an argument on the way to Mother's. I kicked the dashboard—Dean was driving—and I ranted. I can't recall what set me off, that is, my excuse. Maybe Dean noticed a beefy farm boy on the street in one of the small towns we drove through, or perhaps he neglected to ask me if I was feeling my AZT when we stopped for lunch. What really upset me was that I was taking a man home to visit Mother. Honestly though, I didn't realize that then. I told Mother that I was bringing a friend. I suspected she'd assume the friend was female.

Dean laughed. Good-naturedly. He didn't say one unkind word. Not even when I made fun of his family by calling them *The Cleavers*. I was hateful, and I wanted to make him hurt too. Dean didn't understand why I hadn't told Mother, and reminded me that it had been my idea to take him along. I'd have been miserable leaving him in Chicago. Bob might talk him into going out. Then he'd meet someone and talk to them. And I'd be history. I was afraid he was human even though he'd showed no signs of duplicity. I didn't trust myself; why in the world would I trust him?

We drove into town a little after 11:30 P.M.—holding hands across the armrest. Dean had to let go, at the stop light on the edge of town, to shift into first. After he went through the series of gears, he took my hand again. The streets were deserted; no one was up to see me enter town with a boyfriend instead of a wife. We pulled into Mother's driveway; the porch light was on, but the lights in the house were off. I hoped she'd stay in bed, wait until morning to meet Dean, but at the sound of our car doors slamming, the light in the kitchen came on.

When Mother opened the back door, I noticed that she'd had her hair done. She didn't look surprised, and when I introduced Dean, she managed a smile. She wasn't exuberant—as when she met Cynthia—but she was pleasant, and I was grateful. She asked if Dean would like coffee. "There's a pot on the stove I can reheat," she said. Mother and Daddy could drink coffee right up until bedtime, but I'd have had a better chance of sleep after a gram of coke. We walked into the front room, and she sat on the couch, where she did her quilting, and gestured for Dean to take a chair. "How was the drive?" she asked.

"We got a late start," said Dean. "By the time we came close to Ohio it was dark. It looks beautiful—from what I can tell."

"Dean's from Massachusetts," I said.

"You're on vacation?" said Mother.

"I moved to Chicago five months ago," said Dean.

"He moved in with me, Mother. We're roommates."

"When are you going back?" said Mother.

Dean looked at me, wrinkled his forehead, and grinned, as if to signal that I should take this one. I told Mother that we had taken Monday off and didn't have to leave until then at noon.

"We bought the flower shop together, Mother. We're partners," I said. "Now that we're owners, we can't stay away too long."

"You're probably tired," she said. "Chris, your friend can sleep in Mae's room." She got up from the couch. "Are you boys hungry? I made a meat loaf; I could make you meat loaf sandwiches."

"Terrific. I'm starved," said Dean. I agreed, and when Mother went into the kitchen, Dean gave me a look sideways. He'd promised not to say anything about sleeping arrangements, but he had also threatened to sneak into my room. I told him that even if I brought a woman home Mother would have put us in separate rooms, but the last time that Mae and Charlie visited she'd actually allowed them to sleep together even though they weren't yet married.

Ordinarily when I came home, no matter how late, Mother would stay up and talk for a while, but that night she excused herself and went to bed. Dean and I sat quietly at the table as if the kitchen were bugged.

"She's going to be tough," said Dean. Then he used his fingers to brush a strand of hair off my forehead.

߬•९

Dean didn't sneak into my room and I had mixed feelings about that. Saturday morning I got up late and found him and Mother in the kitchen.

"We decided not to wake you," said Dean.

"Blueberry pancakes? You made pancakes?" I looked at Mother.

"Dean made them," said Mother, with a smile. "He insisted."

"What a brownnose," I said later, on the way to see Steve. "What did you talk about?"

"You, of course."

"Does she act like she likes you?"

"She's a little cool, but she warms up when she talks about you. She considers you very successful. She said she was worried at first, when you quit Bradley."

"But now that she sees I'm not starving, it's okay."

"Something like that."

We drove through the elm-lined streets; Dean said that New Harmony reminded him of a town in a Spielberg movie, and that it would be a great place to raise children. I'm not so sure. Goats perhaps, but not children.

On the way to see Steve, I worried about what Dean would think of Steve and what Steve would think of Dean. What did it matter? If they hated each other, why should I care? Why would that affect my life? And Mother too. Why did I care what she thought of him?

We pulled into one of the many empty parking spaces on the Court House Square and got out of the car. Schroeder's was on the northeast corner; this would be the first time I'd gone inside since high school. I drove by at least once every time I went home, and a couple of years ago, I passed as Steve came out of the store. Anyone normal would have yelled hello from the car, pulled over, and parked. Not me. I accelerated and turned my head. Too much time had elapsed. It would be awkward to reestablish contact. Going to the reunion—even if I had hid behind Cynthia—was a bold move. Putting myself in a situation where I had to answer embarrassing questions about why I'd never gotten married had been difficult.

But it occurred to me as Dean and I opened the door that the gay issue wasn't my only problem. Steve had long suspected that I was gay—and still wanted to be my friend. Perhaps he was attracted to me because of it. Pam didn't care either and was anxious for me to come and see her kids and their house. So why was it so difficult for me to pay this visit? Was I afraid he would look at the two of us and try to imagine what we did in bed?

That's why I haven't been more creative in my life. I'm too afraid of being perceived as different. I should have worked with flowers years ago. I should have majored in horticulture. I wasted those years at Bradley with people like Stanley. All those years with people who detested what I was—what I am—was a form of self-hate. Laughing at the Rock Hudson jokes was masochistic behavior. For what? The money and the security? Those weren't good reasons. I can't express how much I regret that it took finding out I was positive for me to change my life. How different things might have been.

No one really knows how much time they have left. In that sense I'm no different. People with AIDS are no different. The only difference between my dad and me is that he was in his sixties wondering how many more breaths he'd take, and I'm thirty-eight wondering how many I'll take. How many more before I contract some obscure illness? It's not healthy to be so often reminded of one's mortality at an early age. Watching Daddy struggle, just to sit on the edge of his bed, I wish I'd asked if he was afraid to die, I wish I'd asked if he worried about what it was like. But he never seemed frightened. For all the things I hated about my dad, I can't say he complained. Because he didn't. Even during the hospitalizations and the respiratory infections he joked with the nurses. The young one, the redhead with the heavy drawl, said, "I like taking care of your daddy. He's a gentleman." She was right. He never questioned his disease or talked about how unfair it was. He seemed to accept his emphysema almost as if it were a cold or the flu. It was more difficult to dislike him after he became ill. No, that's not fair. He was easier to love. At the end he looked translucent against the white sheets.

Steve hadn't expected me. He stood with a woman in front of a sideboard and turned around when we entered the store. He said something to her and softened the intensity of a halogen lamp, then rushed over and threw his arms around me—right there in the store. I had to push away so he would stop slapping me on the back. He called my visit an excellent surprise, and said Pam would insist on me coming to dinner. How long was I staying? And why didn't I say I was coming? He glanced at Dean with the same brightness. Not in a nosey way, just: I haven't figured out who you are but I guess you're with Chris and any friend of Chris's...Then Steve said, "You must be Chris's boyfriend," and before I could introduce them they'd done it themselves and had shook hands. "Jesus, wait till Pam finds out," he said. "She'll be freaked." He explained that Pam had to go to Steve Junior's school over some problem, and I considered his use of the word freaked.

꙰•꙰

"Do you sleep in the same bed?" The child peered into my eyes. Hers, yellowish brown and too closely set, didn't flinch. Why had she asked me, when it was Dean going over the top with charm and adolescent humor?

Dean answered. "Sure, we sleep together." He leaned forward from the couch to hoist her onto his lap.

"That's none of your beeswax," Pam called from the kitchen. "Is she being a pest?"

"A big pest," said Dean, "I've caught a giant cockroach." He tickled her vigorously on her dirty belly, and she shrieked in a voice that grated. The image of an insect with probing antennae came to mind, and I wondered if Dean's description might offend Pam.

We sat in a family room, separated from the kitchen by a wall of open shelving. The shelves held few books, and instead were stuffed with toys of every shape, color, and size. I'm amazed by how much children have. Not that I was deprived of material things as a child. I had plenty: a Schwinn bicycle, a G.E. transistor radio, a View-Master—and after I began carrying papers in the fifth grade—a coin collection. I wasn't obsessed with possessions. For Christmas and birthdays I asked for books. But Steve and Pam's house amazed me. Their family room was not a place for adults—though I suppose Steve enjoyed the Nintendo too—it was strewn with stuffed animals, board games, video tapes, dolls, a giant worm with wheels, building blocks, Legos, drawing boards, coloring books, tricycles, and trucks. Miniature trucks, large trucks, trucks to ride on, radio-controlled trucks, trucks to be held in the palm of the hand, fire trucks, milk trucks, dump trucks, ambulance trucks, garbage trucks, contemporary trucks, antique trucks, futuristic trucks, trucks from Venus, trucks from Mars, and trucks from Pluto. Hundreds, perhaps a thousand dollars, had been spent on trucks. And now there were only two children.

Through the sliding patio doors, in the yard, a sand box over-flowed with toys, and an expansive swing-set was surrounded by even more. The above-the-ground swimming pool was covered for the winter; otherwise I imagine it would have been filled with rafts and floats and balls. Pam came into the room, wiping her hands on her apron. She told the little girl, Tess, to go upstairs and get ready for her bath, and apologized that her daddy wasn't home to help. Then Pam apologized to us. Steve tried to close early on Saturdays, she said, but was seldom able. Dinner would be ready when he arrived. "I hope he remembers that Stevie is at Kevin's," she said, and I concluded that she was merely thinking aloud.

"I'll help Tess with her bath," said Dean. "I help with my nieces and nephews." Pam protested—she couldn't impose on a dinner guest—but Dean stood up with Tess in his arms. His comment about his nieces and nephews prompted Pam to ask him about Boston and how he compared it to living in Chicago. As they talked, I could see that she liked him. Everybody does. He has a sweet face. A perfect face.

Pam directed him to the upstairs bathroom, told him where to find the towels and Tess's pajamas, then asked me to keep her company in the kitchen. Mother had sent me the clippings and a letter when Steve and Pam's middle child died, and even though it had occurred more than two years ago, it was one of the reasons that I had decided to attend the reunion. At the time I didn't call or write to Steve though. Mother had written, saying that it was *a tragedy for a three-year-old to get leukemia*, and then called to say that she'd sent flowers and included Mae's name and mine. At first I got upset. I hadn't gathered the courage to get tested at the time, so there wasn't a day that passed without me wondering when I would get sick and die. I faced death every day. Personally. But Mother never mentioned AIDS and all the deaths it had caused.

Ryan's death had been mentioned only in passing at the reunion and I had the impression that night that they preferred at least for an evening to pretend it hadn't happened. Although Cynthia told me late on the way back to Chicago that she had discussed it with Pam in the powder room at the Country Club.

"You must really miss him," I said.

"He was a completely different child," said Pam. "That's what affects me the most. From the minute they're born you realize they're their own person. An individual. You know?

"I love Tess and Stevie, but it doesn't lessen my pain for one second—or the feeling that it was my fault, that there was something I should have done that I didn't." Pam's voice got higher, and I began to think about what I should do if she cried. "But life does go on, I know that, and I try not to burden people. It does me good to talk, but Steve mostly resists talking about it. He puts it out of his mind I guess. I don't know."

Pam avoided looking at me, but I watched as the ridges in her forehead and the wrinkles around her eyes deepened. Her cheek muscles pulled at the corners of her mouth to force a smile, but her lips curled down in anguish. Not that the pain that gays were experiencing was trivial, but briefly I wondered if there is any grief in the world that can compare to that of a Mother's for a lost child. Pam's expression, her mask, was without comparison. I've seen gays speak of a friend's death while suppressing a smile, suppressing elation. It seemed wrong to me, and that they were somehow lacking in character. Now I know that the elation comes from the joy of survival.

An episode of "Nova" dealt with drought in Central Africa. An elephant herd migrated to find water. When a baby elephant becomes too sick from thirst and hunger to continue, the entire herd falls behind and waits while the Mother tries to prod it forward. The calf keeps falling at its Mother's feet, and eventually after the herd has waited for quite some time, they continue on without the baby—or the Mother, who chooses to stay behind with her child. I had the misfortune of watching this show after a night of cocaine and broke down and wept for several hours.

My life, as I had lived it, seemed meaningless compared with Steve and Pam's. While they were raising a family—and facing the death of one of their children—I spent my weekends in clubs, snorting coke and drinking, chasing boys—and sleeping with as many as I could. I met a guy one night in Equinox, when I was high. He revealed that he'd been a brother in the seminary, in Cincinnati. He didn't talk about his past or beliefs readily, but after we started talking about Ohio and I asked why he hadn't become a priest, we got into a discussion of God—or at least his interpretation of God and the church. I asked how he justified the church's attitude toward homosexuality, and the Pope's in particular, and he didn't have a satisfactory answer. I persisted: "Just why did God make us gay?" I blurted. "Why?" I shouted. He replied that he thought we were "God's special, creative people." If that was the case, and I must admit I liked the thought, my life had been a zero. And that was my fault. No one else's.

"Dean's sweet. Where did you meet?" asked Pam. We laughed about her rhyme, then I told her how he had come because Bob had been transferred and that he liked the idea of experiencing a different part of the country. She wanted to know if Mother liked him.

"She's polite," I said. In truth, Mother was reserved. Because Dean isn't obvious, she was confused. Since she has always judged people by their looks, it would have been difficult for her to dislike anyone so handsome. Steve came in the door a few minutes later with Steve Junior and that ended our conversation about Dean and Mother.

At dinner Steve suggested that he and Pam would like to come to Chicago, after the holidays, and visit. Pam hurried to finish chewing her mouthful and said: "I'll ask Mom to take care of the kids." I was pleased that he and Pam wanted to spend time with us. It seemed to legitimize my relationship with Dean.

❧•❧

On one of my prior trips, I noticed that a gym had been opened in an abandoned store on the square. I'd been tempted to work out, but as the space was situated on the opposite side of the square from Steve's store, I thought I might run into him and decided against it. Dean and I didn't get around to going on Saturday, and when we stopped on Sunday we found the gym closed, so I suggested that we go for a hike in the country instead—along the banks of Dooley's Creek. After the big meal that Pam had cooked the night before—fried chicken and mashed potatoes—we needed exercise. It was warm for November with the sun shining in a cloudless sky and, with Mother at church, I made up a picnic basket of turkey sandwiches and drinks. When we got back, Mother was making Swiss steak for dinner.

Our going to Steve and Pam's pleased her; on Sunday she was considerably warmer. During dinner she asked Dean how he liked Schroeder's house and told him that New Harmony's most prominent citizens lived in that part of town. After we finished eating, she brought out the quilt she was making. Dean remarked effusively about the tiny stitches, saying he could hardly believe it was all handwork, and Mother radiated good humor. She went to her sewing room and came back with a box. She removed another quilt, big enough for a queen-sized bed, and spread it on the floor. It was a magnificent design of interlocking, harvest-yellow circles on a Prussian blue, patterned background, edged in black.

"This is the Irish Double Chain quilt. It won `Grand Champion' at the county fair."

"You didn't tell me you won Grand Champion," I said.

"You don't care about quilts. Don't pretend in front of company that you do," said Mother, with a wink.

MEMORIES

I undress, open the bed, and throw the quilt across the sheets. I adjust the pillow, try sleeping on my back, then my side, then my stomach. For hours I dredge up the memories. I can't write this. I can't do this.

ຂຂຂ Chapter Fifteen

THANK GOD FOR DEAN. Without him, I wouldn't have had the courage to buy the business. He wanted a "romantic" Christmas, and we discussed going to New Bedford, but though we envisioned staying for two or three days at the most, we finally decided that there was no way we could go. First was the flower shop. Either we ran it right, or we sold it. And then there was my apartment, our apartment. After we painted and refinished the floors, we got new linens and towels, bought some new stoneware dishes and flatware, and picked up some great pieces of used furniture to refinish. Dean admitted that he would probably have returned to Boston to live when Bob left, if he hadn't met me, but insisted that he was more content than he'd ever been. We were driving down Wrightwood one afternoon when he noticed a round, oak table with four chairs in the window at Caroline's Collection. He pulled over immediately and parked and rushed inside, and we ended up buying the set for the kitchen, plus a small secretary for our bedroom and a teak coffee table for the living room.

Dean has passion. The apartment looked more inviting than I ever imagined. Without a roommate—a lover—I'd never had the incentive to fix it up. At times, when I'm alone, I stand in the middle of the dining room and run my hand across the lacquered surface of the restored table and I look into the living room to study the shadow of the palms against the white, clean walls and I turn and look into the kitchen to admire the way the track lighting reflects in the gloss of the black tiled floor and I smile. I decided: there was no place like home for the holidays.

Some of the money we'd spent on the apartment and to buy the shop had been borrowed from Dean's father, and we were going to need quite a bit of working capital to get through the holidays. There was more to running a business than I'd foreseen. Joey's bookkeeper finally returned my call and told me that he wasn't a bookkeeper—he had merely done Joey's tax return—and I gathered it hadn't been a happy experience. The books Joey promised were never produced, unless a few scraps of paper with rudimentary sales figures and a cardboard box of receipts and scrawled notes could be called books. Once we struck our deal, Joey disappeared and seldom stopped by. I phoned him a few times, to see how he'd handled a couple of problems with suppliers, but I got his answering service. He had tried for so long to convince me to buy the store—with assurances that he'd be around afterwards to advise—that I felt betrayed. Not that Dean and I needed him that often. It was the principle. Joey was avoiding me, and I suddenly realized that our friendship had meant nothing. He hired me to make his life easier. Any idea on my part that he liked me had been foolish.

It never occurred to me that he might be too embarrassed about his behavior to want to see me, until Lenny started talking. He came in the shop frequently—to gawk at Dean. No one could accuse him of being subtle. One Monday afternoon when Dean and I were in front, Lenny brought in a friend and I overheard him say: "I told you they were stunning." He also asked me about Joey, with a grin and flared nostrils, making it clear that he knew plenty. I didn't act surprised or curious; I mentioned that I hadn't seen Joey for a couple of weeks. Lenny said: "Stop in Cuffs sometime. She'll be in back on the pool table."

Four days after that, on my way into the Loop, I stopped by Joey's apartment. He'd sold his condo and bought a town house in Sandburg Village and, as I stood at his door with my finger over the peephole, I realized that if he had still lived in his twentieth floor apartment I would never have been able to get past security. One look confirmed what I had known: he was on a binge. The weight alone I could excuse—but the dark swelling under his eyes and his voice, so hoarse and scratchy...I told him about my problems with the store license and that I was on my way into the city to renew it. Joey shifted his weight back and forth from one leg to the other and peered past me as if he expected someone. He said I'd get things worked out, and then began to close the door. He didn't even ask me in, saying that he was under the weather and that his place was a mess. I stood on his steps, staring at the closed door, wishing I hadn't stopped.

The problems with the license started because Joey hadn't bothered to renew; apparently he was so sure I'd take over the store that he hadn't concerned himself with details. It's more difficult to reinstate a lapsed license than to get a new one, and although I'd left Dean alone in the store for what I hoped would be at most two hours, I spent most of the entire afternoon and didn't get back to the shop until after five. We had our first heavy snowfall and traffic was congested, so I took a train home. Even the crowded subway didn't bother me; I was so anxious to show Dean the name I'd chosen for the store that I clutched the paperwork in my hand all the way home. *Vale de Flores.* Portuguese for *valley of flowers.*

I walked in the door and stomped the snow and slush off my feet. The store was empty; Dean was behind the counter on the telephone. I took off my coat and went up front. I could tell by his expression and the way he nodded and alternated between "uh huh" and "yeah" that he was talking to someone with a problem. Was it Bob? Had there been a change in his condition? Had it escalated, or deteriorated? It turned out to be Mae.

We closed the shop and drove to Union Station. The round trip took three hours. On the way home, Mae tried to be lighthearted—she even told a joke about a Polish cheerleader—but I knew it was difficult for her to ask to stay with us until she found an apartment. I knew in her voice the minute she said "hello." She didn't have had to say she wanted to come over. It's so easy to observe someone you love, and make judgments about what they should do. Most of the advice people give, or are given, is from a distance—with perspective. I'd been telling Mae to watch what Charlie did and forget what he said. Logically I think, she believed me, but emotionally she hadn't been ready. I still wasn't sure that she was ready. But, it wasn't for me to decide—and there was nothing I could do to make her change her schedule. When Mae was ready to take care of herself, when Mae was ready to change her life, she would. I could support her, I could give her advice, I could listen, but I couldn't force her to make a decision until she was absolutely and certainly ready. We put Mae in our bedroom. Dean insisted: "You can't expect a pregnant woman to sleep on a hide-a-bed."

A week later her story came out. I assumed Charlie had hit her; I pictured him punching her in the stomach. My horrific imagination came from watching too many made-for-television movies. Mae admitted that he had pushed her against the wall, but he had done something even worse. One night when Dean and I got home from work, I opened the downstairs door and detected smoke. We hurried up the staircase and into the apartment. An attempt to mask the odor had been made—with a pine-scented deodorizing spray. Without taking off my coat, I went into the kitchen and found Mae standing at the stove, sprinkling paprika on a pot of mashed potatoes and holding the telephone receiver in her free hand. The cord stretched the length of the kitchen, from the telephone, which was mounted on one wall to the stove, which stood at the opposite end. Mae looked up and attempted a smile.

"I'll talk to you later," she said into the receiver, and paused again. "I've got to go," she said, at last. "Yes, I'll think about it." She walked across the room and hung up.

"Who was that?" I said.

"I made pot roast," said Mae.

"So I smell. Who was that?"

"Please, Chris. Don't start on me tonight," said Mae.

Dean came quietly into the room and said: "What burned?"

"Apparently Mae feels our diet lacks carcinogens," I said, "so she burned the roast."

Dean gave me a disapproving look, moved over to Mae, and put his arm around her. "Let's put the food on the table. You can tell us about it," he said.

I cut a piece of roast and put it in my mouth. How could I make him understand that, although I love my sister, I couldn't give her any more support than I already had? Why should I have to be constantly stressed over her bizarre behavior? She had totally forgotten me after she got pregnant, but the moment the problems with Charlie recurred she came running back. The meat was incredibly tender despite the burned flavor. Mae is an excellent cook and seldom spoils dinner.

"It's good, Mae. It really is," I said. "Surprise me. Tell me you killed Charlie and we're eating the murder weapon."

"That's not funny," said Mae, but she smiled. "I am almost ready to consider that," she said.

Dean looked at me, eyes wide, chewing slowly as if not to disrupt Mae's train of thought. She'd spent a long time on the telephone with Dean that first night, complaining in a general way about Charlie—how he came home really late after work and was always too tired to take any interest in the baby and that sort of thing—but she had never since revealed what specific event had sent her in such haste from their apartment in the fifth month of her pregnancy. Dean and I had lain awake several nights speculating, and at the supper table that evening we were both anxious to hear the complete story.

"I've been getting strange phone calls," she began. "At first they were hang ups and I thought they were wrong numbers. One day a girl tried to talk to me and she knew my name."

"Tried?" I said.

"She's Polish and doesn't know much English." Then Mae got all teary-eyed and her voice quavered.

"Mae," I said, "please don't drag it out. Charlie's got a girlfriend, right?"

She blotted her eyes—they were already red and irritated when we got home—and nodded. "The girl's brother came on the phone and asked me if they could come and see me that afternoon."

"You let them?" said Dean.

"I said I was busy and hung up. But the boy kept calling back, three days in a row. He said it was real important but he wouldn't give me details over the phone. 'Please, you will speak with my sister?' he said. 'It is important about Charlie.'" Mae looked at me. "At first I thought about saying something to Charlie, then I thought how much you don't like him and how lately he's always off somewhere with some weird excuse—and there was something about the boy's voice that told me I should see them. He sounded sweet and gentle and upset."

"At their house?" I said. "I don't think that was a good idea."

"We met at a restaurant on Taylor Street."

"That's better." I said, and Dean agreed.

"Is she Charlie's girlfriend?" said Dean.

"When they came through the front door, I couldn't believe it. She's a lot younger than me and real pretty."

"Mae, you're pretty," said Dean.

"That's not what I mean. We're both pregnant: she's five months and I'm almost six. And she says Charlie's the father."

"Charlie's a bigamist?" said Dean, sounding incredulous.

"No, no," said Mae, "they're not married. You have to be married for it to be bigamy." Mae kept composed; she seemed past crying, but she looked humiliated.

"It's a little like having twins," I said. "What are the odds of something like that happening?" Then I remembered she'd been on the telephone when we came home. "And you're still talking to the son of a bitch? I suppose he's trying to deny it. This is finally it, isn't it? You are finally through with him, aren't you? For God's sake say he's history," I said.

Embarrassment was one reason for my harshness. I couldn't imagine this happening in Dean's family. It gets back to what I said about perspective. Mae had lost hers. For a second I was nauseous: I could be just as foolish where Dean was concerned. I too had lost perspective. Who was to say that later things wouldn't take an ugly turn?

Dean loves me. The attraction was largely physical in the beginning, but things are different now. When I say different, I mean strained. We still have sex almost every day. We masturbate together, really. But sometimes when he touches me I feel the tension. Perhaps I'm too tuned into him. I worry that he's thinking: Do I have any cuts or scratches or lesions on my hands? When I first caught cold I wouldn't let him kiss me on the lips. That's common courtesy. I accused Dean of running to the shower after we climax, and he laughed, but admitted that he's careful not to get semen on his skin.

AIDS has brought out the best and worst in people, the way any crisis does. Lenny came in the store again last week and said Tim was convincing Arvo to draw up a will. He also said Tim wasn't taking any chances: he was selling Arvo's jewelry—ring-by-ring, chain-by-chain. I told Dean, soon after we got together, that I was positive. If he wanted to abandon, that was the perfect opportunity. Bob told me about two friends of his in Boston who have been devoted to each other for thirteen years. Both are H.I.V.–positive, but one is younger and still healthy and the other has AIDS and is so advanced that they gave up on him at the hospital and sent him home. The younger boy is caring for his sick friend with limited help from a nurse who comes in during the day. The lover has to connect an I.V. containing his medicine and nourishment each morning before the nurse arrives and another in the evening after she leaves (they cost a thousand dollars each), then he has to change his friend's diapers and bedding. Most of the time his friend is so feverish that he doesn't know where he is, but the boy tries to keep him comfortable with alcohol rubs and sponge baths. He is watching his friend die and wondering if he will suffer in a similar way—but without the care of a lover. The dying man owns the house, and according to his will his partner is to inherit it, but the parents of the man with AIDS, who haven't contributed to his care or been to see him since he was diagnosed, have hired an attorney and he's been sending letters about the will that the boy doesn't understand. Bob also said he went to a service for another friend whose older brother was a fundamentalist minister. The brother gave the eulogy; he spent an hour talking about the sin of homosexuality with the church full of gays. Bob said he wanted to walk out, and when he told me the story, I said I would have. At the service they put all the gays on one side of the church and the straights on the other side. They should have had ushers ask: *Friends of the deceased or friends of the family?* And everyone, it seems, can point to a case where after a boy gets sick, his lover leaves. Some people aren't strong enough to stay, and others are selfish. They don't want to give up the party and bar life. If the situation were reversed, I'd like to think I'd be as honorable as Dean.

Our bedroom was off-limits much of the time. Dean and I had to knock before entering to get clean underwear out of our chest-of-drawers, and with us sleeping in the living room we didn't have any privacy either. That put an additional strain on us, but I could have tolerated the situation for a while longer—if only Mother hadn't come. She'd been planning to help Mae get a room ready for the baby, and even though Mae insisted that she had moved out on Charlie forever, Mother still came.

It had been difficult enough to cope with Mae, pregnant and sick half the time, for a week. But once Mother arrived—although she did the cooking and cleaning—conditions became intolerable. Dean did not complain, but the tension of us all bumping into one another at every turn was more than I could bear. My cold got worse. We worked long hours at Vale de Flores, the weather was frigid and wet, Mae still talked on the telephone to Charlie, and Mother wouldn't support me when I refused to allow him to come over to the apartment—although Dean agreed with me. How could she consider continuing with him? I hated to see Mae sobbing and exhausted from lack of sleep.

Mother slept with Mae in our bedroom; that didn't change things much, but it was almost necessary to make a schedule for using the bathroom. Like living in a trailer. One night I went out onto the back porch and down the back stairs to the alley to urinate. It was bitter cold, close to zero, but there was no wind. The packed snow squeaked under my feet like dry ice as I crossed the yard. After I finished peeing, I stayed there in the dark alley. The sky was clear and the moon was about three-quarters full, but the street light next to the garage had burned out. I looked back across the shallow yard into Clinton and Angelo's kitchen. Their lights were on. I would have knocked and gone in for a visit, but they were in Hawaii for the holidays. Their friend, Rob, was house sitting; I saw him at the table using a rolling pin, and I decided he was making Christmas cookies. The lights upstairs in our kitchen were out. I thought about walking to the grocery store for cigarettes, but I only had a pocketful of change.

I had looked forward to the evenings alone with Dean after we finished redecorating. He bought two inexpensive light timers so we didn't have to come home to a darkened house. At first we were excited about Christmas, but now we hadn't gotten around to buying a tree. I shook, feeling the cold for the first time and then my eyes teared and I began to cry. That's when our kitchen light came on. Seconds later Dean came out onto the back porch. "Chris," he called, "are you out here?" I wiped my eyes on the back of my sleeve and answered. "What are you doing?" he asked, and I could see the movement of his head as if he were trying to locate me in the darkness. My spirits were buoyed; he had missed me. He wanted to know if I had worn a jacket, then said: "Stay where you are; I'll be right down." He went back into the house, and after a minute came out onto the porch in his down coat, carrying mine on his arm. He closed the kitchen door behind and descended the stairs three-at-a-time in his usual fashion. He ran across the yard to me and held the coat open. "You came out here in a sweatshirt. What are you thinking?" he said.

"What does it matter?" I said. "I'm dying anyway."

"Chris, everybody is dying—"

"Not now. I can't take any of that philosophical crap," I said.

"Look, AIDS is just as much of a factor in my life," said Dean.

I exploded. "I'll bet you wouldn't trade places," I screamed. He tried to take hold of my arm and comfort me, but I shook him off. I cried, then swallowed wrong and started to cough. I coughed until I choked. He meant that AIDS is a dominant factor in his life too. He can't ignore the fact that his lover is H.I.V.–positive. His friend, Bob, is sick now; he's lost friends; I've lost friends. He meant that we're all H.I.V.–positive in the gay community. We're all touched by it. We're all frightened.

"I'm sorry. It's not you. I can't stand having them here," I said. I expected Dean to disagree, to remind me that they were my family, that they needed me. When he didn't comment, I initially felt that he was disappointed in me, so much so, that he was at a loss for words.

"What do you think?" I said.

"It's crowded; our place is small," said Dean, hesitantly.

"But what?"

"It's not my place—"

"It's yours as much as it's mine," I said.

"I mean it's not my place to say anything. They're your family. Give it a couple more days," said Dean. He put his arms around me and we stood silently in the alley for a couple of minutes. "Don't get upset when I tell you this," he said.

"Tell me what?"

"Last night I didn't sleep well and woke up about three. I heard someone; first I thought it was Mae, sick or something. Then I heard the hardwood floors creaking. Instead of creaking in back by the bathroom, the noise got closer, toward us in the living room. I panicked for a minute thinking it might be someone who broke in. The creaking was slow and steady—like whoever it was either wasn't sure where they were going or were trying not to make much noise. I tried to decide what I could use as a weapon if I had to, but kept still. I pretended to be asleep, opening my eyes only slightly into slits and watched the doorway. Then I saw that it was your mom, in her robe. She got to the door and stood there; she didn't come in; she stayed at the entrance and looked in at us. I'll bet she was there not moving for at least five or six minutes," said Dean. "Watching us. Just watching."

The next night about eight o'clock, when the four of us sat around the kitchen table together, I blurted out. "I feel guilty having to say this," I said, "but Dean and I don't have room here for you two and to be honest I have my own problems." I stared at the vase of purple irises in the center of the table until I got the courage to look at Mae, then at Mother. Mae's hair was stringy, her roots dark, and Mother looked as if she'd been slapped. "Mae, don't you have any pride?" I said. "I understand that you might hate yourself so much that you let Charlie push you around, but I would think you'd have more consideration for the baby."

"You sure have some dandy ideas," Mother said. "The baby needs a father. And don't worry, I'll leave. I don't see how you could understand—the way you are."

That's when I lost control. I slammed my fist on the table. "The way I am? You don't know anything about me. You're too narrow-minded. I'm dying. That's how I am. But at least I'm not killing myself like Mae is. At least I think enough of myself to be with someone who loves me."

I always fantasized about the moment when I confronted her with my homosexuality. I felt that I might have overestimated her disgust because of my own fragile ego and heightened sensitivity. I was just paranoid, I told myself. But Mother had never been ambivalent about her feelings on sexual ambivalence.

She got up from the table, walked into the bedroom, and closed the door. Mae began to cry, and I tried to soften what I'd said without taking anything back, though I realized that it was too late to be tactful. I'd inflicted a potentially fatal wound. Dean looked astonished. That's the only word that describes his expression. He went into the living room for a while and sat alone. I figured he was ready to pack and flee the asylum. After twenty minutes or so, he came out and knocked on Mother's door and called in to her. I was surprised she let him in.

I talked to Mae rationally and calmly. I apologized for pounding the table and yelling at Mother. But I told Mae that I seriously wouldn't have any more to do with her if she went back to Charlie. "I didn't want to admit that I needed AA," I said, "but I did." Truthfully, Dean was more the reason than AA that I backed off the drugs, but I didn't tell her. That would be like saying: Find another man, Mae; that'll solve your problems.

Mae used to excuse Charlie by telling me how sweet he really was. She'd say something like: I know you think he's a monster, but he's got problems too. That night, though, she seemed honestly to be trying to understand her behavior—and to explain it.

"I talk to him because I still don't believe it has happened," she said. "I talk to him to try to make sense of it. I'm the one he married," said Mae.

"That's makes you the unlucky one," I said, "not the Polish girl." I convinced her to talk to Cynthia—to get a woman's perspective—and Cynthia convinced her to go home with Mother to have the baby. Cynthia showed her that she needed time to think things over—away from Charlie. Mae said that Cynthia touched her stomach and, when she felt the sturdy kicks, said: "The baby could be next." After that, reality kicked in for Mae. Charlie could no longer assuage her or persuade her that he wasn't an unbalanced and violent person. Mae now comprehended the seriousness of his problem—and the degree to which she had contributed to it. The baby did make the difference. Mae was going to be a mother. After she told me that she had decided to follow the Cynthia's advice, I told her to take a couple of days to get her things together. I told her it was a new beginning.

I wouldn't have had the nerve to confront Mother if it hadn't been for Dean. Thank God for Dean.

ಖಖಖ Chapter Sixteen

THE WBBM WEATHER REPORTS promised another major snowstorm. It was warmer now, above freezing; the air was thick and wet as I walked back from making the bank deposit. I closed the door to the store and saw Dean, up behind the counter, talking to a big guy whose back was towards me. At first I thought it could be someone from the health club, then my heart made a series of irregular beats. Was it a stranger, flirting? I walked behind the counter, put my papers down and pretended to organize them, and sneaked a look. The man smiled and asked why I didn't say hello. His leather jacket was open, to reveal a weighty, gold chain—and his bare chest—and he wore a haircut that featured shaved sides and an inch or more of tight curls on the top. From a distance it almost resembled a knit cap. Norberto was darkly tanned—I recognized his voice immediately—but the face was much fuller. He wasn't just beefy; he was pumped on steroids. I've always liked the muscled look, but I'd been attracted to Norberto because of his sculpted features, curly hair, dark eyes—and his natural, athletic physique. Now his neck came up out of his jacket like a tree stump, and his head was so swollen that the inflated flesh crowded his nose, eyes, and mouth together in the center of his face.

"You didn't know me, man." Norberto laughed, and I said a silent prayer of thanks that he hadn't called me baby.

"You've changed," I said, and then looked at Dean. "Norberto used to work here," I added. How could I direct the conversation so that it wouldn't be apparent that I'd been intimate with Norberto? "Did you come looking for Joey? You can probably can reach him at home."

"I don't need to see him. He wasn't a friend. I came to see you," said Norberto.

"Great. Well how are you? Are you still living in Los Angeles? How's your daughter? I'll bet she's grown." I shifted my gaze to Dean for just an instant; he glared at Norberto.

"I thought sometimes you maybe talk to Lydia," said Norberto. "I ain't seen her and I want to tell her I'm working for Corey Raffin now." Norberto's serious look widened into an orthodontic-enhanced smile. "I'm his assistant. He's in town for business, and we're staying at the Ritz Carlton. Nothing but first class, baby."

I told Norberto that I hadn't seen or heard from Lydia for months and couldn't understand why he hadn't been in touch. This was not the same person. There was something unseemly about him. Something unsavory. Norberto was too slick, too cocky, too grown up. He had a hustler, drug dealer mien. Then I thought of my encounters with him and the times I had masturbated with him in mind. Though I'd known he was a user, he had retained a certain vulnerability and an aura of innocence. He'd been a beautiful boy.

"Can I talk to you in private?" Norberto took hold of my arm, and I glanced at his hand. It was puffy and depilated. Norberto was hardly hirsute, but apparently even the fuzz on his hands was too much.

"Dean's my lover," I said. "You can talk in front of him." Dean's eyes narrowed into slits and the muscle in his jaw tensed. He'd never showed any sign of jealousy before, and I enjoyed it despite my discomfort.

"Walter is back from afternoon deliveries. I'll go help him," said Dean.

Before I could protest, he slipped into the back. I was relieved. Who knew what Norberto was going to say?

Norberto motioned me out from behind the counter and walked over behind the carousel of greeting cards. I followed him, trying to imagine what he wanted. Certainly he wasn't going to ask for money—he'd found a new source for that—and I doubted he was going to repay the $500 he'd borrowed before he left for California. Maybe he was going to ask me to get cocaine for him, although I thought if he could get steroids, he didn't need my help getting illegal substances. He took my forearm and pulled me close. I peeked over my shoulder toward the back room. He was wearing Chanel for Men and his breath smelled like Binaca.

"You're looking buff, man," he said, sounding only slightly insincere.

"I can't shake this cold; we've been really busy in the store," I said.

"No, baby. You're pumped. Hey, I been working out hard too, man," he said, suddenly slipping out of his jacket. He spun around. "What do you think?"

My first impulse was to laugh and say something sarcastic. You're working out? That's great. You look so healthy. Truthfully, I felt like I was talking to a stranger. The bottom half of the store window was fogged over, but through the top half I could see that large flakes of wet snow had begun to fall, while inches away a shirtless, bronzed, and giant-sized Norberto flexed for me. He gave me a double-biceps pose and I wondered for a second if he was going to take a bottle from his hip pocket and ask me to oil him up.

"Corey's having a party tonight and you're invited. Your friend too." Norberto nodded toward the back.

"We have 300 orders to get out before the weekend," I said, "but thanks anyway."

"Come on, baby," he said, draping his forearms over my shoulders. I felt the weight of his upper body as he leaned into me. "I told Corey I'd invite some dudes. At the hotel. There'll be tons and tons of blow. I promise, man." My expression changed, involuntarily, as gravity tugged at my face. Dudes and blow in unlimited quantities, I thought. Norberto reached down and squeezed my ass. "Don't tell me you don't party no more."

"What time?" I asked. "And what room number?" Not that I had any intention of going. I'd come too far for that. Now that I had someone, I couldn't take the chance of losing him. But I wanted to get Norberto out of the store as quickly as possible.

"I'm leaving for the gym," said Dean. I hadn't heard him come up and I jumped feeling at once guilty and foolish with Norberto standing so close.

"It's starting to come down pretty hard," I said. Of course I knew he loved to train and that the weather didn't have anything to do with his going to the health club. Besides, I'd already told Dean that I didn't plan to work out and we agreed that he would take an hour and a half and go before it got too late. After working all day with a cold I was simply too exhausted to throw weights around and then go home to sleep on a hide-a-bed. Since we'd taken over the shop, Dean and I had switched to working out in the evening after we closed, because we had to be in Vale de Flores by six-thirty each morning and I promised myself I'd be ready to work out again as soon as Mother and Mae left for Ohio. "I wish I felt like training with you," I said.

"Right," said Dean.

"Norberto has invited us to a party. At their hotel," I said. "I told him you weren't much for parties."

"Go if you want. Have a nice time. I'll see you at home." He didn't look me in the eye and, before I could say anything, was in the back and out the door. It would be an exaggeration to say he slammed it, but he made more noise than usual.

"So great, man. You're coming. You're going to like Corey. He's got class. He likes elegance." Norberto pushed out his lips, an affectation that he had apparently picked up in LA.

There are still moments when I want to deaden my nerves and experience euphoria. Having a partner has made me realize that there is no easy formula for happiness. As a boy, I blamed my mother and my father for my unhappiness. When I worked at Bradley, I blamed my malcontent on the fact that I had to live a secret life. After I quit, I blamed my unhappiness on the fact that I was alone. After Dean, I blamed my H.I.V. status. Blaming doesn't change anything. What does it matter really who's to blame? I regret that I wasted so many years doing something that I didn't consider fulfilling. I regret that my father and I didn't get along. I even occasionally still regret my homosexuality. And I regret that I didn't tell Mother sooner. I regret living so many years in the closet. But regret, like placing blame, is a waste of time.

"I might stop by," I said.

"I need a favor, baby." Norberto put his palm on the back of my neck and touched my forehead with his forehead. I took a step backwards. "Ask Lydia to come and meet you."

"I thought you didn't know where she is," I said.

"I think she's at her mother's house."

❧•❦

People like Norberto confuse me. I don't understand sexual ambivalence. Norberto prefers women, but he enjoys the attention he gets from gay men and is not an unwilling sexual partner. He's turned on to the money and the attention. The power is a high. He thinks he's in control.

Later that night, we got the full force of the predicted storm—it was our second heavy snowfall of the season and it fell on top of the nine inches still on the ground.

Norberto admitted that Lydia didn't want to see him—that's why he needed me to help, why he gave me Lydia's mother's phone number.

"She has respects for you," he'd said. "If you ask her to meet you here, she'll come."

"Are you going to make her feel better, or are you just going to make yourself feel better?"

"I can give her cash for the rent and things for Celia. I'm making good money now. I'm not working in no lousy flower shop. You should see me, Chris; it's wild—I drive a big old Ferrari."

"Since you have a great job and are doing so well, why don't you take her back with you?"

"Later. I plan to do that."

"Why not now?" I pressed.

"Be reasonable; I'm staying with Corey till I get my own place."

"In Corey's room?"

"What is this, man? I got my own room. Let me live my life." Norberto averted his eyes and slapped his thighs. His face contorted; he seemed close to losing it. I knew he was lying, and he knew I knew. Norberto probably wasn't allowed the luxury of losing his temper. Suppressing ones feelings takes its toll.

"I didn't mean to pry. I'm only worried about you."

"I know. I like you too."

I agreed to call Lydia and ask her to lunch, and I promised not to mention Norberto. I was to convince her that the invitation was my idea. Norberto told me to make sure she came without Celia because he wanted to come into the restaurant after we were seated and surprise Lydia. He wanted a romantic setting. Later I decided that it was unrealistic to pretend my call had nothing to do with Norberto, so I vowed to say that I'd seen him and that I wanted to talk to her about him. Norberto wanted to show his appreciation by taking me into the back room, but I told him that I was with Dean.

"Don't I turn you on, no more?" he said.

I could have said *yes* and been done with it, but I said: "You're too big. I think you look better when you're leaner."

"I'm going to get bigger," he said. "There's lots of dudes bigger than me in L.A."

❧•❧

I walked the three blocks to the el because Dean had taken the car. The snow increased despite the falling temperature, and the wind gusted across the platform forcing me to take stand in a corner for shelter. I wondered why the others were heading into the Loop. It was the time of evening when southbound trains were mostly empty, while those northbound were full of people who had worked late. Normally I loved weather of this sort; it reminded me of those times coon hunting with Daddy. To be out in the howling wind, dressed in a heavy winter coat, hat, gloves, two pairs of socks, and a scarf is to feel really alive. It's exciting to face the cold head-on instead of hiding inside a warm house. On this night though, my coat was not heavy enough, I had no scarf or gloves, and the wind rushed through every crack to get at my chest and back.

The train stopped, and the doors opened. I followed two girls into the car and took a seat just ahead of them. I slid over to the window and next to the heater and pulled my coat more tightly around my neck. I had a headache and leaned against the window, not bothering to see if it was oily from other heads. I could have dozed off in a second, with my head against the glass and propped up on one elbow.

I exited at Grand and State and began the walk to Michigan Avenue. I proceeded, in spite of gale force winds off the lake, with a determination that I have trouble even now understanding. I made it to the Ritz and into the elevator and up to the lobby without pause. I spotted the house phones and trudged across the Oriental carpet and picked up the receiver, moving by reflex. If I could have looked down on myself from Heaven and seen my figure, stooped, leaning into the wind, and walking down Michigan Avenue, then entering the elevator, mechanically selecting the correct button, and arriving just in front of the telephones to lift the receiver and ask for Corey Raffin's room, I believe I would have concluded that the person who behaved in this manner had no will of his own. The phone rang twice. Someone picked up, but I didn't reply. I hung up and looked at my watch. Then I dialed our apartment. No one answered.

Tension and anxiety drove me to Norberto's hotel that night. And desire. Desire to be free from Mother, free from responsibility, free from failure, free from monotony, free from AIDS, free from shame—if only for a few hours, if only for a night. When our machine came on and I heard Dean's voice, I listened through till the end and hung up without leaving a message. Then, I picked up the house phone again and asked for suite 4700.

"Yes, what is it?" The voice sounded angry already at having had to answer the phone twice in succession.

"This is a friend of Norberto's," I said.

I heard the receiver being put down and voices in the background and then: "Chris, I knew you'd come."

When I got off the elevator and turned the corner I saw Norberto at the end of the corridor waiting outside the door to meet me. When I reached him, he stepped forward, gave me a body hug, and slapped me on the back vigorously. He had white powder smudged under one nostril.

We went into the suite, entering the bedroom first and then the connecting living room where the so-called party was going on. Norberto introduced me to Corey, who smiled widely as we shook hands but stopped short of licking his lips as he looked at me. He was probably only ten or eleven years older than I am, but wasn't aging well and had never been pretty. He was very short, very tan, and very made up, and I could see the pattern of frizzy plugs in his hairline.

"I'm pleased you could come," he said. "Your friend, is he coming too?"

"He's not too much for parties," I said.

"This is a friend of mine from Florida." He gestured to the corner and the big blond, who I had recognized upon entering the room, came forward.

"Hey, stud. Small world, huh?"

It was Tulsa, the Entertainment Engineer.

"I see you two know each other." Corey grinned.

"You know him?" said Norberto, grinding his jaw.

I started to explain, but Corey interrupted: "Put your claws away, and let our guest get settled before you start your interrogation. And get him a drink, please." Then Corey looked at me and said: "Latinos are so jealous." I told Norberto I'd have soda water, and when he went over to the bar, Corey patted the cushion. "Sit here. You may have to help me keep the peace. I'm afraid Norberto doesn't approve of my bringing Tulsa up for the party."

"I have that effect on people," said Tulsa, and then he chuckled. As soon as I sat down, Tulsa came over and stood in front of me. His shirt was unbuttoned and he rubbed his bare belly. He had beautiful, smooth skin, but his abs had lost the definition that I remembered. "I'm going to get you this time," he said. "Can Chris have some Special K?" He addressed Corey far more reverentially than he had dealt with Darren, and I chalked this up to hustler's intuition. There was a quality about Corey that I can only describe as menacing.

"No thanks," I said. "I don't want any. Maybe later."

Tulsa straddled me and sat on my knees. He put his hands on my trap muscles. "It's great, man. Have you ever had K? It's like a forty-five minute popper. Until you go in the K hole," he laughed.

"Chris likes coke," said Norberto, handing me the soda water. "Let him have some coke, Corey."

Corey put his arm on the back of the couch and began to massage the back of my neck. "Chris, can have whatever he likes," he said. "So, how do you know Tulsa? Have you worked together in the past?"

Norberto eyed Tulsa, astride my knees, but when the big blond slid down onto my lap and began to grind his hips on my crotch, Norberto stepped forward as if he planned to put a stop to things. With all the distractions, I hadn't caught the gist of Corey's question.

"Worked together?" I said, realizing that Corey had assumed I was a hustler. "No, we've never worked together," I said. "Tulsa, you're too heavy. My legs are starting to go to sleep. Does anyone have a cigarette?"

"I think I've been insulted," said Tulsa, getting up off my lap. "I may have to drown my sorrow in some cocaine." He went into the bathroom.

Corey took his hand away and started talking with me, in a less derisive tone. He asked questions about what I did for a living, whether or not I was a native of Chicago, where I had traveled. He even asked for suggestions of restaurants he might enjoy. Had I judged him too harshly?

Norberto and Tulsa made frequent trips to the bathroom, and I took note of each and every one. Tulsa concerned himself with the music, fiddling incessantly with the CD player and stereo components, while Norberto stayed close to Corey and me. He sat in the chair directly across from us and tried to become a part of the conversation, but Corey steered to topics that excluded him: Had I seen the French film, *Entre Nous*? Had *City of Angels* made it to Chicago? Norberto attempted to move things back to a place where he could participate: "You should see Corey's big old jet. How much did that thing cost again?" Poor Norberto. He got sloppier by the minute.

"Freshen my drink, Norberto," said Corey, holding up his glass. With Norberto busy at the bar, he dropped his voice. "We're taking the plane to Palm Beach for Christmas and New York for New Year's. Why don't you come along?"

"We have a houseful," I said. "My mother and sister are staying with us." I thanked him and thought about how I had just said we have a houseful. Norberto brought back the drink, and I excused myself to go to the bathroom.

I turned on the light and found the coke—in a large hotel ashtray on the marble dressing table. I pulled back the chair and sat down, but for the first time in my life was afraid to do any and just stared at it. In the past I would have told myself I'd do a line to get my energy, but now I knew I couldn't do just one. The choice seemed clear. Do it, and get sick, do it and lose Dean, or don't do it. I took out my gas credit card and poked at the powder. If Dean had been in New Bedford I believe I would have done some right then. I got up, took a piss, and put the card away. Then I sat in the chair again and took out the card.

Norberto knocked on the door and called in to me. He knocked again. "Chris?" When I answered, he said: "Everything cool?" I got up and opened the door. He gave me a coke leer. "Did you do some blow?" he said.

"A little," I said. I walked back into the room, and Norberto followed.

"It's great shit, isn't it?" He slapped me on the back.

Corey smiled and motioned me over to the couch, but I stayed where I was. Why had I come here? And why was I staying? Why couldn't I leave?

Tulsa came up from behind and put his hands on my hips. I moved, and he followed. He rubbed himself against my ass. Norberto was apparently high enough now not to care. Corey sat on the sofa like The Buddha. He was drinking a little, but wasn't doing blow. He was composed, in control. He'd probably brought Tulsa up to choreograph the evening.

It was cold outside, but inside it was Miami. Bloated Norberto kept grinding his jaw, Tulsa kept trying to turn things sexual, I kept slipping out of his clutches, and Corey kept watching us all. He crossed his right leg over the left, at the knee, and dangled his Gucci loafer from his silk-stockinged toes. I thought about how I would feel if Dean went to a party alone—whatever the circumstance, whatever the reason. I missed him. I missed him so badly that I ached.

Again, I twisted out of Tulsa's grasp. "I'm going," I said.

Norberto's mouth dropped. "What's a matter, man? You can't leave now. Have some more *droggas*." When I stepped forward, he took hold of my arm.

"Thanks for the LA hospitality," I said, not bothering to look at Corey. "And Tulsa, what can I say? It's always a pleasure." Tulsa called me a jag-off and strode into the bathroom, but Norberto, who still had a hold on my arm, followed me toward the bedroom.

"Just a minute," said Corey. He looked as comfortable as an overweight house cat nestled there on the couch. Slowly, he got to his feet. I thought perhaps he might slap me with his soft hand, melodramatically, as actresses did in his cheesy movies. "Do me a favor." He walked behind the bar and bent over to pick something up. I heard glass clinking together. He came out and handed me a plastic trash bag filled with empty bottles, crumpled potato chip sacks, cigarette butts, and paper towels. "Take the rest of the garbage on your way out," he said, and thrust it at me.

Norberto followed me into the hallway. "Baby, don't leave me with them," he said. He looked naive and helpless, the way I used to think of him.

"You're a big boy, Norberto," I said, and looking at him, I had to smile. Crossing the lobby I thought of witty remarks I could have made in response to Corey. The perfect put-down to the almost-perfect put-down. But that only happens in sitcoms.

ഇഇഇ Chapter Seventeen

I TOOK A TAXI to the health club. I wanted to call home before leaving the Ritz, but the lobby phones were in use and I didn't want to wait in case Norberto or Tulsa decided to follow. Going to the hotel was absurd, but I was thrilled to have refused an opportunity to stay, and the realization now that Dean meant more than an evening of drugs cheered me tremendously. All I could think about was getting back and telling Dean about what I'd done—or rather what I hadn't done. I rolled down the window and wiped the perspiration off my forehead with my fingertips. I wasn't too concerned about my cough because it was a tickling cough in my upper chest and throat—from sinus drainage.

I neglected to ask the driver to wait and hurried into the club. It was almost 11:30 P.M., and closing was at midnight. I'd had no idea of the time. A blonde with permed hair worked the desk. She wasn't sure who Dean was, but when I described him, she said: "Oh, the real good-looking one. I think he already left."

Her remark about Dean's appearance was a stab in the groin— perfectly timed, perfectly placed. He could have anyone, but wanted me. And where had I been all evening? I rushed back past the desk and hurried down the stairs.

There are two pay phones in the entry alcove at street level. Mae picked up after the first ring. It occurred to me that she might have weakened in her resolve and had been waiting for Charlie to phone.

"Dean called over an hour ago looking for you. Where have you been anyway?" she said.

I hung up and went outside into the cold. The idea that Dean might be angry had always been in the back of my mind, and now the full range of his possible reactions dominated my thoughts. He'd go to a bar. He'd meet someone. He'd go home with him. They'd fall in love. He'd tell me it was over. They'd move in together. I pictured him on top of a beautiful blond boy, looking into his eyes. I thought about the slant of Dean's eyes and his lashes and the teal green of his irises in the early morning light of our bedroom. How heavy his lids were when he was turned on. How he smiled when we finished.

I walked west on Diversey and north on Clark. The streets were busy with restaurant patrons now that the snow had stopped, but the temperature seemed to be dropping further and the wind had picked up. A Mexican boy was shoveling the walk in front of *Le Crêpe*, but the snow immediately drifted behind, covering his tracks. It was the hour when the bars became noisy and crowded, although they wouldn't peak until around 1 A.M., and when I reached the intersection of Clark and Halsted, I walked faster in spite of my headache, deciding that Dean would be in Scream. He'd be standing at the end of the bar. I'd come up from behind and surprise him. I'd scratch his head, kiss his neck.

Dozens of boys were going in and coming out when I arrived. I squeezed through the door, past the cigarette machine, and by the people waiting to check coats. I maneuvered through the crowd and to the rear bar. I saw the back of a head of black, wavy hair next to the exposed brick wall, and I pushed through a circle of boys talking among themselves. "When he farts, dogs howl for blocks," said the one with the spider web tattoo on his neck. The circle screamed in laughter. The remark had apparently been directed to the stocky boy, and he tried a comeback, but laughter drowned him out. When I was about fifteen feet from the end of the room, Dean turned around. I stared a little too long at the hatchet nose and pointed chin and my heart rate quickened. He had already met someone; they had already left. I circled the bar, searching systematically. I saw Dean everywhere, but as I approached the vision dissolved.

I went across the street to search the new leather bar. I didn't think he'd be there, but I figured it wouldn't hurt to look in since it was close. Smoke swirled in red, hazy light. I bummed a cigarette from a fat man in a leather vest then made a circle of the front room, but when I started to go through the doorway to the second room, the shirtless boy in chaps blocked me with his arm.

"Leather or no shirt," he said.

"But sir, I have leather trim on my Nikes," I said.

"Sorry," he said, frowning.

"Can I look in, at least, to see if my friend is inside?"

"Sure, take your shirt off and have a look."

I stripped off my coat and shirt. I made a quick pass of the two back rooms. The bar wasn't yet crowded. Only inveterate leather queens came early; mainstream gays went to video or dance bars first, and then came here after they were drunk or high.

I'd been sweating and felt chilled with my shirt off, so I didn't stay in the back very long. Dean wasn't there anyway. I was tired and decided to go home. There were too many gay bars in Chicago to search them all.

Others were always in the right place to get the taxis so I walked home, thinking that Dean would be there by the time I arrived. I couldn't wait to get into bed. I crept up the outside stairs onto the porch and unlocked the entry hall door. Clinton and Angelo's mini blinds were open, and I looked in at the Christmas tree that the house sitter had put up, then stepped inside our door and began to quietly climb the stairs. Our apartment lights were out and the house was still, but the reflection from the neighbor's rooftop Santa display kept the room brighter than usual and the first thing that caught my eye was the small, decorated tree in our dining room. Had Dean gotten it? Or had Mae and Mother? I looked in the living room. The hide-a-bed was closed. I heard the refrigerator kick on in the kitchen and went in to get a glass of orange juice, then took it back into the front room. It was over with Dean.

I couldn't sleep and sat on the edge of the bed. Our relationship hadn't lasted a year. I'd never have another lover. I thought about places we'd gone. The time we walked to Lincoln Park. We went inside the conservatory, and later strolled through the zoo. There were thousands of huge bumblebees pollinating the canna lilies in the park. It was early on a Sunday morning; we were the only people out, and there was little traffic. We crouched near the flowers and watched. Up close the bees sounded like World War II bombers. Dean laughed when I said that if we had a video camera we could shoot our own episode of "Nova".

Why had I driven him away? I undressed, opened the hide-a-bed, and threw Mother's quilt across the sheets. I got in, fluffed my pillow, and tried sleeping on my back, then my side, then my stomach. For hours, I dredged up memories. The warm afternoon when we toured the Frank Lloyd Wright houses in Oak Park. The quiet moment in front of the Van Gogh self-portrait, with just our shoulders touching. Eating hotdogs and popcorn at Wrigley Field when the Reds scored twice in the top of the ninth and went on to win. The night after our trip to Lake Geneva, when he told me he loved me. The Whalemen's Chapel in New Bedford. I even included our trip to New Harmony in my nostalgia. My head hurt. After Dean, life would not be as rich or as full of purpose. Having known him, had ruined the prospect of life without him. I was proof: We don't appreciate what we have until it's gone.

❧•❧

Mother shook my shoulder. I hadn't set the alarm; I had no intention of worrying about the shop. Annette was working full-time during her Christmas vacation and she could handle things until I got there.

I felt somewhat better, which is not to say I felt good. I stood up next to the bed and rubbed my face to stimulate the circulation. Then I remembered. In the summer the sun's rays are diffused and softened by the trees around the house, but during Chicago's winters the rays slice through the cold air with an alien angularity and harshness. Like shards of broken glass, the sun came through the window and lit the square patch on the floor where my feet were planted. The hot shower spray relaxed my neck and shoulders, but the steam made me cough. I didn't want to give Mother reason for concern so I kept the water running until I could stop. My phlegm was wet and yellow; I figured my cold was breaking up at last.

I sat at the kitchen table. I only wanted coffee, but Mother fried eggs and made toast. Mae was shopping for baby clothes, and since Mother had already eaten she sat across from me and watched while I chewed and swallowed.

"I'm sorry I yelled the other night," I said.

"We're leaving this weekend," said Mother.

"It's the best thing for Mae," I said. "She's got to get away from Charlie's influence."

"What time did you come home last night?"

"Late."

"Dean didn't come home, did he?"

"No, he didn't."

"He called over and over last night, looking for you. I'd like to know what's wrong."

"Dean won't be coming home."

"It's a crime how you never keep any friends."

"Thanks, Mother. You always say something to cheer me up."

She was right. I never trusted people enough to keep them as friends—or lovers. I knew Dean would eventually leave, for one reason or another. People get bored with their lives and when they're ready for a change, they make it. Husbands leave their wives after forty years of marriage, because the eggs are too runny and the toast is too dark. Dean and I met; we were attracted to each other; we moved in together. When things got heavy, he left. No legal or financial complications. We'd sell Vale de Flores and split the money, and then we'd be finished.

I drove past the leather bar and shook my head. The windows were blacked out so no one could see in. The flower shop was three blocks north. I thought of the street between the bar and Vale de Flores as a straight line. A continuum. At one end: night. At the other: day. Responsibility; escape. Fantasy; reality. Like two doors. Pick one.

When I drove past the shop, I saw Annette inside. For an instant I considered continuing on, but there wasn't any place to go. I turned the corner and drove into the alley. The delivery truck was gone, and I checked my watch.

Annette said, "good morning," but without looking at me. I assumed that she was angry because I was late.

"Walter's not back from morning deliveries?" I said.

"Walter has the flu," she said. "He called my apartment late last night."

"Where's the truck? Who went to the Mart this morning?"

She looked at me as if it were a dumb question. "Dean. He should be back any time."

"He came in?" I said, but it wasn't really a question. It was a statement I made to myself.

"He was back from the Mart by seven. He made a second trip; he said we needed more inventory for Christmas."

I almost dropped my car keys, but before I could get specifics, a customer came through the door. Annette rushed more quickly than usual to wait on her. I stood there watching, hoping it would be a quick sale and I could find out more, but as soon as Annette finished another customer replaced her. I didn't want to interact with people so I went in back to pay bills. We still had Joey's manual bookkeeping system which involved posting invoices to different accounts on a large, metal board with pegs that held the accounting pages and carbonized checks in place. The board is two feet wide and cumbersome. Dean had wanted to purchase a computer system.

I cleared off the desk and took the board down from the top of the filing cabinet and set it up, then went in front to get coffee. Annette was still with the customer and I filled my cup and returned to the back. I had my favorite kind of pen—a rolling writer with a wide tip—my coffee, and the bills, which I had arranged alphabetically a day earlier, were on my left in a neat stack. I have to work when I'm upset. After Mother and Daddy argued, Mother took out a quilt.

Daddy left the house. Mae gets completely crazy—she can't brush her teeth until things are settled. The last time I visited Dr. Jacoby, I pressed: How long did I have?

He said I was being rash, but didn't make light of my status. He smiled and put his hand on my shoulder. "Chris, you don't have pancreatic cancer," he said.

But I didn't let him out of it so easily. "What's the longest anyone has survived?"

"Michael Callen has been diagnosed for ten years," he said. "He wrote a book."

Afterwards I was depressed for a day or two. Dean asked what was wrong. He knew, of course, but encouraged me to talk. He was always supportive. "Ten years with today's medicine," he said. "They'll continue to find new treatments. In a year, it'll be twelve years. In two years, it'll be fifteen," he said. "The idea is to buy time." Then he would remind me that Salk was working on a vaccine and I asked him, as I always did, what good a vaccine was for people who already had AIDS.

A friend of Bob's in Boston is going to spend his remaining time seeing the world. Bob may go along. I could have been happy at Vale de Flores with Dean, with enough time off to go to New Bedford now and then, plus a couple of weeks in Hawaii or the Virgin Islands each year. I put my head down on the desk. I dreaded the moment when Dean came back. Annette had stayed up in front—avoiding me. I wondered if Dean would want to move immediately and how we would settle our financial matters? He'd have to stay at least through the holidays. I tried to conjure up a scenario where he had wronged me, but couldn't come up with anything remotely convincing. When I heard the back door open, I blotted my eyes on my shirtsleeve. I glanced back to see that it was Dean, and then continued posting invoices. He didn't say anything while he unloaded the truck, which took about ten minutes, and after he carried the last of the new ficus and schefflera trees to the front, he stayed out there. I figured he was checking to see if Annette and I had talked.

I posted first one invoice then another. My stack of paper grew and still Dean stayed in front. With each additional bill I wondered: Will he stay up there? Will he leave again? Will he interrupt me? Will he want to stay friends? I didn't want to be friends. And where had he slept? I imagined Dean putting his arms around someone else. The thought of him kissing another man made me wallow in self-pity. Then the door from the front squeaked open.

He walked up behind me, but I kept looking down, kept making entries. He stood quietly for a second or two, and then said "good morning," but without touching me.

"Chris, are you okay?"

"I think I'm having a nervous breakdown," I said. "I think I'm going crazy."

"We've already established that you're crazy. How are you feeling?"

I turned around to look at him, he smiled, and I lost control. I put my face in my hands and bawled. I made noises like a wounded animal. Dean stepped forward and put his hands on my head. He brushed my hair with his fingers and rubbed. He massaged my scalp while I howled. He didn't try to talk or try to get me to quit; he let me cry for as long as I wanted. When I would think I was about finished, I would cry louder— mechanically—for specific thoughts no longer materialized.

I don't want to die," I said through the sobs. My head was plugged and I immediately regretted saying this for it sounded like yet another plea for sympathy. "I have to get a tissue."

"Sit still," said Dean. He walked to the bathroom and came back with toilet paper. He handed it to me and pulled over the other chair and sat next to me.

"I don't want to lose you," I said.

"That's funny, because I got the impression you were trying to get rid of me," he said.

"I went to Scream looking for you last night."

Dean took my hand. "Let's be honest. You knew I wouldn't go to a bar, just like I knew you would. Did you do cocaine?"

"No," I said.

"You look like shit, your head is clogged, and you're coughing. You should be in bed. You're going to kill yourself. You don't need to blame AIDS."

"Are we breaking up?" I said.

"You piss me off. I love you, Chris. Do you want to break up?"

A SUMMER AFTERNOON

Life arrives in the middle of a summer afternoon. I'm eleven years old when I plop down on the floor at the top of the stairs. On the landing, between my sister's room and mine, I open the issue that the mailman just delivered. Of all the magazines that Mother takes, it is my favorite. About halfway through, I start reading an article about Hitler, but stop on the word at the top of the second page that I've never seen before. *Homosexual.* I run downstairs to get the dictionary. The article says Hitler may have been homosexual. Blood fills my fingers as I turn the pages; it's as if I'm being stung by millions of bees all over my face and neck as I read the definition: Of or having sexual desire for persons of the same sex. I stare at the word. A housefly, large and slow and with an iridescent, green back, lands on my hand and rubs its front legs together. I put down the dictionary and put away the magazine and go back up to my room to lie down. Through the open window I hear my sister and her friend on the front porch, talking about boys. Downstairs Mother comes home with the groceries. She calls for me, but I don't answer. I turn over on my side and put my arms around my pillow and watch the shadows of tree branches flicker on the wallpaper.

ಬಬಬ Chapter Eighteen

DEAN COULD HAVE GOTTEN indignant, could have preached to me when Norberto showed up, could have insisted that I not go to Norberto's party. But he didn't. He worked out; he picked up the flowers; he carried boxes; he smiled at customers.

He convinced me to ask Mae and Mother to stay for Christmas. If I made Mae's departure too traumatic, he said, she'd be tempted to go back to Charlie. "She's at a turning point—and we can manage," he said. He talked to Mother for an hour and a half the night of my outburst. She didn't want to talk about me being gay, he said, but she was concerned and saddened by my health. She had put her quilt aside, and taken Dean's hand, and said: "Believe me, I do love him." After that night Mother and I didn't make eye contact. We hadn't embraced full of good cheer and insight as so often happens in the movies, and a part of me was relieved. She asked questions about the pills I took and referred to my cough, but it was the questions she didn't ask that made me edgy. Years of conditioning had left me with a sense of shame, and I simply didn't feel comfortable with the issue being a matter of public information. The issue being *homosexuality*, and the public being *Mother*. I didn't sleep for fear that she would stand in the doorway again, watching. If Dean had been a woman and my wife, I wouldn't have felt comfortable having sex with her in the next room.

Dean does have faults. He does things that irritate. When we re-decorated the apartment according to his plan, I yelled at him because he gloated each time someone came in and complimented us on the place, as Clinton and Angelo had. Dean grinned impishly and said: "I told Chris it was too dark to use color."

We have trouble choosing movies because Dean doesn't like Hollywood. He prefers European films. He won't consider seeing anything with Arnold, Sylvester, Dolph, or Patrick. And he refuses to use their entire names. He says they're not actors; they're porn stars. "You want to watch porno? Let's look at one of your tapes."

When we went to the Art Institute he discussed the Impressionists as if he were the *Chicago Tribune* art critic. "I studied design at Rhode Island," he said. "I'm qualified to hold Manet's work in higher esteem than Renoir."

I find Dean almost arrogant where matters of taste are concerned—and I had to adjust—but I must say that I don't consider his tendency to condescend as a character flaw. It's my best attempt to illustrate his negative qualities. Dean is honest, considerate, industrious, thrifty, brave, clean, and reverent—and Lassie was less faithful—but he's involved with someone that I'm not sure I'd put up with. He said: "You'd do the same if the situation was reversed." Would I? I am so attracted to him that I might feel just as passionate if I found a boy's telephone number in his pants pocket, or if he spent mornings at the gym and afternoons at the beach, or if Lenny said he saw him with a muscular young blond. Dean laughed. "If I were an asshole, you'd find something physically unattractive about me," he said. "You'd say I have too many pimples or something."

"You don't have any pimples," I told him.

He said: "You know what I mean."

When Dean revealed that he spent the night at Cynthia's and Louie's, that he had called then gone to discuss me, I said, "Louie was home? How did he treat you?" But I didn't really care about Louie. I suddenly saw myself as an errant child whose parents were so distressed and so confused and so out of options that they had no choice but to visit the school psychologist.

Cynthia and Dean stayed at her kitchen table until one o'clock talking and drinking coffee. Dean told her he loved my passion, but that it sometimes frightened him. Cynthia said, "Chris can be spiteful when he doesn't get his way, but I've never seen him so focused or content. He needs you." And then I realized that he'd gone to see my best friend because he cared about me—and needed me. He too could be insecure. My going to the party had shaken him—understandably.

I'm glad that I left Corey's suite when I did. I'm glad I broke the pattern. Maybe I didn't like seeing Norberto or Corey together, or maybe the Natalie Cole CD turned me off. Maybe I left for Dean—or maybe for me.

I went home after we talked and spent the afternoon in bed. I didn't feel much better the following morning, but I forced myself to go into the store. It was Christmas Eve Day and we'd be swamped. Dean wanted me to see the doctor, but I insisted that I had a cold, or at worst, a mild case of the flu. I was ashamed to let Dr. Jacoby see me.

Two policemen came to the store, after lunch, asking about Norberto. Had he kidnapped his daughter or beaten up Lydia? The police weren't eager to give details and would only say that Norberto had been involved in an altercation at the Ritz and that charges might be filed. Do they have a course at the Police Academy to train cops to use unnatural language? I explained that Norberto used to work in the store. "Who told you to come here?" I asked.

"When was you last in contact with Mr. Perez?" the shorter, heavier cop said.

"I stopped in the hotel where he was staying."

"And that was when?"

"A couple of nights ago," I said.

The taller cop had been walking through the shop looking around. He came back to the counter and said: "You must do pretty good here. What's your lease cost you?" He took off his left glove to adjust his crotch and coughed as if he were checking for a hernia.

I started to answer, but the short cop spoke again. "And that would be Wednesday, December the twenty-second?"

I looked back at him. "Yes," I said.

"And you haven't subsequently seen or talked to him?"

"No. Look, what has he done?"

"We have reason to suspect he caused some damage on the forty-seventh floor at the hotel."

"In the room? What kind of damage?" I said.

"He broke a mirror in the elevator bank, tore an ashtray off the wall, and toppled a potted plant," the short cop said.

His partner wandered off again, over to our display of poinsettias, and was busy turning pots to check prices. He whistled softly, then adjusted himself again, and said: "Jimmy, get a load of these prices. You can get these same poinsettias at K-Mart for eight bucks."

"I've never known Norberto to be violent," I said. "Someone saw him do this? He was a guest of Mr. Raffin at the hotel. Haven't you talked to him?"

"If you hear from Mr. Perez, please give one of us a call at the precinct. He handed me the slip of paper with two names and a telephone number.

"Sure, but let me ask you something. How do you know Norberto tore the lobby apart?"

"A wallet was found with his Illinois driver's license and a man fitting his description was seen leaving the premises. Give us a call if you hear from him. A merry holiday season to you."

Dean came back to the store after four o'clock, and I called Cartier to see what time they closed. I had barely enough time to get there and buy his gift. I had picked out a ring with three interlocking bands of gold—each one a different shade: pink, yellow, and white. On one of our Sunday afternoons we'd gone window shopping down Michigan Avenue, and when we spotted the ring in the Cartier window, Dean went wild, so I decided right then to make it his Christmas present.

I told him I had errands as I left the shop. We were getting ready to close—Walter had already gone home and Annette would handle the last of the shoppers while Dean cleaned up. I told him to take the car, that I would take the subway, and meet him later at home.

I love Michigan Avenue at Christmas. I planned to check out the window displays after buying the ring and I had every reason to be in a good mood as I headed for the train, but instead, for reasons I didn't understand, I was depressed.

I boarded the train and took a seat by the door. If someone had seen Norberto by the elevator, why wasn't he caught then? Why did they really suspect him? Did the cops know about the drugs? What had Corey said? A picture of him whispering about Palm Beach came to mind. Had he given them my name? I awoke in Jackson Park. With a raging headache, it took all the effort I had to get down the flight of stairs and back up to the other platform. Not much new snow had fallen, but the wind swirled it in the air. I sat on a bench and drew myself into a ball. Just inside the turnstile, a tall man stood drinking from a bottle wrapped in a paper bag; he wore several layers of ragged clothing and his head was turbaned in heavy scarves. The northbound train arrived and I walked on. From my seat I watched the man stumble toward the train, but the doors closed, leaving him at the station.

I regained consciousness on my back on the floor. My body blocked the doorway, and at least two people stepped over me to get out of the train before a black kid helped me up. He had perfect, white teeth and his eyes were as dark and clear as two polished buckeyes. I thanked him, insisting I didn't need further help, and actually found my predicament humorous. He might have thought I was a drug addict, and I've no idea how many others ignored me as if I were no more consequential than a bag of rubbish. When I saw the name of the station—Clark and Division—I realized that I'd been unconscious for at least twenty minutes and I didn't wait for the Fullerton stop before exiting. I went to the pay phones, trying to avoid sudden or rapid movement: I didn't want my inflamed brain to be slammed unnecessarily against the inside of my skull. Mae answered, and I wrapped my scarf around my head and ears.

Mother has a crinkled photograph of me on Daddy's lap when I was four. We had a red vinyl-covered chair in our living room and he used to rock me and comfort me when I had the measles, chicken pox, or a croupy cough. In this picture though, I don't have a cold or a cough or a fever; in this picture I'm not ill. In this picture it's an ordinary evening just before bedtime, and I'm dressed in flannel pajamas. The picture makes the pajamas look light gray, but I remember clearly that they were a soft, pale silver. In this picture I have an impish smile, with the corners of my mouth turned up, and I'm leaning back against his chest, but there's something more than pleasure in my smile. My expression is exultant. I look completely thrilled peering into the camera, and my father's expression is sublime. In this picture, there's such rapture: two human beings so peaceful, so completely in harmony with each other that I shake my head trying to consider how we got to where we were before he died.

So many times I've considered that photo. When Mother showed the album to visitors as she did on that first occasion when Cynthia came home to visit, or when the house was empty and I took it down myself from the shelf in the hall closet and gazed at it in the silence of the living room. The rocking chair is gone, but I sat in the same spot and tried to identify the moment when our attitudes changed. At what age did I first disappoint my father, and what was it that changed his smile, broad and proud, to the scowl he made whenever I got too upset or too emotional? I can look at the picture for hours and never tire of those smiles.

In the vestibule between the parking lot and the Jewel entrance, I sat on the floor against the front of one of the newspaper vending machines. The woman said I had my face in the palms of my hands. She said I looked up when she came through the automatic door with her groceries. She said that for an instant she thought I was homeless, because I asked her for change to make a call. But when she gave me a quarter I reached in my coat pocket and pulled out a dollar. Then she said she asked if I needed help, if I were all right. Apparently I called her Mother and told her I was sick. I got to my feet, but ended up leaning against the wall next to the phone.

"Mother," I said, "would you call Dean for me," and I recited the number. One minute, she said, I seemed clearheaded and then I'd act anxious. Mae didn't know what the woman was talking about; she thought it was a prank. The woman hadn't been able to get me to tell her my name, but because I kept talking about Dean, she decided that was my name. Dean wasn't back and Mae said Mother got on the line. Mae said she took the address down, hung up, and ordered a cab.

It was Mother who picked me up. She and the woman got me into the taxi and Mother took me home.

శుశుశు Chapter Nineteen

EVERY SATURDAY—in August when the pavement asphalt bubbled and in January when ice covered the gravel—he drove down Locust Street to the New Harmony Pool and Billiards Parlor. He promised to have only a few games. He didn't wager on quarter horses or professional football and never went to Las Vegas, but whether it was gin rummy or checkers or pool, though he didn't risk large sums, he always played for money. Once he started, if the smallest amount was involved, he'd play through dinner and into the night. When he was with other men, Daddy never looked at the clock.

I didn't watch him or his friends and they paid no attention to me; I stayed in the back and to the side of the large room. I wasn't much taller than the table when I ran my hands over the kelly green felt and tugged at the interlaced leather pockets and put blue chalk on my fingertips. I racked the balls and rolled them across the felt, but didn't learn about the game: I couldn't hold the cue properly. The hall had oily, worn wood floors, and a single, hooded bulb was suspended over each table from the high ceiling, leaving other areas of the room in darkness. Dozens of brass spittoons were placed at intervals against the cracked plaster walls. The cuspidors were heavy and bowl-shaped and had fluted tops in the form of a shallow funnel with an opening in the middle, and when the men spit, the saliva hit the banded top and ran slowly toward the opening and into the bottom.

The third Saturday, I discovered a closet in the back of the hall with a deep sink containing rags and mops and cleansers. I brought a spittoon to the closet and emptied the saliva and tobacco juice and poured in cleanser and scrubbed until I had removed the crusted residue from the inside. I polished the outside with Ajax, making the brass so shiny that I could see my reflection, then did a second and a third. I made a game of cleaning the cuspidors, pretending to be in charge, pretending it was my duty to keep them spotless. One by one I carried them to the back until I'd cleaned them all. The next week, I started over.

Cowboy, lanky and loud, wore Western boots and a Stetson. He stood on the sidewalk in front of the hall one afternoon when Mother and I walked by. He whistled at her and said: "What's a matter, beautiful? Cat got your tongue?" I asked her what he meant, but she didn't answer. Daddy and Cowboy talked about fighting, but never did. They went to the alley in back of the pool hall one time, and everyone followed them outside, but they only faced off and shouted at each other. The Saturday after, Cowboy saw me bringing one of the cleaned spittoons out of the mop closet. He'd never spoken to me, though I often watched him, but he grabbed onto my arm and yelled to my dad in front of the five or six others in the hall that day. "Hey, Dale. You raising a little housewife? He do the washing and ironing too?"

My father's face turned red and he threw down his pool cue and took me home. I asked what I did wrong, and he walked faster. Mother was surprised to see us, but Daddy didn't mention Cowboy and neither did I. I didn't go back with him for several weeks and, when I did, he told me to keep my hands off the spittoons. Mother gave me books to take, and I read the Hardy Boys and Nancy Drew each Saturday after that. If they still make spittoons, I'll buy some for Vale de Flores to use as planters—for Boston fern or Mother-in-law-tongues.

Before we had our first television, Mother subscribed to *Life*, *Look*, *Redbook*, *Ladies Home Journal*, and *Readers Digest*. They were her contact with life outside New Harmony, since we didn't travel and Daddy didn't care for movies. She tried the recipes in the magazines—recipes with names like Hungarian goulash, Spanish rice, and Italian spaghetti, although the ingredients for all the dishes were rather standard and unexotic: hamburger, tomatoes, and onions. During the summer I met the mailman at the edge of our porch when it was time for her copy of *Life* to arrive and I always read the magazine before she did.

Mother had gone to the grocery store the day I brought the mail into the house and took the July issue upstairs. I sat on the landing at the top of the staircase, in between my room and Mae's room, turning the pages. About halfway through I came upon an article about Hitler. There were several pictures—one of him with his hand outstretched to a cowering German shepherd and another of him with his mistress, Eva Braun. The article described how Hitler had married Eva Braun and then committed suicide with her at the end of the war. In the next paragraph the author, citing references and opinions of psychologists, stated that Hitler might have been homosexual. I stopped reading. I closed the magazine and walked downstairs and put it in her rack next to her chair then went into her bedroom where she kept her dictionary. I read the definition—*Of or having sexual desire for persons of the same sex*—and stared awhile at the word, until a housefly, large and slow and with an iridescent green back, landed on my hand and rubbed its front legs together.

I climbed the stairs and went into my room and looked out my window onto the front porch. Mae and her friend, Sally, were playing with dolls. "Is Bobby your boyfriend?" Sally asked. I lay down on my bed, and a few minutes later Mother came home with the groceries and called for me, but I didn't answer. I put my arms around my pillow, turned over on my side, and studied the shadows of tree branches flickering on the wallpaper.

A starving, yellow kitten came to our back door, and I asked to keep it. Daddy didn't look up from his plate of fried liver. I asked again. He put a forkful of onions in his mouth, and chewed for a moment, and said: "No." I waved my hands and demanded a reason, and when he didn't provide one, I balled a wad of white bread in my fist and threw it in my plate.

I'd been asking for a dog for two years. I cut pictures of cocker spaniels out of magazines and pasted them in a scrapbook. "When you show you can take care of Humphrey we'll talk about getting you a hound," said Daddy.

After I hurled the bread onto my plate he didn't reach across his to slap me or drag me from the table; he sent me to my room. I flung myself on the bed, put the pillow over my head, and held my breath. Fourteen-year-olds do leave home, but I wasn't one of them. I removed the pillow, took a breath, and looked at the plastic curtains with the large, patterned flowers at my window. Mother had hung inexpensive ones in the bedrooms, saying we could only afford cloth drapes in the main rooms. I got up from bed and clutched the plastic in my fists and pulled them to the floor with the rods intact. I stripped them off the rods, wadded them into balls as I had my bread at the supper table, and stuffed them into my wastebasket. Daddy never discovered the crumpled drapes. Mother did. An hour later, she came into my room with a sandwich and glass of milk. It had gotten dark outside and I was reading from a book of dog stories. The ceiling light was off, so the only light I had was from the table lamp next to my bed. Without curtains, the window reflected the outside blackness, making the sparsely furnished room even darker. Mother tapped on the door before coming into the room, and I glanced up from my book. She stared at the uncovered window for a moment, and then looked over at me on the bed. I looked back. After a moment she said: "I brought you a sandwich; I told your father it was liver." Neither of us mentioned the curtains that night, or at any other time, and a week later, she began making new ones. "I found some material on sale," she said. The background was my favorite color, blue, and there were drawings of kittens jumping, playing with twine, rolling over, and chasing their tails. Daddy never saw the curtains. He never came to my room, and Mother worked on them during the day. The material wasn't on sale, because I showed it to her one afternoon when we were in Woolworth's, and the sandwich she brought me was leftover meat loaf that she'd taken from the freezer and heated in the skillet.

Mother wanted to go to college after finishing high school. She wanted to be an English teacher. She taught me to read before first grade and gave me my first lessons in arithmetic. My dad could read and write, but left school in the eighth grade. Mother made clothes for me and Mae and knitted sweaters for us. She insisted that Mae and I eat the right foods and have balanced meals. She made us take vitamins and put cod-liver oil in our milk. She put it in milk to disguise its taste, but it made the milk turn yellow ochre and we could still smell the oil.

I took Colleen to my senior prom. We double-dated with Steve and Pam. Daddy had just gotten a new Ford Galaxie, but I hadn't asked to borrow it because Steve wanted to drive. When he failed calculus and had to enroll for summer school, his father postponed his graduation present and told him he couldn't use his car either. His father owned the only Mercedes in town, and Steve enjoyed making an entrance. Colleen's parents were driving to Cleveland that weekend, and Pam's parents had an aging, rusted Chevrolet, so the four of us now planned to take Steve's mom's Volkswagen.

Mother and Mae were preparing dinner. It was a few days before prom weekend, and I stood next to the counter discussing the plans with Mother while she sliced potatoes. Daddy came home from work and over to the sink to wash his hands. He stood bent at the waist to ease his breathing.

"Schroeder's kid flunked calculus?" he said, inhaling through his mouth. "What did you get?"

"An A," I said.

"Did he still get his Mustang?" said Daddy.

"He doesn't get the car until he graduates," I said. "After summer school."

"And Mr. Schroeder won't let him drive the Mercedes to the prom either," said Mae.

"How are you getting there?" said my dad.

"In his mom's VW," I said.

"You're driving a toy to the country club?" said Daddy. "Take the Ford."

"Really?" I said.

"It's got more room than a Hitler-mobile. It's got more room than a Mercedes."

The Galaxie was his last new car. He left work less than six months later. At the time we had never heard of emphysema, nor had our neighbors. They didn't carry health and medical at the plant, and even after he qualified for disability, there was barely enough money to make the mortgage and the car payments.

He wanted to keep working, but it took considerable effort simply for him to climb steps and walk up inclines. He fired kilns until he was no longer able. They moved him to another job, but he said he was no better than a janitor. Once he was diagnosed, the doctors told him he had to quit work altogether because he was failing so fast. When Daddy told our neighbors that it was emphysema, Mrs. Epley said "at least it ain't TB," and when Daddy repeated her statement at home, Mother said, "They can cure TB." Then she called Mrs. Epley a *fool.*

But the Saturday of the prom, Daddy hadn't yet been diagnosed. Mother came to my room to tell me that he was washing and waxing the car. It was two weeks old. Mother was concerned that he'd overdo it—he needed weekends to rest—and I went downstairs to help. The Galaxie was dark, metallic blue with white interior, white sidewalls, and had a strip of chrome along each side. Daddy sat on the coping with his feet in the street, breathing hard but smiling. "It's magnificent," I said. "I'm glad we didn't get the Galaxie 500; it has too much chrome."

When he was admitted to the hospital for the last time, I drove down from Chicago. I told Mother I couldn't take any time off, but Stanley told me to take all I needed. I told Mother I had to save my days off for when Daddy died—to help her with funeral plans.

Mother and I stepped quietly into his room and found him sleeping. The bed by the window was empty and I asked her why Daddy wasn't in that one so he could have better light and a view. Mae said he hadn't been in any condition to enjoy seeing outside. He had lost his appetite and developed pneumonia. I put the planter basket of pink hyacinths on the side table, next to his pitcher and water glass, then walked over to the edge of his bed and looked at him. He was grayish white, and in spite of the oxygen tube in his nose, his mouth was open. I watched the movement of his chest rising and falling. He made a low, groaning noise each time he exhaled as the wind passed over his vocal chords. He lay on top of the sheets; I watched his fingers twitch. His feet were smooth, white, and hairless—swollen like doll's feet—and his legs jerked. He was sixty-two. His sagging cheeks and chin were covered with stubble. I hadn't seen how white his beard had become because he never went unshaven—he said he couldn't stand to feel his whiskers on the pillowcase. I turned to Mother and whispered: Is he in pain? She covered her mouth with her fingers and nodded, and I watched her eyes mist. That's when he took my hand and held it. I turned to look down at him again. He tightened his grip. "Look what the cat drug in," he said, his voice husky with phlegm.

He was better on Saturday. Sunday he improved and I took Mother home, early in the afternoon, so she could rest. Then I left for Chicago.

I drove west out of town and north toward the interstate, passing the gravel road that led to Dooley's Woods. It was a sunny, spring afternoon; there were still several hours of daylight left, so I stopped in the middle of the pavement, put the car into reverse, and backed up until I reached Dooley's Road again. I sat behind the steering wheel for a minute or two, then turned left onto the gravel and followed the road over the hill, down through the gully, and into the woods. When I reached the clearing at the top of the ridge, I pulled over to the side and shut off the engine. Past the open field on the right, the woods began again, but denser and more rugged. There was a weathered, rickety gate across the entrance to the field, chained and secure, with a NO TRESPASSING sign nailed to the top slat. I got out of my car, studied the sign briefly, then climbed over the fence and started my walk across the newly plowed earth.

There were additional signs on the wire fence at the beginning of the woods, which I took note of as I climbed to the top. I caught my trousers on the barbed wire and tore a small hole in one cuff when I jumped to the ground. I picked up a branch next to the base of a dying elm, to use as a walking stick, and headed into the woods. It was twenty minutes before the terrain began to slope downward, and probably another thirty before I came to the overhanging rock wall where our fire had been that night in January, so many years before, when the coon took refuge in a rabbit hole. I made a place in the grass and lay down with my head a few feet from the base, then peered up the side to the treetops. It's a place I've returned to several times over the years, but on that particular Sunday it was smaller. I stayed in that position, on my back, for a long time and eventually fell asleep.

When I finally got back to Chicago, late that night, I heard my phone ringing as I climbed the stairs. Even before I walked into my apartment and picked up the receiver I knew it was Mother. "Daddy's gone," she said.

ಬಬಬ Chapter Twenty

I WAS SO DEBILITATED that I didn't read the newspaper. People hovered over the bed with questions about insurance; nurses and orderlies raced up and down the hallway pushing carts and gurneys; my bed was raised at the head and the foot in such an odd angle that I felt as if I'd been abandoned with head injuries in a ditch. I've always had frequent colds during the winter. At Bradley, I caught every sniffle, ache, and fever brought to the office. Stanley bragged that he hadn't taken a sick day in twenty-one years and came to work coughing and sneezing, with crusted, red eyes and a voice that sounded as if it were coming from deep inside a drainage tunnel and I could practically see the phlegm on the memos he gave me and every time this happened, exactly ten days later, I caught cold.

This time I told myself that it was the rush of the holiday season and after Christmas and New Year's I'd get more rest. Denial is healthy: those who succumb go quickly. Dean blamed himself for not making me go to the doctor's office. But then I hadn't revealed that my temperature was 100.4 degrees—after all that's less than two degrees above normal. When Dean found out, he said: "You're like a dog scratching an open sore." By then I was too weak and scared to resist going to the hospital. Still, I insisted: "It's just a cold. I'm doing Pentamadine." I didn't know there were breakthrough cases of PCP. Then, I blamed myself for not being better informed, and Dean vowed to get involved.

Being positive is not something to announce to strangers—unless you're financially and socially secure like Arthur Ashe and Magic Johnson. Morally, I had an obligation to tell Dean, and telling Cynthia was appropriate—we were best friends—and I didn't hesitate to discuss my situation with Mae, and because of Dean I told Bob and learned that he was doing ddI and ddC. But even among gays, there's an attitude. I don't want people waiting for me to cough, looking for lesions, anticipating the weight loss.

Clinton and Angelo came to see me. I thought they were staying in Hawaii for New Year's, but Dean saw them get out of a taxi a couple of nights ago. In his rushing between Vale de Flores and the hospital he'd almost forgotten to tell me. Clinton was thinner, and his tan had a yellow cast. He looked exhausted—and not simply from jet lag. They brought me chocolates. Dean said it was inappropriate, because chocolate temporarily shuts down the immune system. When Clinton turned to put the box on the table against the wall, I couldn't help staring at his baggy slacks; he didn't have any ass left. He walked over to the window and looked outside. Angelo stood at the foot of my bed, peering into the hallway.

"So Dean's taking care of the shop while you're gone?" said Angelo, as if I were on a business trip.

In all the years I'd lived above them, nothing had been said about our status. "We have reliable help now," I said.

"That's good," said Clinton.

"Yeah, that's good," said Angelo.

"I thought you were staying in Hawaii for New Year's," I said.

"We got homesick," said Angelo.

"Are you going to have your party?" I asked.

"I don't think so. We hadn't planned on being here and it's only two days away."

"A New Year's Eve without Clinton's surprise evening of drag?" I said. Clinton looked out the window again and said he didn't have anyone in mind to be. Then he turned back and forced a smile. If he lost any more weight he could dress as The Duchess of Windsor.

❧•☙

Cynthia came this morning. She invited Dean and me for dinner, and I asked what Louie thought about her plans.

"He's all for it," she said.

"He is?"

"He thinks you're witty—and he likes Dean a lot."

I couldn't remember a single thing I might have said that Louie would consider witty.

Cynthia said they'd been talking, and Louie was beginning to understand. I suggested getting together for a movie and coffee first, when Pam and Steve came up to visit; with six of us, Louie would be more inclined to think of Dean and me as simply another couple. That's when Cynthia rubbed my arm and said: "You and Dean are not just another couple; you're two of the sweetest people I know."

I didn't avert my glance and I didn't comment on the weather and I didn't tell the joke the nurse told me: What's black and brown and looks good on a lawyer? I took her hand and squeezed it and looked her right in the eye and said, "Thanks. Really. Thanks for everything."

Dean said that Stanley called and invited me to his New Year's celebration. He's changing to a daytime party to watch the Rose Parade and football games. Dean didn't tell him I was in the hospital.

Gays have a fantasy that on the same day at the same time every gay in the world would announce their homosexuality. Imagine every congressman, every CEO, every television and movie actor, every accountant, every farmer, every attorney, every producer, every florist, every pilot, and every priest and every nun and every second baseman and every country and western singer and every doctor announcing themselves to the world. Being sick must have affected me in the same way that being pregnant affected Mae. Playing this game with Stanley no longer mattered. I called him the same afternoon at the office. Then I called Beth at home and told her that I'd told Stanley that I was H.I.V.–positive, and that I was in the hospital with PCP.

≈ 275

I heard Stanley's breathing on the phone and I heard him light a cigarette, but he didn't say much—just that that he was sorry to hear I was sick, and then: "Marty and I are in the middle of a meeting. Got to go." He hung up.

Had I made a mistake? Complicated matters? I told Beth that I liked him—and that's true. He had the right to know; in his way he'd been a friend. I don't expect he'll come to visit, but Beth came and we talked for over an hour. "He's afraid of what people will say if he has a homosexual friend," she said. "I don't believe he would have told me you called." She patted my hand, then said: "We'll talk. I wouldn't worry too much about Stanley. He has a few hang ups, but I think he respects you. If he doesn't, it's his loss."

If it was up to me, I'd have Beth put up for sainthood.

҈•҉

The hospital is the last place I wanted to spend Christmas Eve, but with the I.V.s of Pentamadine and rest I was better by Christmas Night. Now it looks as if I'll be able to go home for New Year's and finish my treatment on an outpatient basis. Dr. Jacoby says one more week ought to do it. He wants me to try Dapsone now; the possible side effects are nausea and vomiting—and there is the potential for liver damage, but all things considered, I suppose I'll do it.

Except for when I was born, I've never been in the hospital. The room smells of disinfectant. The bed is plastic with an artificial wood-grain. There's too much chrome in the room and it's too chilly. Hospital rooms are cold, like doctors' offices; the air moves swiftly. The walls are lifeless, pale green, and the view is uninspiring. I'd prefer to look out on snow-covered trees and hills that slope down to a thawing stream. I'd like to hear galoshes squeaking on the ice and children laughing as they make a snowman. All I see is a row of grim, gray stone houses, and the ambulances as they speed through the street. There's no incentive to get well in this place; the only incentive is to get out, because it's prison. Bottles of fluids hang from upright stands and plastic tubes go into all the body's openings. If there aren't enough openings, new ones are made with syringes and catheters. The flower arrangements are already stale and artificial. Too many kinds are forced together in the same arrangement: unnatural groupings never found in nature. The notes on the cards are awkward and forced. I've never written to anyone seriously ill. And how bizarre it is to see visitors' faces. They don't like coming here because they are looking into their own future, looking ahead to the day when they lie in this hospital bed. They enter the room as if they expect a team of doctors to jump out from behind the door and say: "We want to perform a few tests as long as you're here."

Norberto called—about half an hour after Beth left. I never called Lydia. I can't be his protector any longer. He hadn't heard from Corey, but assumed he ran off with Tulsa. Norberto said, "He was going to put me in a picture, man. Is my skin too dark?" Corey sent him on a drug run, and then checked out of the hotel. Norberto hasn't heard from the police; I'm sure they wouldn't have known to come and ask questions without information from Corey—who I'm sure probably sent a lackey to the hotel to handle things and implicate him. I sympathize with Norberto, but that's all. I told him he was a beautiful color.

Mother and Mae are leaving for New Harmony tomorrow. Mother's probably uncomfortable with the prospect of explaining why to her friends. I told her that people don't hide their problems as much these days, and as a result, find they're not so unusual.

I'm afraid that's not true with AIDS. God, I hope I don't ever have to go back to New Harmony to live; I hope I don't have to go back to New Harmony to die. It might seem like I'm doing the pragmatic thing by wanting it to work with Dean. But if anything, I've reacted against staying with him—out of pride. I don't want to be a burden. But nothing is certain. He could be hit by a bus. He could develop pancreatic cancer. I may end up taking care of him. Dean says that is implicit in any relationship, and that he lives for the day. He refuses to worry about tomorrow.

I get emotional when I think about Mother coming after me in a cab. We still hadn't talked about me being gay. The way I exploded at the table was not the way I fantasized it would be. I wanted to sit with her on the banks of the Ohio or the Lake Michigan shore, and take her hand. I wanted to explain that there wasn't a single thing that anyone could have done to change me. Dean says she needs to meet other gay parents and wants to take her with us to New Bedford on our next trip.

This morning I told her I get to go home tomorrow, and that Dean and I are going to have a quiet dinner at home to celebrate New Year's Eve. She removed her coat and draped it over the chair next to my bed and sat down. "Thank goodness you're feeling better," she said. She reached in her shopping bag and pulled out a book of crossword puzzles and a garden magazine. I smiled and then we both stared up at the television. We sat without a word until the Oprah promo. A typical show—this one dealing with incest. Mother got up and drew the curtain. Then she sat back down in the chair, glanced through the open door into the hallway, and turned to me.

"We did the best we could as parents. Look what some do. Nobody molested you or Mae."

My gown had gotten twisted; I straightened it and pulled the sheet up over my chest. "I know. Have you had lunch?"

"I know you think it was our fault."

"Your fault?"

"You being the way you are."

"Gay? Being gay isn't my problem. Hating myself is my problem. How can a two hundred pound man with calloused hands justify slapping a child? Imagine how humiliated you'd have been if he slapped you." Mother didn't answer, and I didn't have to look into her tired eyes this time to know they were tearing. "Can't you admit that was wrong?" I said. "Why couldn't you both accept me the way I was? Why can't you now?"

"I do love you. I'm the way I am too. I thought I was supposed to discourage you from playing jacks and jumping rope."

"Why?" I said. My voice had gotten a little strong so I took a breath and leaned over to pour myself a glass of water. Mother took a tissue from her purse and blotted her eyes. "I used to wonder if I were adopted," I said.

"I wanted you to have friends and get married." Mother blew her nose, and then looked at me suddenly. "Don't be ridiculous. You look just like Dale when he was young."

"I have Dean," I said.

"I try to understand, but I don't understand."

"You won't get it in a couple of weeks."

"It's just that I worry that I could have done more, and now with this horrible disease—"

Mother didn't finish her sentence, and though she made very little noise, she put her face in her hands, and her shoulders shook violently. I slid out of bed and sat on the edge and took hold of her wrists and pried her hands away.

"You did the best you could, Mother. Leave it. We can't change the past, Mother." I leaned over and put my arms around her shoulders and rested my head against her.

The nurse came in to give me my pills. I got back on my bed and introduced him to Mother, relieved by the interruption. He saw Mother's wet, red eyes and immediately reassured her that I would be leaving the hospital in time to celebrate New Year's Eve at home. She smiled and thanked him. After he left, she said: "Is he studying to be a doctor?"

"He's a nurse, Mother. He likes being a nurse."

"Do you remember the time you and your daddy went fishing?"

"The only time we went fishing. What was I, eight?"

She nodded. "He got you the fishing pole for your birthday, I got up early and made pancakes, and then you went off together before the sun came up."

"I wanted a bicycle. Like the one Steve had."

"We couldn't afford a bicycle."

"That's what he said. He could afford to play pool." I peered at Mother for a few moments, but when she didn't come to his defense, I went on. "I couldn't have a cat, but I had to feed his greedy coonhound." She looked down at her lap and clasped her hands together.

One evening when I went inside the kennel, Humphrey rolled over onto his side and put his leg up to expose his crotch and thumped his tail lazily against the ground. This was the way he always greeted me, with a show of respect, an acknowledgment that I was master. I kicked him solidly in the groin, and he let out a sharp, surprised yelp.

"He got you a bicycle the next Christmas."

"Did you talk him into that?"

"He didn't even tell me until a few days before; he was afraid I'd spill the beans. He took me out to the garage one night to show me where he'd hidden it up over the rafters. I should have told you, I guess. I never seemed to do anything right when it came to you two. The fishing pole was my idea; I thought it would be good for you to spend time together."

We stopped to get night crawlers, then drove to Dooley's farm and walked several miles to the river, and he never talked. I was tired before we reached his favorite spot. He didn't show me how to bait my hook or use the pole. So I collected rocks and shells and went into the woods to pick flowers. I found wild, white violets and jacks-in-the-pulpits and mayapples and trilliums.

"You make him sound like a heel."

"He didn't like me. He never touched me."

"You were never interested in anything he did."

Until the backyard boxing bout, I enjoyed his Navy stories. During meals on the ship, they held their bread up to the light to pick out the bugs. In the Navy a man always had a bed to sleep in. Daddy went past the open door of the ship's galley one afternoon and saw the fat, hairy cook with his arms immersed in potato salad. This story I heard again and again, and it never failed to reduce Daddy to shaking, crying laughter as he described the cook in his soiled undershirt and up to his elbows in mustard and mayonnaise stripping the excess off his each forearm with the alternate hand. Daddy always ended his story, after regaining control, by saying: "I sure didn't have no potato salad that night."

I smiled, and then said to Mother. "I liked hearing about when he was in the Navy."

"He was proud of his boxing; I expect he thought it would give you a little more spunk—make you confident."

"Boxing is barbaric; even as a child I knew that."

"He didn't have an easy life. He hated his work, he started getting sick before he was fifty, and we never had enough money. He could never tell me he loved me either, and he never said he was sorry about anything, but I knew he was. I know he loved you kids and I know he loved me. But he was scared. I know he was scared."

My father told us a story one evening. The son of a friend at the plant had stolen a motorcycle and called a week later from Florida. My father laughed and said, "The boy's just like his old man."

Dean said he and his dad went fishing, they went to Red Sox games, and they went bowling. My dad boxed, hunted, fished, hated cats, and got me for a son. I liked being alone. Dean's dad went to all of his football games, but Dean is still gay. When he told him, his father said: "What? Do you think I'm stupid? I know. I don't get it, but I know. For me, when I see a good looking man and a good looking woman in the corner of a room, I don't see what you see in the man, but what do I know?"

Perhaps my father would have taken me more seriously if I'd stolen a motorcycle. Mother got up to leave and bent over and put her arms around me and kissed me goodbye. "When are you and Dean coming home next?" she said.

∾•⋐

I picked up the phone expecting it to be Dean or Cynthia. I hadn't expected Dean's parents to call me. His mother was on one phone and his father was on an extension. Frank spoke first. "Get out of that fricking place, cause we're coming out. We got it all worked out. Dino didn't tell you?"

He hadn't, and it was already arranged—even the plane tickets. Dean's parents would spend a week in the store—to get familiar with operations—then Dean and I would fly to St. Croix for two weeks in the Virgin Islands while they took care of the flower shop.

"It's our Christmas present," said his mother. "You boys deserve it; the sun and ocean air will do you good."

❧•❧

Dean has such a different temperament. He's calm and doesn't use his arms or hands—even during a heated discussion. And he doesn't raise his voice. The first time we got into an argument I thought it meant he didn't care that much about me. I asked if he was on Lithium. His lack of animation makes him appear in control. He knows what he wants. He enjoys a routine, he's not easily bored, and he doesn't care for crowds. So his anger came as a surprise. He came into the room when Dr. Jacoby was making rounds. I was in the chair working a crossword puzzle. He didn't smile when Peter said I'd be going home the next day. "But if you don't change your ways," said Peter, "you'll be back too soon." Then he smiled. "You have people who care and you're hurting them." After he left, Dean asked me to walk with him to the lounge.

There was a haggard boy visiting with a man and a woman that I took to be his parents. When we walked past, to the opposite corner, I heard him say something about Compound Q and shake his head. We sat down, and I joked about getting the chairs for our apartment—they had wooden armrests and were covered in canned-pea green vinyl—but Dean only frowned.

"You talked to Dr. Jacoby?" I said. Dean nodded.

"And I talked to your mother. We shipped Mae's things home and I took them to the airport."

"Thanks for taking care of them."

"Is that why you want me around? Do you think I'll stay, no matter what?"

"I love you. I like being with you."

"Do you think I'm going to be an enabler?"

"I told you how I feel."

"Don't play stupid, Chris. I know you did cocaine at that boy's so-called party. I won't stand by and watch while you kill yourself."

Dean might be bluffing. Who knows how much a person will take. I don't intend to find out. I don't want to hurt Dean and I don't want to kill myself. Getting pneumonia, mild as my case was, scared me. Jolted me. My T-cells are probably below 200 now. The CDC is changing their classification: anyone below 200 will be classified as having AIDS. Maybe I'm below 200. Maybe I'm a PWA.

Dean told me to stay where I was and not move. He had a surprise. He put on his coat and disappeared down the hall and was gone for about ten minutes. When he came back into the lounge, he carried a large package wrapped in black, glossy paper and tied up with a white, satin bow. I never had a chance to get Dean's ring. He handed the package to me, and I felt something move inside and heard a whimper. After I removed the bow and stripped away the paper, I peeked inside the kennel door at the small black puppy with the one white paw: a Portuguese water dog. He looked out at me and thumped his tail against the side of the case.

"Merry Christmas," said Dean. "He's ten weeks old."

❧ • ❧

I push my dinner tray to one side and look through the window. The evening sky is dusty pink—the color of a faded rose—and the leafless maple, framed in the opening, reminds me of a charcoal sketch against a pastel background. The wind grows stronger. The window is close to my bed, and I can see that it's warped, which prevents it from closing completely. The imperfect fit causes the air to whistle as it passes over the cracks. Frost has formed on the corner of the glass and condensation has run onto the sill and frozen. I pull the blanket to my chin, and then put my arms underneath and against my sides. The sky dims; the wind gusts. I look at the tree again. A sparrow lands on one of the branches, then immediately flies away, and the limb rocks as if the bird's quick departure and not the wind caused it to sway. I feel drowsy, then sleep unexpectedly for several hours—a black, dense sleep—not accompanied by body movement. I sleep as if paralyzed. My arms don't flail, my legs don't jerk, my eyelids don't flutter.

When I open my eyes, I have no idea where I am. I am surrounded by blackness. I don't know if it's night or day. I don't know the month or the year. There's nothing to anchor me in time or place. I'm not conscious of any odor or aroma, the air is completely still, and there is no feeling in my body. It's as if I am packed in insulation, as if I am floating in the world. No outside sensation. Gradually, I become aware. First, my arms resting against my sides, palms flat against my thighs; my breathing slow, rhythmic; my chest rising and falling. Breath being expelled. The blood running through my veins. The thump of my heart. A hum, no a ringing in my ears, almost an electrical sound, steady and even. Then, I become acutely aware of my body. I feel no pain, no pressure, no headache, no clogged arteries or nasal passages. My body is machinery, perfectly lubricated, perfectly milled. The parts function with precision. I don't fight the feeling. Luxurious. I don't sit up abruptly or try to figure things out; I don't try to get grounded. The feeling is enough. Eventually, I regain an awareness of my surroundings. I feel the sheets with my hands; I move my head slightly to the left, then to the right. I take a deeper breath and shrug my shoulders and feel the wool blanket against my cheeks and chin. I rub my feet together and find that they're warm and dry. My body is the correct temperature—a thermometer would indicate 98.6—not a tenth too high or low. The aroma of disinfectant comes to me slowly, the distant sound of another patient's television filters in, and then slowly the sound of the wind picks up again outside my window. Sensations of an outside world return. The day, the month, the time. The time. Never have I experienced such a heightened sense of my body. Ideas and concepts take shape again.

But they're not intrusive. Dean, Mother, Cynthia, Mae, winter, December thirtieth. The day. I begin to recall the events of the recent past: Norberto, the episode on the subway, and the pneumonia. I smell the arrangement of lilies on the dresser, and remember Vale de Flores. I think of the pneumonia. None of it matters. The serenity and peace of my sleep have not been replaced with dread or fear. Memory returns, but does not intrude. How I got to be the way I am doesn't matter. All the issues I've spent my life trying to control, trying to figure out, are unimportant. It no longer matters. I'm alive; that what matters. I am responsible for me. Dean is not responsible for me, Mother is not responsible for me, and it doesn't matter what my father did or didn't do. I'm not thirteen or twenty or forty or fifty or sixty. Now is all that matters. I'd rather have five years or ten years of joy than a lifetime of fixing blame. I'll jog along the lakefront at sunrise, I'll read Dickens and Tolstoy and Faulkner, I'll listen to the thunder during rain storms, and I'll fill our kitchen with the smells of *sopa de pedra* and *broa* and *flan*. I'll listen to Sibelius and Brahms and Mahler and surround us with orchids and amaryllis and daisies and tulips. And I'll take my dog, Humphrey, for a walk through the snow-covered streets.

I have a lover. I'm still here.

About the Author

RONALD ALEXANDER is a Pushcart-nominated author whose fiction, poetry and essays have appeared in journals including *The Chattahoochee Review, Confrontation, Columbia*, and *The James White Review*. His work has been performed on "Word Theatre," his novella *Romanze for Martha* was a finalist in the St. Andrews Novella competition, and his novel *The Final Audit* was published by Hollyridge Press. Mr. Alexander lives in Venice California with his Labrador retriever, Cub.

Acknowledgements

I am indebted to many for their interest in and support for *Below 200*. Thanks to Linda Chacon, Virginia Smith, Chris Harvey, Anamyn Turowski-Allen, and Robert DiFrancesca for reading the early drafts. I am grateful to Peter Amsden, PA and the late Dr. Robert Jenkins for their medical and technical information. Much obliged to Ethan Canin and my fellow MFA classmates at Columbia University for their suggestions and critiques. And finally for his blue pencil and attention to detail, I thank my editor at Hollyridge Press, Ian R. Wilson.